ORDER

R. L. MEDINA

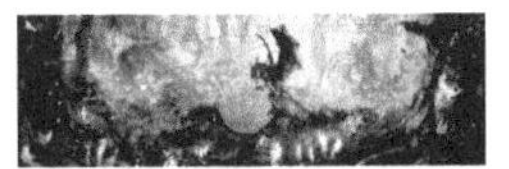

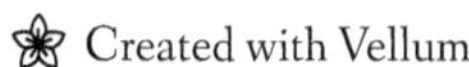 Created with Vellum

For my family. I'd be lost without you.

1

———

VALERIA

A rabbit. Easy prey. Let me kill it.

I dismissed the voice of my inner wolf. *We don't need food at camp, and I didn't come out to hunt.*

She made an irritated noise in my mind, reminding me it had been a while since I let her loose. I hadn't been hunting since... Elijah left.

His face flashed in my mind. Dark, mischievous eyes and smooth, brown skin. My throat turned dry. We always hunted together and let our wolves run free, but now it was just me, and as many times as I'd tried to explain his leaving to my wolf; she didn't understand.

She ached for him, still believing he was coming back. I wasn't so sure. The curse changed him, broke him beyond repair. Elijah wasn't the same carefree, reckless boy we'd grown up with.

None of us were the same. Not since the world had fallen.

Fighting the wave of sorrow threatening to rise at the memories, I continued my walk. The woods helped me center myself.

It was the only place I could be both human and wolf equally at the same time.

I could pretend the last six months never happened.

That the mysterious worldwide disease targeting only the youngest never happened. That the witches hadn't cast the spell that was supposed to stop it, which instead killed everyone. Everyone but us—those stuck between childhood and adulthood.

Alone in the woods, I could pretend that Mom, Dad, Jaime, and the others were back at camp waiting for me. Tears filled my eyes. I blinked them away.

I was alpha. The others would think me weak. Too human. What would Dad say now?

Willing the memory of his voice to surface, I held my breath. Only the sounds of the forest filled my ears. Because Dad was dead—and the dead didn't speak.

Banishing my dark thoughts, I glanced up. A full moon shone brightly from a cloudless sky. The smell of Spanish moss and yarrow filled the Georgia air, but there was something else. My wolf stirred, instincts taking over.

We knew that scent. We knew it well.

Blood.

I clenched my fists and urged my wolf to stand down. At eighteen, I'd managed enough control over myself to not transform at every sign of danger.

The unmistaken snap of branches caught my ear. I crouched behind a wide oak and waited. Only shadow pack wolves were supposed to be in the area, but whoever or whatever was out there was not one of us.

My wolf snarled within me. *Human.*

Heavy footsteps sounded. More than one. I sniffed. Three humans.

How did they get past our guard? Anger stirred in my belly.

With Elijah gone, the pack was growing too lax. That would change. I was still alpha, even without my so-called mate. I could still lead them just as well as he had. *Then why don't they listen to you like they did him?* I dismissed the thought as soon as it came.

"Shh. Someone's here." A male voice broke the quiet.

I pressed myself against the bark and held my breath. My wolf urged me to run. *Warn the pack.* I didn't move. Three. I could handle three. If I fled now, I wouldn't find out what they were doing in our territory.

Besides, the pack's safety was all up to me now. I couldn't screw it up.

With a steadying breath, I pushed myself off the tree and onto their path. A gun whipped toward me. My wolf rose to the surface, ready for action.

I reigned her in and held my ground. "This is shadow wolf territory. What are you doing here?"

The guy stepped forward, motioning the girl with the gun back. "We've come to speak to your alpha. Please, we don't want any trouble."

My wolf bristled. *Alpha. Elijah.*

"I am the alpha of this pack." My voice was strong. It was the tone I used to command my wolves.

His eyes widened. I scowled as he sized me up. I knew what he saw—high ponytail and plain face, average height, average weight with a little extra on my hips. I didn't *look* threatening.

The human mocks us. My wolf's voice came, offended for both of us.

I watched as he glanced at his female companions. One of them, the smaller of the two, was bleeding. Her eyes were pained, and her hand gripped her side. The scent of wolf was on her. One of my kind had torn into her flesh. There was something else, too. *Vampire.* Both had used her as their plaything.

My stomach turned at the sight. She couldn't be much older than fifteen.

"Please. My friend needs a healer." He spoke again.

The other girl continued to stare at me, her gun still aimed at my heart. That one was a threat. My wolf sensed her thinly veiled rage and hatred, her desire to put a bullet in me and all those like me. No surprise there. Even at the end of the world, humans couldn't accept us. Despite the sickness that took our families—wolf, human, witch, and vampire alike—and the final collapse of society; hatred and prejudice remained.

We were all the same in their human eyes.

I met her glare. "You're better off taking her back to the city."

"I told you, Drew. They're not going to help us," the dangerous one spoke. Moonlight reflected in her dark eyes. Eyes that were narrowed with distrust.

"Put your gun down, Becca," he said through clenched teeth.

She ignored him.

"Please." The smaller girl looked to me. Her voice was barely a whisper.

Pity filled me. I didn't want to imagine everything she'd suffered, but I couldn't risk my pack's safety.

I shook my head. "You shouldn't have come." I turned to the boy. "She shouldn't be walking and moving with that wound. She's going to bleed out faster."

"We didn't have a choice. Please. Help her and we'll leave."

The other girl scoffed. "How about help her or I'll shoot you."

He glanced at her. "Shut up, Becca."

I bit back a smile, though my wolf's hackles rose at the threat. If they hurt me, my pack would tear them apart, but it wouldn't come to that. I could handle them myself.

"Go back to the city," I repeated.

Shadows fell across the boy's face. Even in the dark, I could see that he was handsome. Strong jaw, sensual lips, and dark eyes. Like the girl. I glanced at her, realizing their resemblance. Twins?

Blood kin, my wolf agreed.

"We can't. It's not safe." He took a cautious step closer to me.

"Drew," his twin warned, her gun steady on me.

His eyes were on me. "Please. We just need a healer."

But my mind snagged on his other words. *It's not safe.* The city? Why would it be unsafe for humans? Had something happened? My heart skipped. Elijah was in the city. I pushed away the fear and dread. He made his choice.

"You shouldn't be here. I—"

"We have no choice! Are you going to stand there and let her bleed out?" His eyes pinned me, an anguished look on his face.

My wolf growled at his outburst, and outwardly I clenched my jaw. Realizing his error, he stiffened. The mask of control and diplomacy returned, but I'd seen it—a glimpse of the unbridled emotions he kept hidden and leashed.

The injured girl wobbled on her feet, face ashen in the moonlight. I could smell death on her.

Yes. Death marked, my wolf agreed.

Her body swayed. The boy swore and reached for her just as she collapsed. Behind them, in the distance, came a howl. The hairs on my neck bristled. Wolves. Red Wolves. Is that who they ran from? Though we were neighbor packs at one time, they weren't exactly friends of ours.

What were they doing so close?

"Please. I beg you. Please." He was desperate.

No. Must warn pack. Leave the humans.

His pleading eyes stared into my soul. I couldn't walk away even though my wolf was adamant we do just that.

"Come." The word tumbled out of my mouth before I could stop it.

There was no time to think it through. No time to regret my decision. My wolf was furious and retreated to my innermost consciousness.

"Thank you." Relief rang in his words.

I turned to lead them through the forest. A bird called, warning of danger. The sound echoed in my ears, high and shrill. My heart thumped wildly. What was I doing? Helping humans? I shook away the doubts crowding my mind.

Too late to go back now.

McKenzie

"They caught another one."

I closed my book and turned at the sound of Kohl's voice. It was a measured tone, one that he was an expert at. No hint of emotion or opinion of how I should respond. The perfect right hand of the queen.

"Human?" I asked.

Candlelight reflected in his gaze. His hazel eyes swept over me, the desire he so fervently tried to hide, rising to the surface. I pretended not to notice.

"No. Werewolf this time."

My eyebrow arched. "One of their own wolves?"

The fire in his gaze died. It was back to business now. "No, I don't believe so, My Queen—"

"You don't have to use that title, Kohl. Not when it's just us."

"But—"

"Please."

He gave me a solemn nod. He, of all people, knew how I felt about hearing that word. A title meant for my sister. Not me. It was never supposed to be me.

I pushed away the thought and sighed. "Not one of their own wolves?"

"No. A lone wolf. New to the city."

"What is he doing killing a stray wolf?"

Kohl shrugged. "Boredom? Because he's a psycho? Who knows what motivates Diego."

My lip curled. First humans and now he was going after other wolves? Would my witches be next? Diego was getting bolder.

"He knows I won't let him kill any more people like this. What is this? A test?"

"Maybe?"

I scoffed. "Just what I need right now. You ready then?"

He straightened. I bit back a smile at my best friend. He was nothing if not professional. Neat, cropped, blonde hair and freshly shaven face. His shoulders were squared, and his stoic stare reminded me of his prim and proper father. Even before the curse, Kohl had been much too serious. An old soul trapped in an eighteen-year-old body.

I stood and smoothed out the wrinkles of my long, red dress. One of the few perks of being queen was the glitzy fashion no one could judge me for now. "Alright. Let's go."

Kohl nodded and waited for my lead.

Pulling my strappy, metallic gold sandals back on, I stood and headed for the stairs. Candles burned, creating shadows against the walls.

Five witches waited on the landing. They bowed and took their place behind me. Kohl had readied them.

Our footsteps echoed through the mansion as we descended together. Though the old building was full of all the surviving witches, it felt empty to me. Death lingered in the halls and every day we were reminded of those we'd lost.

At the bottom, the rest of the coven dispersed, making way for us.

Most of them bowed. Some of them didn't.

I glanced at Kohl and he nodded. He was already making note of the latter. At eighteen, I was the youngest witch queen Savannah had ever seen. If they didn't want me, well that was too damn bad because I was all they had.

All *we* had.

Melody was supposed to be queen. She was the one groomed for it, but instead I was forced to take my sister's place. To become something I never wanted.

The face of the previous queen, Blanca, flashed in my mind. Her haunted eyes, pallid skin, and chattering teeth. Even at the final moment, as the curse took her, she was chanting—casting with every last scrap of magic and energy she had left.

It wasn't enough. She—and all the witches before us—failed to undo their spell, leaving us to pick up where they left, but the damage was done. We were all cursed, and we couldn't bring back our dead. Mama, Daddy, my sisters, and so many, many others.

As I led my warriors through the giant entry way, I met all the vacant stares. My coven sisters and brothers who'd lost just as much as I had. As a whole, we were weak, vulnerable almost, but I would not let us fall.

"Oaktree Square?" I asked Kohl.

"Yes, My Queen. Do you want to take the bikes?" He glanced at my dress. "Or the car?"

"No. We can walk."

There were only so many old vehicles that still ran without technology and siphoning the gas was time consuming. Besides, the square wasn't too far.

Drawing in a deep breath, I summoned the magic. It came at my call, showering me and filling me with its burning intensity. My body trembled at its intrusion. I emptied myself and let it take what it wanted, as painful as it was.

The others did the same. I felt the power grow and strengthen between us. Together, we could do the impossible. Together, we could force the wolves into submission. *But for how long?* I dismissed the nagging thought. Tonight, we would win and that would be enough... for now.

I led them to the square, barely aware of the warm, summer air on my skin. Campfires burned all around the city, filling my nose with the smoky smell. The moon was high and the night perfect for spells. Nature was on our side, I could feel it.

Teens crowded the cobbled streets. The werewolves. The vampires who technically weren't teens anymore, but their bodies had been turned before adulthood, marking them forever free of the curse. Rogue witches who wanted nothing to do with the coven. And the humans who, practically overnight, had become the weakest race. Some wore slave collars as they stood by their vampire masters.

I fought the urge to shudder at the cruelness. It was payback for all the shootings and violence they'd unleashed on the city when all the adults and children were taken by the spell, but not all the humans were responsible. They didn't deserve this treatment.

Everyone, human, vampire, and werewolf alike glared daggers at us. We were, after all, the reason the world had gone to hell.

At the center of it all, against the stone tablet that not so many years ago, my teacher had brought us to see on a field trip, hung a boy—a wolf.

Beside him, looming over everyone, was Diego Garcia, the alpha of the Red Wolves, and the most powerful teen in the city. Well, after me.

His dark eyes met mine and a slow smile crept on his face. "Your Majesty." He gave an exaggerated bow. His long hair fell forward.

Laughter rang out at his mocking.

Magic thrummed inside me, heady and explosive. I could feel it pushing against my skin and seeping from my pores.

I was strength. I was power. I was queen.

"Well, isn't this a treat? Come to see the show?" His hand swept the crowd. "Ladies and gentlemen, Queen McKenzie. In the flesh. Leaving her tower to come mingle with us commoners."

His face hardened. "Us monsters."

The mob jeered. Snarls and shouts filled the air. I could almost taste the blood they so hungrily wanted to spill. Flashlights darted back and forth, and someone had lit a fire in the middle of the park behind us. It was like a scene from some bizarre horror movie. This wasn't the Savannah I remembered.

A pair of brown eyes flecked with gold found mine. The wolf.

Not just any either. *Alpha,* the magic whispered inside me. What brought him into our territory? Where was his pack?

Bruises and gashes covered his dark-brown skin, but his face was stone, his lip curled in defiance. No sign of pain or weakness. Inside, I felt his inner wolf tremble. Not with fear, no.

It was rage.

A silent fury building inside of him as Diego taunted me. Anger not directed at his captor, but at me.

Queen of the witches. Queen of the curse.

2

VALERIA

Ten. Ten more steps and we'd be at the line. It was too late to change my mind now. My pack would smell the blood soon, and then they would come. Jay and Tati—my betas—first. My throat turned dry, words already deserting me. My subconscious turned traitor.

How are you gonna explain this one, Val? You're too weak. Pathetic. Too human. No wonder he left you.

I pushed the thoughts away, refusing to get swept under the tidal wave of regret. My wolf was still making herself scarce; the reminder blunt—you are alone.

"I'm Drew. Sorry, we didn't introduce ourselves earlier."

The human's voice caught my ear.

He carried the injured girl in his arms, the cloth he'd tied around her waist already soaked with blood.

"That's my sister, Becca. We're twins. And this"—his eyes dipped to the dying teen—"is Jen. Our friend. She was our neighbor before..."

He didn't finish. I knew what he meant. Before the spell

went wrong and took everyone except us. Us teenagers. Before the world went to hell.

"What's your—"

I threw up my hand to silence him. We were at the line now. Where were my guards?

Laughter echoed from ahead, making my face flame. Clearly my pack needed a refresher in appropriate protocol for keeping watch. They'd grown too comfortable out here in the woods. Too careless.

"This is a mistake, Drew. We never should have left the others," his twin whispered.

The laughter stopped. I drew myself up and squared my shoulders.

You are still alpha. They have to obey you, even if they don't like it, my wolf encouraged me.

"Put your gun away." I motioned to Becca.

She met my gaze but didn't budge.

"I promise my pack won't hurt you. You have my word."

She scoffed. "I'd rather not take any chances."

My wolf resurfaced, indignant that this human dared defy us.

"Becca." Her brother's eyes narrowed in warning.

"Alpha?" Jay's voice cut in.

I turned to face my beta and his mate. They gaped at us and behind them the rest of the pack crept closer, their whispers carried by the warm breeze.

"Humans?"

"Here? What are they doing here?"

Some had already shifted, their wolves ready to handle this new threat. Becca stiffened at the first growl, but her hands were steady, finger on the trigger.

Jay's face hardened. His wolf was waiting for my command.

"Stand down. They're with me."

Surprise flashed on my beta's faces and murmurs erupted. Jay's eyes shot to mine and though he said nothing, I could read the question burning inside him, burning inside everyone—what are you doing, Val?

I wish I knew.

The injured girl whimpered, the sound soft and pitiful. I winced. Some of my wolves would mark her as prey. I glanced at her. Her eyes were wide with pain. She looked young, couldn't be much older than Jaime. The face of my brother flashed in my mind, making my heart twist. How could I send this girl away? After all we'd lost—our mothers, fathers, sisters, and brothers we couldn't save—how could we allow death to take one more life?

I turned to Jay. "Take her to Cruz. Now. The girl needs a healer." I glanced at Tati. "Go tell him."

She nodded and ran for the healer's tent while Jay reached for Jen. Becca swung her gun at him, making him pause. His eyes flashed silver—the signal his wolf was about to emerge.

Jumping between them, I yanked the weapon from her grasp. She was strong. For a human. Stupid too, to point her gun at the giant beta.

"You want our help? You'll listen to me." I let my wolf's anger lace my words.

Her eyes were murderous, but she said nothing.

"Please. We don't want trouble. Just help our friend," Drew spoke up.

The girl was past saving, but I'd given my word. I nodded for Jay to lead them to Cruz. The other wolves stood, watching the scene with unabashed curiosity and suspicion. Humans were dangerous. Unpredictable. There was a reason Elijah and I moved the pack farther from the city and the human mobs.

I pushed away the memory of the attack they'd launched on

us in our old neighborhood. The violence and blood. Murder. Elijah's revenge on them.

His face flickered in my mind once more. The dark, gold-flecked eyes that always saw too much and his sly smile. I pushed away the image. It was hard to forget him, but impossible to forgive his abandonment. Even if it had been to hunt his sister's killer. The path he'd chosen wasn't one I could follow.

Dismissing the thoughts, I turned to give my orders. "Cameron and Spencer. Back to your posts. Now. Red wolves are in the area. I want four more guards posted. Who's posted at the edge of the woods?"

Jay and Tati exchanged glances.

"Who?" I insisted.

"No one, Alpha. We—I thought it was unnecessary."

Tati shifted nervously beside her mate.

My wolf growled at Jay's admission. He thought it was unnecessary?

I glared at hm. "That isn't your decision to make. Help them bring the girl to Cruz and then you can take first watch."

He nodded. "Yes, Alpha."

The others hurried to obey, but the fact they'd broken protocol still made me seethe. When the humans were gone, I'd have a little chat with them.

They need their alpha, my wolf spoke.

I *am* their alpha.

She fell silent, wisely reading my mood.

I followed the humans and Jay farther into our camp and to the healer's tent. Becca's head swiveled as she took in our layout and my heart skipped. Did I make a mistake? Were they really spies sent out under this guise?

My fist clenched. They wouldn't be leaving until I got some answers.

We reached the large, green and brown tent in no time. Cruz and Tati stood outside waiting for us.

Tati ran to her mate's side, his giant, dark frame dwarfing her. Cruz lowered his gaze in respect to me and glanced at the others.

"Thank you, Jaylen. Tatiana." He nodded at my betas.

His blue eyes darted to Becca and her twin. "Set her on the blankets."

They strode forward and disappeared inside. I moved to follow them.

"Val—Alpha."

I stopped at Jay's address and turned to face him.

"How long are they staying?" His huge arms hung by his side, but my wolf could sense the tension running through him.

"Until I decide they can go."

His lip curled, but he didn't question me. Tati shuffled on her feet beside him, flipping her long hair behind a shoulder.

"Alpha," Cruz spoke.

I met his serious gaze.

He shook his head. "That girl. I can't save her."

"I know. Just... do your best." I mentally kicked myself at the words. Do your best?

"If she dies. What happens to the others? They'll be mad. Blame us. What if they want revenge? What are we going to do?" Jay's voice rose.

I shot him a cool look. "You'll do what I tell you to do, Jay."

He stiffened. "Yes, Alpha."

"Go to your post. And send out a scout. The Red Wolves could be close. Or vampires." I thought about the girl's injuries. Damage done not just by werewolves.

Jay nodded and Tati swore, trailing her mate back to the perimeter. I turned and followed Cruz into the tent. My heart pounded in my ears, the sound echoing Jay's questions as well as my own.

What were the humans really doing here? What was happening in the city? Was Elijah okay?

The smell of death filled my nose as I entered. My wolf didn't like it. Not one bit. Ignoring my instincts to tuck tail and run, I approached the injured girl.

Cruz ripped her shirt, revealing the bloody gash on her side. Deep. It was way too deep for our healer to fix. Drew swore, distress flashing on his face. Becca straightened, her eyes full of resolve. She accepted the truth.

"This will stop the blood and take away the pain." Cruz brought a glass jar over. Crushed flowers and spices filled it.

Without proper medical equipment or the doctors and nurses knowledgeable in how to use it, we were lucky to have a healer. Lucky Cruz's abuela taught him the old ways. Though there was still a limit to what we could do without modern technology. Just another side effect of the spell the witches cast. No technology. No adults and no children. Just us.

Jen hissed as the mixture touched her.

"Ugh. What is that?" Becca covered her nose.

"Turmeric. Honey. And yarrow," Cruz answered.

"And this will heal her? She'll be okay?" Drew continued staring at the open wound.

Jen's eyes met Cruz's. So hopeful. Even after all she'd endured, she still wanted to live. I looked away. The injustice of it made my stomach churn. Six months ago, she was just an average teen worried about high school. Not death. Not a death like this.

"She's lost a lot of blood." Cruz's answer hung in the air.

Becca's jaw clenched.

Drew looked to Cruz and then me. "But you can save her?"

Cruz turned to me.

"We will do our best," I replied.

Becca glared at me, but she didn't say anything. Probably to spare her dying friend and her brother the cold, harsh truth.

A wave of sorrow struck me. For a moment, I was back at the bedside of my dying brother. Jaime. Only twelve. If he'd been thirteen, he would have survived the curse. I didn't know the importance of the ages, but for whatever reason only those between thirteen and nineteen were safe from the spell.

My wolf whimpered, pulling me back to the present.

I turned to Drew. "Did the wolves who did this follow you into the woods?"

He shook his head. "No. Only to the outskirts of Savannah."

"Why didn't you get help in the city?"

Becca scoffed. "Help? What help? Those wolves control every hospital and clinic. They guard all the medical supplies."

Her words startled me. Since when had the Red Wolves taken over? The last time I'd been in Savannah, the human teens were the ones with all the power. I shuddered as memories of the first few months returned.

The fires. Gunshots. So much senseless violence.

Though the witches were the ones who'd cast the spell, all of us were blamed. All of us who weren't human were hunted and killed like animals. Had Diego put an end to it like he'd sworn?

"We couldn't get through. To make it back to our... camp." Drew rubbed a hand across his face.

Cruz returned the jar to its place on the shelf and started cleaning the skin around her wound. Jen's eyes were clenched shut, her body trembling.

"Once Jen is healed, we'll go back," Drew added, brushing the sweaty clump of hair away from Jen's face.

His dark eyes shone with an intensity that reminded me of that sibling bond I'd had with Jaime. That same protectiveness and empathy. My heart twisted in two. Drew thought we could save his friend.

Becca gripped his shoulder and motioned him to follow her. I watched as she led him outside the tent and listened as they exchanged hushed words.

"She's not going to make it, Drew. It's too late."

"You don't know that. The bleeding stopped. They said they'd save her."

"Yeah, well they're lying."

They fell quiet. I turned away, not wanting them to look in and see me eavesdropping. Cruz held a cup up to Jen's mouth, coaxing her to drink and swallow the pills he'd given her. She closed her eyes. The sound of her labored breathing filled the tent. Cruz's gaze met mine briefly and returned to the dying girl.

"You should see this." He motioned me over.

I walked to him and looked to where he pointed. He moved her curly hair away, revealing several bite marks on her tanned neck. Vampire and wolf. My stomach churned at the sight. They'd used her like a freaking chew toy. How the hell had she survived that?

"She's going to turn," Cruz whispered to me.

My stomach rolled. Turning humans had been a thing of the past and only alphas could do it. Most of the werewolves were born not made. The ones who were turned from a bite... the inner wolves that bonded to them were notoriously savage as if the pure human gene called to something darker, something stronger to rise within them.

This is true, my wolf agreed.

Drew and Becca reentered the tent, and Cruz returned to cleaning Jen's other wounds. I stared down at the girl with a silent apology. It would have been better if she'd bled out. Her body wouldn't survive the change. One was bad enough, but two? No one survived two turns.

Anger stirred inside me. Why did they do this to her? What could this girl have possibly done to be abused so badly?

Waves of regret and hopelessness washed over me. The world didn't make sense anymore. We were supposed to make things better, be the next generation that would change everything. It was a good thing our parents were gone.

They didn't have to see the monsters we'd become.

"Could I talk to you? Please?" Drew's voice broke my thoughts.

I whipped toward him and nodded.

He rubbed a hand over his creased forehead. "I'm sorry. I still didn't catch your name."

"Valeria."

A brief smile flickered on his face. "Nice to meet you, Valeria."

Becca glanced at her gun still in my hand and glared at me. She didn't trust me. Well, I didn't trust her either, and she wasn't getting her gun back.

I turned to her brother. "What is it you want to talk about?"

His eyes darted to Becca and back to me. "It's not safe in the city anymore. We have to move our camp. We have to bring the others here."

My wolf growled. *More humans?*

I was already shaking my head. "No. You can't bring them here."

Frustration shone in his eyes. "We can't leave them in the city to be tortured. Like Jen." His voice cracked.

I looked away, not wanting to see his pain.

"Ben isn't going to move the camp, Drew," Becca cut in.

He ignored her, his big brown eyes still imploring me.

"Please. We just want a safe place to stay. We aren't going to hurt anybody."

Out of the corner of my eye, I caught Cruz watching us with interest. The heaviness of our situation weighed on me. It should have been Elijah and I making the decisions, but he'd left it all to me. I should have hated him for it, but I didn't. How could I? The crisis hit him harder than most of us, leaving him a broken shell of what he used to be.

"No. You'll have to find another place. Farther into the woods maybe. But away from the Crescent Pack near the river. Or out of Savannah altogether."

Drew's eyes narrowed. "We can't. Haven't you tried leaving the state? We're stuck here."

His words startled me. Stuck? But hadn't people left when it started? When our phones and screens still worked, showing the same phenomenon was happening everywhere?

"There's some kind of barrier keeping anyone from leaving. The witches couldn't break it," Becca added.

I frowned. "There has to be some place in the city you can go."

Becca gave a harsh laugh. "The city's gone to hell. How do you not know that?"

My wolf growled at her tone.

"Well, you can't stay here."

Drew sighed. "We are better off sticking together. Your pack is small. Most of them don't look like they have any fight in them. We have more people at our camp. People who can fight."

I frowned at his words. My wolf snarled at the assessment. He didn't know what we'd been through. We were fighters. Survivors.

Calculation shone in his eyes and I felt stupid for not seeing it earlier. They'd already cased my camp and hadn't even been there more than an hour. My cheeks flamed.

Humans cannot be trusted.

"We don't need fighters. We can hold our own and the Red Wolves aren't our enemies."

In fact, Diego had been in some of my classes. We weren't exactly friends, but we traveled in the same circles. Back when life was normal.

Jen moaned, the sound slicing through the silence. We turned to her. She was convulsing. Spit bubbled from her mouth.

"What's happening?" Drew rushed to her side.

"She's turning," Cruz answered.

Drew staggered back, distress written on his face. Becca's fists clenched.

Bones snapped. A scream tore from Jen's mouth, the sound sharp and chilling. Her tan skin turned ashen, her eyes sunken. Numbness filled me at the sight. I remembered Mama on her last day. The smell of death so strong, pungent, and offensive. It marked her and there was nothing I could do.

You can't save her. You can't save anyone. My thoughts darkened.

3

MCKENZIE

Wind swept through the trees in the square, the branches shaking under the assault. My magic welcomed it. Nature could be one of our greatest allies or worst enemies. Tonight, it was on my side.

My witches and I were boxed in now. More and more teens streamed out of the buildings to watch what was going on. Funny, really. Not even a year ago, these same people were flipping through TV apps, glued to their phones or video games for entertainment.

Now a public killing is what we looked forward to?

It was barbaric—we were barbaric. It hadn't even taken much of a push for some of us.

"Well, this is a turn out. All of Savannah, here for you, Queen." Diego's voice rose above the noise.

I flinched at his address. It was hard enough hearing Mel's title used by my witches but hearing it from him made me want to sew his lips shut permanently.

His mate, Sylvie, stood close by, scanning the park for danger. She was thinner than when I'd last seen her. Her blonde hair dirtier too. I smiled as her gaze fell on me. Her blue-green eyes narrowed.

Bitch, please. I was the biggest threat to the wolves, we both knew that. The girl wouldn't have time to shift before I struck.

"What are we doing here, Diego?" I turned to the hulking werewolf.

He flashed me a grin. "I give you Elijah Martin. Alpha of the Shadow Wolves. Elijah, you should be honored. Not everyone gets to meet the queen of Savannah. The newly, self-appointed queen, I should add."

A lick of anger curled within me. I was the only one qualified for the position and no one wanted the title now with all the pressure of breaking the curse. The crown was mine by default.

I glanced at the injured werewolf. His dark eyes pierced me with their brutality. He didn't look honored or grateful for my rescue. He looked like he wanted me dead.

So much for me playing hero.

"I thought it was only humans you strung up in the square." My voice echoed, carried by the wind.

Diego shrugged. "I made an exception. An alpha who abandons his pack? Tell me that doesn't sound like something a human would do?"

Snarls and howls echoed. They wanted his blood. Hell, I wasn't so sure the lone wolf even wanted my help, but I'd already come. To leave now would show weakness and I wasn't weak.

"Let him go, Diego."

The crowed hushed. Kohl and the others stepped closer, tightening our line of defense.

Diego folded his arms across his broad chest. "Now, why would I do that? No fun in that, *Queen.*"

I sighed, letting the magic glide over my skin and ball up against my palm.

"Do you want everyone to see this, Diego? Even Sylvie?"

His mate sneered at me.

"Go ahead. Use your magic. Stop me if you can." Diego turned to the crowd. "She'll use magic to keep us all in line, but can't bring anyone back? Can't break the curse?" His voice rose.

Damn him. It was all a ploy.

Angry hisses and murmurs erupted. The idiots didn't understand how it worked and they wanted someone to blame. Diego was giving that to them.

"My Queen—"

I silenced Kohl with a look.

Diego watched us. "You stay locked in your palace keeping your secrets, but what about us? Are we just supposed to believe your word? Some of us will be twenty in a few weeks. Are we gonna die just like all the others?"

Yes. The spell was still in effect. No one made it past their nineteenth year.

"Believe it or not, Diego. My coven and my witches are your only hope. You want answers? Let us do our work and stop with this petty, useless killing and torture."

He shook his head. "We don't want words, McKenzie. We want action."

Fire lit inside me. "Action? Well, then. Here you go."

My body trembled as the energy shook inside me ready to erupt. The burning made me wince, but the pain was fleeting. I released my magic into the wind and smiled as it exploded around us. Colors flashed in the sky.

First, the injured wolf. The wind, infused with magic cracked the stone tablet in half, and he fell to the ground.

Next, it drove the crowd away. Their screams and snarls

were music to my ears as the invisible threads of magic tore at their clothes. Clawed their faces.

Diego and Sylvie glared at me.

My witches joined in, pushing the mob back into the streets with their power. Some of the rogue witches tried to fight back, but their hold on magic was pitiful. Laughable. They skittered out of the square, falling over each other.

"You seen enough action yet, Diego?"

The magic still thrummed around me, buzzing in my ear. I could do so much more.

He gave me a mirthless smile. "You've only proven my point. Stop playing games. We need that cure, McKenzie."

"Then stay the hell out of my way and stop with these stupid outbursts."

Sylvie's eyes narrowed. "You're the one with the outbursts."

Diego held a hand up to her, silencing the bitch.

"Any wolf who deserts his mate and pack doesn't deserve to live. But if you want him, take him."

He kicked the injured wolf from the platform. His large body rolled to the grass and came to a stop. He groaned.

"Kohl." I motioned for my witches to grab him.

I watched Diego and Sylvie as they directed their pack to stay back. There were more of them than us, but we had magic and what I said was true.

We were the city's—maybe the world's—only chance at stopping the curse.

I just had to figure out how.

The coven was in an uproar when we returned. Lips flapped, their whispers echoing off the walls.

"A werewolf in the coven? What was she doing?"

"Melody would never have allowed it."

I lifted my chin, and stilled their tongues with my stare. Kohl and the others carried the unconscious boy behind me, the sound of his scraping boots filled the room.

"Put him in the old parlor," I ordered.

They headed for the stairs. I turned back to face the rest of the coven.

"Reset the wards. I don't want anyone in. And no one goes out. Not tonight."

"But we just set the wards," a witch argued.

My eyes shot to her. "Do it again."

She flushed and bobbed her head in agreement before skulking back into the crowd. I waited for any other complaints, but everyone fell silent.

Good. I hated having to play the queen card. Why couldn't they just do what was needed without me having to tell them every time?

With a final glance back, I climbed the stairs to see to the wolf. The giant mirror hanging in the middle landing caught my eye. My reflection stared back at me. My God. How I'd aged. I looked like Mama. Her face flashed in my mind, making my heart twist. Dark flawless skin, full lips, and laughing brown eyes. Only my eyes didn't laugh. No, my resting bitch face was something I'd inherited from Grammy.

I took a deep breath and blinked away the tears threatening to surface. I was the queen of Savannah and queens didn't cry. At least not when others could see them.

Pushing away the emotions, I continued the rest of the way. The others disappeared with the wolf around the corner as I made it to the second floor. I charged forward down the hall and headed for the upstairs parlor.

A spirit paused and turned at my approach, but I didn't stop. Her translucent form wavered as she let out a stream of muffled words. The old mansion was filled with the lonely apparitions. Witches who'd lived there before and were either too greedy to leave the magical place or didn't know how.

None of them could help me with the curse, so I didn't bother with them. There wasn't time. Diego's words replayed in my head.

We need that cure.

I knew that better than anyone. It was the only thing that kept me going, that kept me holding onto the material world when I'd like nothing better than to follow my sisters into that sweet darkness where grief couldn't claim me.

"My Queen." Kohl's voice snapped me to attention.

The others bowed as I entered the room and backed away from the werewolf. His body was sprawled on the couch, his blood bright against the cream, upholstered sofa. Several cuts and bruises marred his brown skin, but nothing my healers couldn't tend to.

I watched him from a distance, sensing his inner wolf on guard. Though the human part of him was passed out, his wolf could still emerge and take control. A cornered alpha could do a hell of a lot of damage.

"I'm trying to help you. Will you let me help you?"

His lip curled in defiance, but his eyes remained shut. *Stubborn ass.*

"We can heal you, if you want."

He tossed and turned, nearly rolling off the sofa. A growl came from him. His wolf didn't want us any closer. He was on edge, any moment he'd shift.

"Cast a sleeping spell," I instructed Kohl.

His hands flew, summoning enough magic to knock the wolf out. He let the spell fly. It hit its target, the affect immediate.

The werewolf slumped against the fabric.

"Call in a healer, and get me when he wakes."

"Yes, My Queen."

I turned and headed for my bedroom. Magic still lingered on my skin and after the energy I'd spent casting, I needed to rest. I sighed. I wouldn't be able to perform any more experimental spells until I could recover which meant the rest of the night was wasted.

Diego.

The wolf was quickly becoming a bigger and bigger pain in my ass. If I'd known he was going to challenge my authority, I never would have helped him take control of the city. What he'd done to the humans since then was on me. It was my fault, but it was the price I'd been willing to pay to try to save us all.

Without the humans hunting us all to extinction, I could focus on what was important—breaking this goddamn curse.

Pushing away the thoughts, I made it to my room and downed the herbal tea one of my healer's had left for me. The warm liquid burned my throat with its spiciness, the coolness of the mint leaf followed.

I stood and let the magic settle over me, replacing the energy it had taken. Refreshed, I sighed and moved to my desk to pour over more books. It was a tiring existence. Casting, reading, studying, and casting some more. A dull ache filled my head at just the thought of deciphering the ancient texts. I'd give anything to have technology back. It would have made my research so much easier.

Images swam in front of me as I opened another giant tome. Faded pictures of Savannah witches all through the centuries performing various rituals and spells. My eyes scanned the handwritten list of ingredients, heart sinking. I'd studied all the lists already. Even if we found all the necessary stuff, it was still unlikely the spells would work.

The witches before us did something no one had done before. They used vampire, werewolf, human, and witch blood to set the spell. It was the most volatile and powerful spell in the history of witches, and it worked. Just not in the way they, or anyone, expected.

Where the strange sickness came from, no one knew, but it struck hard and fast, all over the globe. No amount of medicine or scientific experimentation could stop the children from dying.

Desperate, the world turned to magic, and magic failed them.

The spell that was supposed to transfer the incurable disease from the kids to their willing adult guardian backfired. Instead of killing the chosen parent or guardian, it took every adult and the kids still died. Only those of us in between survived. To make it worse, technology flat out stopped working, and we were forced to live like cavemen.

Thankfully, we still had our magic, but for how long, I didn't know.

We would need magic to stop the spell the others had cast. From what I gathered from Blanca, the queen before me, I needed the blood of someone older to reverse what they'd done. Someone older than the nineteen years the curse stretched to. But where was I supposed to get that? Even the vampires, who were stuck permanently at the age they'd turned, didn't have anyone older than that among them.

If I didn't find a way to stop the spell, we'd all be gone eventually except the bloodsuckers. The world would be theirs forever.

Hopelessness washed over me. Were we the only witches left in the world? The coven erected a barrier around the city and woods in the hopes of stopping the curse, but it didn't work and now we were all trapped. Without technology, there was no way to know if others survived outside of Savannah. How could I, alone, reverse what a hundred covens worldwide had done?

"Kenzie." Kohl's voice startled me.

He stood in my doorway, his shoulders relaxed. We were alone and hearing my nickname made me feel almost normal—the girl I'd been before.

"Is he awake?"

Kohl's eyes met mine in the mirror above my desk. The warm glow of the candle turned his skin golden. He nodded.

"Still angry?"

He nodded again, eyes dipping to the open books in front of me. "You should rest. I can question him."

I smiled, but the reality of our situation stung. Not so many months ago, we'd been making the most of senior year and applying for colleges. I thought I had time before my coven duties took my focus. Time for just me.

"What are we going to do about the wolves?" Kohl moved to my lounge chair and sank into the brown cushion.

My smile faltered. "What can we do?"

He pressed his fingers together and held them to his lips in thought. The face he made for every school test and complex spell.

"We could drive them out of the city. To the woods."

I scoffed. "There's too many of them."

"We could ally."

I gave him an incredulous look. "With who?"

"The humans. The rogue witches. Some of the smaller wolf packs."

"The humans? Do you remember what they did?" I shook my head.

He frowned. "We would keep them in check this time."

"This is crazy." I pulled the hair tie from my wrist and pulled back my long, thick hair, pretending not to notice his eyes following my movement.

Even with the window open, my room was a hot box. All

the candles we had to burn for light didn't help. What I'd give to have air conditioning again.

"We could ask the vampires for help."

My eyebrow arched at his suggestions. "That's even crazier. Break our agreement with them? We're not supposed to have anything to do with each other."

He shrugged a shoulder. "Fane is no friend of Diego's."

"Yeah and he's no friend of ours either. How do you even know he's alive? He could have been taken with the spell."

Kohl leaned forward in the chair, his hazel eyes conspiratorial. "No. He's alive. The vampires running loose in the city have to be answering to somebody."

"Well, he's not gonna help us. Why would he? Diego's literally delivering humans to the vamps in silver collars. Not to mention our ancient oath that we're bound to. Vampires and witches do not mix."

His forehead creased. "It's worth a try."

I gave him a flat look. "Since when do we count on others to handle our problems?"

A shudder went through me at the thought of calling on the vampire prince. Fane had a reputation among the higher ranked vampires, but even he was nothing compared to his brother, Prince Ryn, who thankfully was still staked, frozen in his coffin waiting for a release that would never come.

Kohl stood, drawing himself to full height, taller than me, but barely.

"We could hex Diego. Make him mute."

I smirked. "He could use a muzzle."

Kohl smiled. Memories flooded back. He'd been my best friend since forever, knew me better than any of the other witches. Kohl was kind, smart, and cute. Why couldn't I return his feelings? What was wrong with me? I loved him, but not in the way he wanted.

I sighed. "Let's go deal with this alpha first."

He motioned for me to lead the way, his shoulders stiffening. Gone was the casualness and familiarity. His formality returned full force. The professional Kohl was much easier to keep at a distance. I pushed my shoulders back. We all had our roles to play, even here at the end of the world.

4

VALERIA

I couldn't watch anymore. Jen writhed and hissed, her bones contorting and skin reshaping. The poor girl's screams and howls ripped through the night air, silencing all. In the distance, my wolf sensed the fear from the forest animals.

"What can we do? Is there anything we can do?" Drew looked from me to Cruz.

Cruz looked to me.

"Give me that gun back. I'm going to put her out of her misery." Becca held out her hand.

Drew whipped to her, eyes savage. "No, you're not. Back off, Becca."

"She can't survive the change in her condition. It would be better to end this now."

"You're not going to gun her down her like an animal. Like Rub—"

Her hand shot out, the sound of her fist against her brother's face echoed in the tent. He recoiled.

Anguish flashed on Becca's face replaced with rage. "Don't. Don't say her name." Her voice trembled.

I watched, stunned as he held his bleeding nose. Cruz handed him a cloth, and he took it silently.

Becca stormed out of the tent, her dark braid whipping out behind her as she went.

"Are you okay?" I asked Drew.

He didn't meet my eyes. "What do you think?"

I didn't answer. Jen's howls broke out once more, her body thrashing wildly.

"She's right, you know. It would be kinder to stop her suffering."

His gaze snapped to me. "Then you do it. I'm not going to kill her."

My eyebrows shot up. Kill her? The thought made my stomach roll. I didn't want to be the one to do it either, but how could we stand there and do nothing? She'd been given vampire blood to initiate the change and the werewolf bite was already turning her.

I looked to Cruz. "Is there something we can give her? To help ease her into..."

He turned to his shelf and rummaged through the bottles and containers. Jen's snarls turned to sobs, the last part of her humanity being torn from her. The sound struck my every nerve.

Drew flinched and turned away. My throat turned dry. I was so tired of death. So tired of the hopelessness of everything.

What was the point anymore?

"Here. This poison will do it quickly." Cruz handed the dusty bottle to me.

I stared at him. He kept poison in his supply? That was unsettling. I gripped the cool, dark bottle and gave it to Drew. He didn't touch it. There was a lost look in his eyes as he stared at his friend. My heart twisted.

"Can't do it, can you, Drew?" Becca stood at the entrance.

She marched over and swiped the bottle from my hand and thrust it at her brother. Her eyes bore into him and even I trembled under her intensity.

He still didn't move. Jen's sobs grew louder, morphing into blood-curdling screams that made my ears ring and my inner wolf retreat.

Becca unscrewed the bottle and strode toward Jen. She threw her twin a dark look. "Coward."

Tears glistened in his eyes. I looked away, pity filling me. I felt out of place, there as witness to their grief, but I didn't want to leave and offend them.

"Not too much. You only need a small drop in her mouth," Cruz instructed.

Jen continued thrashing against the blankets. Her screams quieted. Blood trickled from her open mouth and her eyes stared unseeingly at the roof of the tent. Bones misshapen and skin stretched too thin, it was hard to look at her. At the broken creature she'd become.

"I'll hold her arms. If you like," Cruz offered.

Becca gave him a curt nod.

Drew and I watched as Cruz pinned her frantic arms to the ground and Becca rushed forward with the poison.

She held it over Jen's mouth and dropped it in. Jen hissed. Becca stepped back, screwing the lid back on and Cruz let go of the girl's arms. We waited as the liquid did its work. A gagging sound escaped her followed by silence. Her body stiffened.

Just like that, she was gone.

A shudder ran through me. No one spoke. I didn't dare look at them for fear of coming face to face with their sorrow. I'd seen more grieving, broken people in the past few months than I'd ever imagined seeing in my entire life.

"I'm sorry."

They didn't respond, but I didn't expect them to. Sorry didn't change anything.

"We'll have to bury her in the woods." Becca's monotone voice sliced through the heavy silence.

I glanced at her. "Not here. Farther from camp."

She was staring at the dead body. How many deaths had she witnessed? This was obviously not the first friend she'd lost.

"Do you need help? I can—"

"No. We will do it ourselves," she cut me off.

Her twin nodded, his brown eyes drowning in misery. My heart ached for him and their suffering. Though it was the Red Wolves who'd killed her I couldn't help but feel partly responsible.

They'd come to me for help. *And you failed them. Just like you failed the others and Elijah.*

I squared my shoulders back and pushed down the wave of regret and self-pity. There was no time for that.

"I can show you to a place where she won't be disturbed."

My eyes flickered to Cruz. He stood silently watching our exchange, though his expressive, blue eyes said it all—I wasn't acting like an alpha.

There were other wolves that could take the humans, but I'd volunteered my personal assistance. Why?

Because you don't trust your pack, my inner wolf scolded.

Shame bloomed in my chest. *I do.*

You don't.

She was right, but I hated the fact that Elijah's abandonment affected me so deeply. Made me question everything. Was he even thinking about our pack? About me?

"Thank you." Drew's words scattered my thoughts.

I turned away from them and waited by the exit, acutely aware of Cruz's eyes on me.

"We will have to do it now. Before the smell attracts other wolves..." I trailed off, face flaming.

"You mean before one of your wolves eats her?" Becca's voice hardened.

I glared at her. "We don't eat people."

Some do, my wolf argued.

"Oh, right. My mistake. You just tear them up and chew on them. That's much better."

Her brother gave her a side glance, a weariness in his eyes.

Did she always have such a sharp edge or did the fall of the world do this to her? The curse changed all of us in some way.

"We wouldn't do that. But there are other packs in the area. Wild animals too."

Her eyes glinted, and though she didn't speak it, I saw the insult written there—*wild animals like you?*

"Thank you." Drew stepped in front of her, his face ragged and dirty.

And handsome despite the sweat and grime. My wolf snarled at my wandering thoughts. Ever loyal to Elijah, she had a fit whenever I noticed any other male.

"Do you want me to accompany you, Alpha?" Cruz's question brought my head around.

His gaze dipped in respect.

"No, that's okay. Thanks, Cruz."

He bit his lip and shook his head as if keeping himself from arguing my decision. I knew he was just looking out for me, but his lack of confidence in my ability made me flush.

Would he question Elijah just as easily?

Dismissing the thought, I walked out of the tent and waited for the others. Jay and Tati were back from checking the perimeter. They looked up at my approach and grew quiet.

Others stood around waiting with them and I could sense

their curiosity and hostility. I squared my shoulders and met their stares.

"Their friend didn't make it. I'm going to take them somewhere deeper in the woods to bury her. When we return, they will be staying with us for the night. Tomorrow, they'll be gone."

Jay and Tati exchanged glances.

I bristled. If it were Elijah, they'd obey without question. They were supposed to be my betas too, but they were loyal to him. Yeah, well he's gone, I wanted to tell them.

It was me they would answer to now.

"I will come with you." Jay broke my thoughts.

A statement, not a request. My inner wolf snarled at his audacity.

"That's not necessary. You will stay here and guard the camp."

"Are you serious?"

My hackles rose at his challenge. I was alpha, and he had no right to question my authority in front of the pack.

I let my wolf rise to the surface. "You will stay here."

He scowled under my glare but fell quiet.

The others murmured as Becca and Drew emerged with their friend's body in tow. It was too late now to cover her and hide the transformation. What would they think when they saw it? I didn't have answers for her injuries, and I really didn't want their questions.

Jay saw her first. "She was in the middle of turning." His eyes shot to me. "Who did this?"

My back stiffened. "Diego."

He frowned. "Are you sure? Are you sure it wasn't another alpha?"

Fire sparked inside me. "Yes."

I didn't really know, but I was done with his questions. It

was the Red Wolves they'd been running from, so it was hardly a leap to suspect Diego. Only alphas had the ability to turn someone.

"I want everyone rotating watch tonight. If anyone approaches, turn them away."

Jay's eyebrow arched. "What if it's Diego?"

All eyes turned to us. I hated that part of being alpha. Always being put on the spot and responsible for everyone's wellbeing, but never appreciated for what I did.

"Then tell him to wait for me, and send someone to warn me."

Gazes darted and lips curled. They didn't like my orders. I straightened to full height and ignored the piercing stares. It was too late to change my mind now. Worry gnawed at me and my inner wolf echoed the pack's concerns.

Why help the humans? What about our wolves?

"What do you want us to tell him about the humans if he asks?" Jay asked.

"Tell him I'm taking care of them."

The twins whipped toward me, eyes wide.

"It's just to throw him off your trail." I offered them a weak smile for reassurance.

Drew nodded, but his sister only continued glaring at the gun in my hand.

Watch her, my wolf warned.

Oh, I would. I would make sure neither of the humans were a threat to my wolves before I led them back to camp.

A bird called from the distance. The thick summer humidity clung to the trees and underbrush. Jaime would have been thirteen next month, I realized. A lump grew in my throat. He'd been so ready to leave middle school and start high school, wishing he could skip ahead and now...

I pushed the memories away. It did no good to live in the

past. We couldn't change anything, and grief was like an anchor, once you let it take hold, you'd find yourself sinking deeper and deeper, stuck in the sorrow.

"How far are we walking?" Drew interrupted.

I glanced back at him. "Not too far. It's a sacred place. No one will disturb her there."

Becca frowned. "Not where you bury your dead is it?"

Her twin shot her a look that said, shut up.

My lips twisted at her barely veiled disgust. She didn't realize we would never dishonor our pack by letting an outsider lie side by side with us in death.

"No."

It was a place the witches had used for their mysterious rituals. Strange things happened there, and we were smart enough to steer clear of the place for the most part. My inner wolf didn't like the unnaturalness of it. Her nervousness filled me.

We made it to a clearing where the forest was silent. All the animals skirted the place; my wolf sensed their fear.

"What is this place?" Becca asked.

Her voice held suspicion. She stood next to her twin, body tensed and alert. Drew scanned the tree line with a frown of his own.

Their responses surprised me. It wasn't every human that could sense the magic of the place. I watched their wary faces and wondered what it was they felt.

For me, it was a strange sense of being watched and judged. As if the forest itself had come to life and was weighing my worthiness of being there. There was a strangeness in the air that spoke of something ancient and otherworldly. What it was, I didn't know. The witches never came anymore, and they were the only ones who knew its secrets.

"Are you sure this place is safe?" Drew asked, still glancing around as if he expected an ambush.

"I'm sure. You can bury her here."

"Too bad we only have one shovel. This is going to take all night," Becca grumbled.

Drew frowned at her. "I'll do it."

He looked around for a place to set Jen's body. I helped him move her toward the center. We set her in the grass and backed away.

Becca handed him the shovel and folded her arms across her chest. "We can take turns digging."

Her twin didn't respond but started digging a hole next to the girl's body.

"Why here?" Becca's words startled me.

I glanced at her. "You asked for a safe place."

The moonlight trickled in from the treetops, casting shadows across Becca's face. Her eyes narrowed at me and her lips pinched together. I fought the urge to shudder under her hostility. Images of the angry faces and deadly violence in the city flashed in my mind. We'd barely made it out without losing more of our pack to the human mobs. Were Drew and his sister there too? Among the mobs?

When Elijah insisted he return to Savannah to find the witch who'd killed his sister, I'd been terrified for him. How could he expect to make it alone? Though I understood his thirst for justice, I could never forgive him for choosing it over his pack. Over us.

The heavy thud of the shovel brought me back to the present. I turned to see Drew shoveling another load of dirt.

A warm breeze rippled through the tree branches, the sound sharp and ominous.

My senses were on alert. That feeling of being watched made my wolf shrink back. An enemy we couldn't see was twice as frightening as any other beast.

"What was that?" Drew paused.

He stood straight, squinting into the forest.

"I don't think we should be digging here," Becca murmured.

"Others have done it. Buried their dead here."

She whipped toward me. "Who? Other humans?"

"Witches."

Her eyes widened.

"But your friend isn't human anymore anyway."

A scowl lit her face, making me regret my words. Did the magic of the place not like us burying Jen there?

My hand gripped the gun. Even my wolf was unsure of what was watching us, though she knew it was a threat.

We were in danger.

"Something's not right. We should leave," Becca insisted, motioning her brother to stop his digging.

He stopped. Silence stretched between us. Even the animals had stopped chattering in the distance. My wolf's hackles rose, and her warning rang clear in my mind.

Run.

5

MCKENZIE

The wolf stood by the sofa as we entered. My five best witches blocked the door but dispersed when I approached.

A strong scent of iron—blood—mixed with the burning candles, filled the room. In the glow of the open flames, the werewolf looked fierce. His dark eyes tracked my movement and my magic let me sense his inner wolf rising to the surface.

They were both hungry for violence.

My chin lifted. Well, if they wanted a fight, I'd show them just what I could do. Magic swept through me, sharp and hot. I bit my lip to keep myself from hissing at the pain. As quickly as the sharpness came, it left, settling into the warm energy I was used to.

Kohl straightened beside me and I could feel the magic building around him as well. He nodded at me. Silent assurance that whatever I chose to do about the wolf, he was on my side.

It felt good to have his support.

"Elijah, right? What pack are you from? Shadow Pack?"

He didn't respond.

Kohl raised a hand toward him. "Answer her." His voice was steel.

I grabbed Kohl's forearm and lowered it. He glanced at me, lips thinning.

His loyalty was admirable, but I didn't need his help. The last thing I wanted was for the alpha to let his wolf loose on my best witches. We couldn't afford to lose any more of our strongest casters. That, and I didn't want to have to kill the wolf.

I didn't need his pack coming for us, or another reason for Diego to stir trouble.

"You spelled me." The deep timber of his voice was startling.

Gold-flecked, brown eyes turned silvery blue—his wolf surfacing.

"Your body needed rest and time to recover. You're welcome."

His lip curled. Despite his obvious disgust for me and his nasty attitude, I couldn't help but find him attractive. Tall, dark, and brooding fit him to a T.

"I'm fine now. Release me."

Kohl strode forward, hand raised once more. "Watch your tone, wolf."

The alpha turned to him with a cold smile. "Or what? You're going to cast another sleeping spell?"

I shook my head. Clearly, this wasn't going well and as much as I wanted him gone, I wanted some answers first.

"What are you doing in the city? Where is your pack? The woods?"

He scoffed. "Am I under arrest or something? I don't have to answer to you. You are not my queen."

Kohl's eyes turned murderous. I held up a hand to him, a silent warning to stay back.

I could deal with the wolf.

"This is still my city, and we can make you talk, but trust me, you won't like the way we do it."

He scoffed.

"I'm not letting you go until you tell me what you were doing with Diego."

He fixed me with a chilly gaze. "Isn't it obvious he was about to kill me? I'm not with anyone. I came to find the witch that killed my sister."

My breath hitched at his words. "Who? Who was it?"

"I don't know, but I'm here to find out."

His confession rattled me. A witch killing a werewolf? Why?

"You don't know who it was, but you assume it was one of my witches?"

"I was looking for clues when Diego caught me. You don't own the city. I have a right to be here."

I snorted. "Correction, I actually do own the city. That's kind of what being queen means."

His eyebrow arched. "Seems like Diego is the one running the show."

Irritation spread through me. Is that what everyone was saying now? I was tempted to let my magic loose. Show the wolf what I could actually do, but I refrained.

"I could kill him with a wave of my hand."

The wolf's lips pulled back in a tight smile. "Then why don't you?"

What? Where were these questions even going? My head ached. I was supposed to be the one making him squirm.

"Been kind of busy trying to you know, stop the curse and save the world."

His eyes danced across the room. Trying to calculate a plan of escape? My magic thrummed.

Not gonna happen, buddy.

"Right. And kill innocent wolves while you're at it. Some queen." His gaze shot back to me.

I stiffened. "I didn't kill anyone."

"You haven't made any effort to stop the killing."

Anger curled inside me. Who the hell did he think he was talking to me like that? I literally just saved his life. My hand itched to wipe the stubborn scowl off his face.

Kohl inched forward, the magic stirring in the air around him. I didn't need to look at him to see the outrage I was sure was there.

"You're responsible for everyone your coven has killed. You're responsible for my sister's death," the werewolf insisted.

"We had nothing to do with that."

"A witch killed her. Burned her alive while she was injured in her wolf form."

"Why would we do that?"

His eyes narrowed. "That's what I want to know. Give me the witch who's responsible and I'll leave."

Weariness filled me. There was no talking to him. He was hell bent on blaming us.

"There are rogue witches all over Savannah. It could have been one of them. I'm not going to just hand over one of my innocent witches to you."

A harsh laugh escaped him. "Innocent? There are no innocent witches."

"I'm sorry for what happened to your sister. Truly, I am, but what did you think was going to happen when you came to the city? That you could just go on a witch killing rampage and I would just look the other way?"

He didn't respond.

I sighed. The conversation was going nowhere, and I had other things to do. Still, I couldn't let him wander Savannah and murder my coven.

"Leave the city. Go back to your pack."

His chin lifted, dark eyes piercing through me. "No."

Kohl flexed his hands. His gaze slid to me.

I shook my head. "Then I can't let you leave this coven."

The wolf scoffed. "So, what, I'm your prisoner now?"

"If you won't drop your vendetta, then yeah. You're my prisoner. Kohl will show you to your room."

Kohl stepped forward. The others moved with him, hands raised as magic bounced in the air between them.

The wolf tensed, eyes going completely silver. His skin stretched and bones snapped.

Shit.

Throwing a spell together as quickly as I could, I shot my magic at him. It struck him in the chest as his wolf began to emerge. The force of my power sent him flying back. He crashed against the couch, body returning to human.

Kohl met my eyes. "I could have gotten him."

"I'm faster."

A smile flickered on his face before disappearing. The other witches waited for my order.

"Take him to the room."

They hurried to obey, eyes widening on the boy as his body continued to convulse. He slumped over.

I turned to Kohl. "I want a guard posted outside his door. He doesn't leave the room without my approval. Be careful with that one. He's dangerous."

Kohl nodded. "I'll take care of it, My Queen."

With that, he led the others down the hall.

I sighed and rubbed my aching head. Looks like I would need another tea to replenish the energy I'd lost. Biting back a groan, I headed downstairs to find Cherise, our best healer.

After an hour or so of tossing and turning, I finally drifted to sleep. Then, a knock sounded on my door, pulling me from my slumber.

I groaned. "What now?"

"We have a visitor. He's trying to come in," came a small, delicate voice.

A visitor? Where was Kohl?

Throwing off the covers, I shot up. "Who? Diego?"

Anger built inside me. That wolf was officially starting to piss me off.

"No, Queen. It's Prince Fane. He won't leave."

Fane? The vampire prince? What the hell was he doing breaking the agreement? They weren't supposed to be anywhere near the coven.

"Ugh. Tell him I'm coming."

Her footsteps retreated as I got myself dressed and wiped the sleep dust from my eyes. A million questions raced in my mind. What did the prince want? Why was he here?

For the most part, the vampires kept to themselves except for the few that strolled the city, preying on humans. Our ancient covenant with the vampire royals kept them from attacking my witches. They were supposed to stay in their territory, in the north of the city. Ever since Prince Ryn's punishment they'd left us alone. So why was Fane here now?

Shoving down my weariness, I downed the dregs of my tea and headed for the door. *You better have a good reason for waking me up, vamp.*

Only a few candles were lit in the entry room and the fire was starting to dwindle in the fireplace. The witches attempt to save our resources on both candles and magic. Though my power was weakened from my confrontation with Diego, I couldn't very well face the vampire prince in the pitch black.

I needed to see him at all times.

Summoning my magic, I winced as the pain flashed through me and settled. I flicked my wrist at the dead lightbulb overhead. It flickered on, bathing the room in a warm glow. The magic wouldn't last long, but I didn't intend to entertain the vampire all night.

"Queen McKenzie." Kohl's voice echoed in the room.

He and the two other witches on watch turned and bowed to me. My eyes met my best friend's. His lips pursed in disapproval, but he didn't say anything. I bit back a smile. Kohl. He was more upset about me losing sleep than I was.

"What is it? What does he want?" I asked Kohl.

A very loud harrumph sounded on the other side of the door. "I can hear you in there."

The cultured drawl reminded me of the old south and was startling coming from the youthful looking vampire I remembered. His wasn't a face I'd seen much, but one I'd never forget.

"He says he needs to talk to you. That it's urgent," Kohl answered.

I stepped closer to the door. "You're breaking our agreement. You shouldn't be here. What do you want, Fane?"

"Prince Fane. And I'm not talking to the door. Invite me in. *Please.*"

The hairs on my neck bristled. There was something in his voice that triggered my flight or fight instinct and right now that voice was telling me to kick that vamp to the curb.

"Come back in the morning."

"Now, now, Queen McKenzie, is that any way to treat a fellow royal? You know I like to get my rest in the daylight."

I could hear the smirk in his voice. My face heated with irritation. It wasn't like he couldn't come out in the sun, but it did weaken them, made them slower.

Kohl shook his head at me. "I don't trust him, Queen."

A snicker sounded. "Are you that frightened of one vampire? I'm flattered."

I sighed. "Just let him in. Make it quick, Fane. Unlike you, we sleep at night. Like normal people."

The door opened and my witches stepped back, our magic thrumming in the room. I moved to the couch and sank onto the cushion. My heart pounded as I watched the vampire waltz in.

He was tall and slender, looking every bit the prince he was. Raven hair fell to his shoulders and framed his pale, heart-shaped face. The contrast was striking, but not as striking as his ice-blue eyes. His lips quirked into a knowing smile that made me flush with annoyance.

Walking toward me, he completely ignored my witches. His long legs were encased in black denim and moved much too gracefully to be natural. My eyes snagged on his opened, black, button down that revealed way more of his toned chest than I cared to see. I snapped my gaze back to his face.

A small smile played on sensual lips and he arched a dark elegant brow.

I sat up straighter, refusing to let him have the upper hand.

"Aren't you going to offer me a seat? Or a glass of—"

"We don't serve blood here," Kohl cut him off. He came to my side, shoulders stiff.

Annoyance flickered on Fane's face, but he didn't respond to my friend. Instead, he stood above me, holding me captive with his beautiful, cold eyes.

"Wine is what I was going to say. I prefer red," he drawled.

I gave him a flat look. "Sit down, Fane."

"You didn't say prince."

Heat crept up my neck. He was getting on my last nerve.

His eyebrows continued to arch in challenge. It was way too late in the night to be playing games with me. Before I thought better of it, my hand lashed out and I used my magic to pull him to the chair in front of me.

He landed hard, his eyes widened in surprise. That made me smile. The two witches stood behind him and Kohl moved closer, towering over me.

A low rumble sounded from Fane. Laughing? Was he laughing? Anger flared in my belly.

"They said you were a feisty queen, but no one told me how alluring you were." His gaze roamed over me, making me bristle.

Heat flooded me as he undressed me with his eyes. I immediately regretted the thin tank top and skirt I'd thrown on.

Kohl stepped forward, but I was faster. I let my magic shoot forth once more, pushing Fane and his chair back. The wood scraped along the carpet a few inches.

Pain sliced through me. I really needed to stop with the magic.

Lifting my chin, I met his gaze. "What do you want, Fane?"

Clearing his throat and straightening his shirt, he smirked at me. "Remind me never to compliment you again."

I shot to my feet, patience evaporating. "You have one second to tell me what the hell you want or I'm kicking you out."

He scoffed. "One second? That's hardly reasonable."

Glaring at him, I turned to walk away.

"Leaving so soon? But then you won't get to hear what I have to say and trust me, you want to hear what I have to say."

"Doubtful."

"It's about the barrier," he spoke in singsong.

The barrier? What the hell did he know about it?

I heard him rise, his clothes rustling, but I didn't turn back to him.

"Ahh. I thought that might interest you, but obviously this is a bad time. I'll show myself out."

The smugness in his voice made me want to unleash more magic at him, consequences be damned. But I refrained.

"No." I slowly turned around.

He was still standing there, having the audacity to look amused.

"No?" he repeated, cocking his head.

My eyes narrowed. "Tell me what you know, and then we'll let you go."

A deep rumble of laughter erupted from him and I fought the urge to strike him with my magic again.

"Stop wasting our time," Kohl interjected.

I glanced at him in surprise. The mask of coolness had slipped. That was a sure sign of the vampire's ability to annoy that even Kohl—the most self-controlled person I knew—lost it with him.

Unfazed, Fane sauntered closer to me and smiled. Who did he think he was? I'd seen him maybe twice in my whole life and had never officially met face to face, but he acted as if we were close friends.

"My brother requests your audience."

The witches behind him gasped. Kohl scowled. I blinked at Fane, stunned. Prince Ryn was awake? How? When?

A sliver of fear crept up my spine. I'd heard the rumors of the heartless vampire—all the things he'd done before he was staked and frozen as punishment for turning one of our witches.

Ryn was their next king, and I'd hoped the curse meant he'd stay in his coffin forever or be taken along with the other vampires who'd been over nineteen when turned.

Fighting off the nerves, I frowned at Fane. "You woke him? He was supposed to be staked for two more years."

"I didn't wake him. I don't know who did, but he's up. And he wants you."

An icy rush of fear filled me. Beside me, Kohl tensed, an actual growl escaping him.

"Me? What for?"

He smiled. "He has a proposition for you. Innocent, I swear. Unless... you're into something more—"

"I'm not."

Fane shrugged. "It's something about the barrier."

My eyes narrowed. "What does your brother know about the barrier?"

I didn't have time for his games, and I definitely didn't have time to seek out the deadliest vampire in Savannah. What he asked would break our ancient agreement. It had to be a trick.

"Well, that's something you'll have to ask my dear brother. He doesn't tell me all his... secrets." Fane smiled.

His fangs protruded, making my heart race. I shoved down the panic threatening to rise. We were in our coven, we had magic. We were safe. The light above died without warning, submerging us in darkness.

Crap.

6

———

VALERIA

*R*un. My wolf screamed inside me.

But it was too late. A powerful force rolled through the clearing, making me stumble back.

"What the?" Drew's voice broke out over the whipping wind.

"Leave the body," I shouted.

His head snapped to me. "What?"

I motioned for them to follow. "We have to get out of here. Just leave the body."

"No. I can't just leave her out here."

Becca glared at me. "You said this was safe."

"I was wrong."

Without waiting to see if they followed me, I ran for the trees. My inner wolf was filled with terror, and that chilled me. There were few things that scared her that bad.

What was happening in the forest?

All around us, the birds sprang from the branches, taking to the sky with a sharp cry. In the distance, animals yipped, squeaked, and scurried away. The leaves whipped in a frenzy, pulled by some invisible force.

Drew and Becca ran toward me. The body was nowhere to be seen.

I paused. Would it stop now?

"What was that?" Becca demanded before she'd even caught up.

Drew's eyes were still wide in fear. He didn't speak.

"I don't know."

"You don't know? Isn't this your territory? How do you not know there's a freaking... whatever that thing is?"

Becca's words made me growl. I didn't need her to point out my shortcomings. We were there for her. To help her.

"Shut up. Listen." Drew held a finger to his mouth.

My wolf stilled within me. There was a strange wail and snapping of bones. What the—?

A howl echoed from the clearing. I tensed. How? No one was there... I would have sensed them. The only thing left behind was the human and she couldn't have made the sound.

"Is that... Jen? Becca's words echoed my thoughts.

I shook my head. Impossible.

Another howl ripped through the sky and the unmistakable sound of footsteps pounded toward us. It was too late to run. I called my wolf forward and sprang into action.

My body shifted. Pain flared hot as I turned.

Alarm came from the others, but they weren't the threat. My senses heightened in wolf form, I watched the edge of the trees.

Something was coming. Something unnatural. Unwanted.

I would kill it.

A half wolf, half vampire appeared, still wearing the skin of the dead human. I snarled.

It spotted us and sped toward us at an incredible speed.

Large fangs jutted from its mouth, and fur lined its once fleshy skin.

Not even proper wolf, it couldn't shift fully.

My claws sunk into the earth, ready to spring. Wild, yellow eyes met mine.

It dove.

My teeth sank into its neck, breaking through skin. A sour taste filled my mouth making me release it.

Wrong. All wrong. I heaved.

It thrashed, blood gushing from its neck. Snarling and hissing, it came for me again. I leapt out of reach. My tail swished. Eyes focused on the monster, I watched and waited for her to attack again.

Before it got the chance, a gun fired. The sound shattered around me, piercing my ears. A bullet struck the hybrid right in the chest. She stumbled back with the force and let out a piercing howl. Another bullet followed the first, and then another.

Ringing filled my ears and the ground spun around me.

She fell to the earth. I padded closer to inspect it. A ghastly scent enveloped her, making me skitter back.

Blood. Death.

It's over. You can retreat, my human commanded.

With a final howl of victory, I did just that.

Coldness swept over me as I shifted back to my human form. My body trembled as I pieced together what happened. The taste of rancid meat and blood filled my mouth, making my stomach roll. I was going to need a lot of toothpaste to get that taste out.

"Here. Your clothes." Becca's voice snapped me to attention.

Heat spread through me as I grabbed them from her and held them up to my naked body. I didn't have time to undress before shifting so the fabric was torn. Holding up my shirt like a towel, I glanced around. I'd have to hold it together with my hand until I could change.

"Take my shirt," Drew said.

His eyes averted, he handed me the T-shirt from his back. I turned my back to them and pulled it over my head. The smell of his sweat and soap washed over me making me flush. It was still warm from his body. He wasn't much taller than me, so the hem barely covered my ass. With my wolves, it didn't matter. We were used to seeing each other in the bare flesh, but standing with the humans I couldn't help but redden with embarrassment.

Ignoring my mortification, I went to stand with the others and looked at the dead body. Becca's shots had made their mark. Chills crawled up my spine. Silver bullets. That was twice now she had to kill her poor friend—twice in one night.

Sorrow bloomed in my chest. What kind of future would the poor girl have had if things had been different?

"So, are you going to explain what the hell happened here?" Becca's hard voice caught my ear.

I turned to her. "I can't. I don't... this shouldn't be possible."

"Maybe the poison didn't work," Drew offered.

My eyes dipped to his bare chest, the sight startling. He was much broader than he looked with a shirt on.

My wolf growled inside me. *Not our mate.*

I whipped back to the dead body, trying to hide my furious blush. Had he seen me looking?

Becca glared at me. She'd noticed.

Holding my head up, I turned to them. "We should head back to camp."

Branches snapped in the distance, the noise alerting my wolf. Someone was coming. I motioned for the twins to get behind me and stay quiet.

Jay. What was he doing there? His eyes widened when he saw me. My face flamed, but I met his stare. Thoughts tumbled in my mind. Yeah, I'm wearing the human's shirt. So, what?

"What happened?" His words came harshly.

My eyes narrowed on him. "I told you to stand guard."

"Luke is on duty now." He stared at me. There was no hint of repentance for disobeying my order. My wolf snarled. *Unacceptable.*

I shoved him hard against a tree, letting my inner wolf lash out. The sound of his back slamming against bark echoed around us. He didn't fight back, but I didn't like the hard look in his eyes. Silver replaced brown.

My lips parted in a predatory smile. "Do it. Shift. See what happens."

He stiffened underneath my hold, his eyes returning to their mocha brown.

I released his shirt. "Go back to camp."

His eyes darted from me to the others as he straightened. I could tell there was something he wanted to say, but he didn't dare speak it now.

With a quick nod, he was off. I watched his broad frame disappear back toward camp. I felt the eyes of the humans on me and turned to face them.

"What do we do with... where should we bury her?" Drew's voice broke the silence.

I glanced at the poor girl and shook my head. "Just bury her here."

"Are we really going to pretend like this didn't just happen?" Becca frowned at me.

Her twin stopped, shovel in mid-air. "Which part?"

She grunted. "How about where Jen came back to life and tried to kill us?"

He continued his work, muscles on full display as he swung. I averted my gaze and looked to Becca.

"The poison must not have been effective."

Her lips thinned. "She was dead. I helped carry her out here. There's no way she—"

"What do *you* think happened, Becca?" her brother cut her off.

Pausing, he stared at her, one eyebrow arched.

"I don't know what happened in the clearing, but something did. I felt it. Something was off. And Jen... there's something about that place. You said witches were buried there?"

I nodded.

"Maybe there's dormant magic then too? Something that could—"

"What? Resurrect a body?" Drew scoffed.

My heart skipped. It couldn't be that. It had to be the poison. If there was something powerful left behind wouldn't it have resurrected the witches there too? Why Jen? Why now?

Drew frowned at me. "What do you think?"

I shrugged. "I don't know. I'm not a witch."

Questions filled my mind. Was it because she had been in the middle of her transformation? Or was it the poison? Maybe it didn't actually kill her to begin with?

None of it made sense. Tomorrow. Tomorrow, I could deal with it. I was too tired now. My body, though it hadn't been present during the fight, felt bruised and broken.

The aftereffects of the change.

I sighed, wishing I could sink into a hot bath. Or curl up in a real bed.

Elijah, what would you do? I dismissed the thought, hating that I was missing him. What could he have done differently, anyway?

I helped Drew finish digging the grave and waited as they

placed her monstrous body in it. A shudder ran down my spine as she disappeared under the dark earth. Hopefully for good.

Watching as they said their final goodbyes, I tried to block out the memories of those I'd lost. Silently, they followed me through the woods, their grief a heavy blanket around them. Guilt racked me though I hadn't delivered the killing blow.

Another life lost. When would things get better? Would the world ever be safe again?

Back at camp, I changed into my own clothes. Worry gnawed at me as I replayed the events over and over in my mind. I couldn't have any of my wolves wandering in that part of the forest. As late as it was, I was going to have to call everyone together to warn them.

There would be questions.

Questions I didn't have answers to, and I didn't want to give the others any more reason to lose confidence in me.

And what about the humans?

I turned over my wolf's question. What did I do with them? Send them back to the city in the morning was the best option, but Drew's request to return with his pack made me nervous. We couldn't let them stay with us.

Dismissing the thoughts, I hurried out of my tent and went to find Jay and Tati to call everyone together.

Drew and Becca found me first. My eyebrows raised as they made their way toward me. Why weren't they in the spare tent I'd given them?

I waited for them to catch up. Irritation prickled at me. What did they want now?

Becca stood, stone faced while her brother offered me a tentative smile, that made my annoyance turn to guilt. They weren't like the other humans in the city who'd hunted us. His kindness was genuine. I was sure of it.

You are too trusting, my wolf warned.

I ignored her.

Drew cleared his throat. "Valeria, we wanted to talk to you."

"Can it wait until morning?"

He glanced at his twin and back to me. "Well, I was hoping to discuss it tonight."

I scanned the camp for my betas. Were they on patrol again? Where were they? I didn't see their faces among the various pack members gathering around the fire and shooting curious looks our way.

My lips pursed at the fire. Was it a good idea to let it burn tonight with the possible dangers we'd just found? Or was everything back to normal now that Jen was buried?

"Valeria?" Drew's voice tugged at me.

I turned to face him. "Just tell me then. I need to gather my wolves together."

He gaped at my brusqueness but quickly recovered. "There's talk of a union between all of us who are against Diego. We're trying to get something established. An alliance. Before we left, our leader Ben, was going to present it to the queen. Get the witches on board too."

I blinked at him. "An alliance?"

Drew nodded. "To restore some order. Stop all the fighting and killing."

"And how would this alliance do that?"

Determination lit in his eyes. "It would show the Red Wolves we have the upper hand. There would be consequences for breaking the allegiance. We could set things back to normal, or as normal as they can be."

"You mean with the humans in control again?"

He cringed. "No. We would all have a say. A vote."

I laughed. "What like a democracy?"

His eyes narrowed. "Why not? It worked before."

I rubbed my head with my palm. "Yeah but we had laws

then. And police, judges, and jail. How are we going to keep order?"

"The same way as before. With force."

My gaze flickered to his twin, who remained silent, face devoid of emotion. Was this some kind of trick? Or did he mean to make my pack this 'force' he was talking about?

"And who would make all the rules this time?"

"We all would. We all would be equals."

It sounded nice, it really did, but it wasn't that simple. There was no way Diego, or any werewolves for that matter, would agree to take orders from a human. It was too late to salvage what was left of equality or civility.

This was the end of the world. Everyone for themselves.

"Yeah. Good luck with that."

Drew scowled at me. "Do you want things to get worse? Because that's what's going to happen. No one is going to be safe."

I frowned.

"Even here, you won't be safe for long if the wolves start spreading. Or the vampires."

I shrugged off his warning and stared out at the woods. We would have to double our patrol. Make sure no one strayed too far from camp.

"Don't you care what happens to your pack?"

My back stiffened at his accusing tone. Inside, my wolf was ready to leap on him.

"I'm trying to help you." His voice rose with desperation.

A snort escaped me. "Help me? I can take care of my pack without your help."

"Not for long," he insisted.

Anger curled inside me. Who did he think he was to judge my leadership? I was just as good of an alpha as Elijah. Better, even. I never left the pack.

I couldn't. They needed me.

And you need them.

Dismissing my wolf's words, I walked away.

Drew started to follow me. I sighed. Why couldn't he just go and leave me alone? Becca stopped him with an outstretched arm and a shake of her head.

"Please, Valeria. You have to listen. It's not safe," he called after me.

Several of the wolves glanced up from their spots. His words stirred looks of suspicion and curiosity. There would be more of that when I gathered them together to tell them what happened. Doubt prickled at me. Was that a bad move? Was keeping it a secret from my pack the right thing to do to keep them from worrying? I honestly didn't know and not for the first time, I wished Elijah were there to make all the hard decisions again.

Just be the alpha they need.

I snorted at my wolf's message. How? How was I supposed to do that? Sighing, I pushed away the thoughts and went to find Jay and Tati. I'd have to at least tell them and hope they didn't have a million questions for me. Or any arguments.

7
___

MCKENZIE

Kohl was first to light the candles. The flames flickered as Fane moved about the room. I exchanged a look with my best friend. Vampires were fast—especially royals. I didn't like not being able to watch him and it had nothing—absolutely nothing—to do with his looks, as intriguing as they were.

"I'd love to stay and swap pleasantries, but the night is short, and my brother doesn't like to be kept waiting. I'm sure you've heard the juicy gossip about him and his temper."

My stomach churned. I had. The prince of darkness, they called him. Heartless heir. I pushed down the memories of my sister's anger at what he'd done to her best friend. And the humans he'd drained...

Before I could respond, Fane swept out of the room, the air whooshing at his movement. It wasn't until the front door opened and slammed shut that I registered his leaving.

I glanced at Kohl. His face held the same grimness I felt. The other witches, Blake and Alex, gaped at the spot where the vampire had been.

Weariness filled me. "Well that was... weird."

Kohl grunted. "Suspicious. What would the vampire know about disabling a magical barrier?"

His eyes were narrowed in calculation. I shook my head and stifled a yawn. My head was pounding, and my body too weak to figure out the prince's dastardly plans. That would have to wait until the morning.

"I don't know. But I'm going back to bed. Can you—"

"Reset the wards? Yes, My Queen," he answered immediately.

Worry lines creased his forehead as he watched me. I gave him a grateful smile and said goodnight to the other two witches. My legs felt like lead as I climbed the stairs back to my room. Whatever few hours I had left of the night, I hoped I could actually sleep. Tomorrow I would need all the energy I could get.

Morning came way too quickly, but after two cups of Cherise's miracle tea, I felt ready to take on the day. First thing was to talk to the werewolf. Holding him in my coven was a risk I'd rather avoid. We definitely didn't need him freaking out and trying to escape captivity, but I couldn't bring myself to hurt him or waste magic for a hex.

Scarfing down breakfast in my room, I got dressed and readied myself for another interrogation. Kohl met me outside the wolf's guarded room.

His eyes searched my face, worry written in his features. I gave him a bright smile that he returned.

"You ready to deal with him?" I nodded toward the door.

There was nothing but silence coming from the other side, but I was one hundred percent sure the alpha could hear us.

Kohl grunted. "Of course. Would you like me to handle this? You could get some more rest."

I rolled my eyes. "I'm fine, Kohl. Let's do this."

He sighed and knocked to announce our presence. "Open the door." His tone turned serious.

Only silence returned.

I frowned. So that's how it was going to be, huh?

Kohl looked to me, expectantly.

"Go ahead." I motioned him to continue.

He threw up a hand and unleashed some magic. The door burst open. Kohl walked in first and waved me in.

The smell of sweat and pine assaulted my nose as I strode forward. Without air conditioning, the rooms grew stuffy in the summer heat.

I stopped in my tracks. He sat on the edge of the bed, shirtless with only his scruffy looking jeans. Scratches covered his naked, muscular chest, but the injuries were already healing.

Kohl glared at him. "Where's your shirt? Put it on."

The alpha stared back at him. "I was about to do just that when you two barged in here."

His eyes flicked to me. I glanced away, spotting his T-shirt rumpled on the floor.

He took his time standing and retrieving it. Kohl huffed beside me as we waited for him to dress.

"Did you sleep well, Elijah?" I asked pleasantly.

He shot me a flat look.

I sighed. Clearly, this interrogation was going to go as well as the last one. *How effin-tastic.*

I pointed at the untouched breakfast on the side table. "You don't like eggs?"

A tight smile spread on his face. "What makes you think I'd eat anything given to me by a witch?"

Kohl stiffened. I touched his wrist lightly, a subtle order to stand down.

"It's not poison, if that's what you're worried about." I returned his cold smile.

"Are you going to give up the witch who killed my sister?"

I blinked at him. "What? Like I told you already, none of my witches are responsible."

He scoffed.

Biting back a groan, I tried to come up with some kind of solution. I wanted him gone, but I didn't want him loose in the city. What was I going to do with him?

"What happened to your pack?"

He just stared back at me, dark eyes burning with anger.

"You don't want to talk, fine. Drop this vendetta against my coven and you're free to go."

"I want the witch who killed my sister."

I gaped at him. Is that what all this was about? Revenge?

"How do you know it was anyone from my coven?"

His teeth flashed. "It happened here in the city."

"There are rogue witches all over Savannah."

"Aren't you responsible for them as well? Are you or are you not the witch queen?"

My lip curled at his accusation. "I don't know who killed your sister, but I'm sorry."

A storm raged on his face. "Sorry? No. That's not good enough."

"What do you want from me? What did you think you would happen if you came here?"

"I want justice."

My eyes narrowed. "You mean you want revenge."

"A life for a life."

"I'm not going to hand over one of my witches to satisfy your anger. If you know the witch who is responsible for this, I can set up a trial. We—"

"No. No trial. I want them dead."

"I'm not going to sentence anyone to death without hearing the whole story."

His face darkened. "You'll protect the guilty?"

Irritation flared hot. We were going around in the same circle. So pointless.

"We could hex him. Make it so he can't kill a witch. Or if he does, he's cursed," Kohl cut in.

I frowned. "I don't know..."

"We can't keep him here forever."

Kohl was right, but I didn't like it. There were other uses for our magic, and I hated to waste it on him.

The wolf's eyes flashed to silver. "I'm already cursed, remember? We all are thanks to you and your fu—"

A blast of magic shot around him, grabbing him by the throat. I watched, stunned as Kohl held him in the air. His arms and legs flailed, but his face remained murderous.

Almost as murderous as Kohl's.

I spun to my friend. "Release him."

His jaw clenched, but he obeyed. The werewolf fell to the ground in a gasping heap. A snarl followed and the unmistakable crack of bones.

Not again.

I threw my arms up and blocked him as he shifted and leapt for us. Rage, hot and burning, radiated from the wolf and if it weren't for the invisible barrier I'd cast, he'd be tearing out our throats.

"Yeah, this isn't working. We're going to go. Maybe when you've calmed down, we can reach a better agreement," I shouted over his growls and snapping jaws.

I motioned Kohl out and pulled the door closed before letting my barrier fall. Kohl locked it. Inhuman snarls echoed and the wood trembled as the wolf rammed it over and over.

"Well, that went... about as well as we could have hoped." I sighed.

"We should hex him." Kohl frowned.

My eyebrow arched at him. "We don't have unlimited resources for that, Kohl. Who knows if our magic will run out? Besides, he's not worth it."

"It hasn't run out so far."

I glanced around the hall to make sure we were alone. "True, but it could happen and then..." My words died on my lips.

There was really no telling what would come next if we lost magic. We'd be as helpless as the humans. But none of that mattered if the curse remained, anyway.

"I think I need another tea." I blew out my breath.

Kohl nodded. "I'll tell Cherise."

My eyes burned as I poured over the ancient books. Despite my tea, my head continued to pound, and I'd only attempted one spell. My warning to Kohl replayed in my mind. We couldn't afford to keep using permanent spells. Casting for short term things was easy and didn't take much, even the weakest witch could do those types of spells. But the ones that were longer term like hexes or curses, those required a lot of juice.

I stood from my desk and stretched my arms above my head. Pain spread through my limbs. I needed a break. The meeting with Fane kept flashing to the forefront of my thoughts. His chilling eyes and beautiful face. Gorgeous until he opened his foul mouth.

Prince Ryn was awake. I didn't like knowing he was up and about, doing who knew what. What did he know about the barriers? Could it possibly be true? If there was a way to break through and escape Savannah... then what?

Maybe I could find other witches. Powerful ones that could help me break the curse. The thought alone brought tears to my eyes. It could be the answer to everything.

But what if he lied? From our brief encounter, I suspected it was more of a trap than a solution. Breaking our oath to meet with the vampire prince? Yeah, I wasn't that desperate... yet. The agreement was there for a reason. I couldn't put my coven at risk.

A knock on my door startled me out of my thoughts.

"Come in."

Kohl entered with a grim look.

I sighed. "What now?"

He walked in and handed me a small, red envelope.

Taking it from him, I frowned. "What is this? Who would send a letter?"

My eyes widened as I read the fancy script on the corner. *Prince Ryn Trahaearn.*

"A letter?" I turned it over and glanced at Kohl.

"Guess Fane wasn't lying," he muttered.

I touched the strange black seal before tearing it open. My heart thudded as I pulled out the folded note. The cream paper was thick and crisp with an elegant, inked design at the top of the page.

"Fancy," I muttered.

Curiosity and dread filled me as I unfolded the note and scanned it. Kohl stood behind me, peering over my shoulder to read it as well.

"He wants to meet."

Kohl grunted. "I still don't trust their reasons."

I reread the letter and shook my head, feeling the same suspicion. Why wait all this time if he really knew how to leave

Savannah? Why break our truce now? What was in it for them? What were they hiding?

"Should I respond?"

Kohl folded his arms across his chest, a scowl on his face. "Only if it's to tell them to go fuck themselves."

My lips twisted in a wry smile. "Kohl."

He shrugged. "You know how I feel about bloodsuckers."

I winced. Yeah, I did. Poor Kohl. His great aunt had been turned by one of them ages ago. He'd seen firsthand the destruction they brought and the cruel games they played.

A memory of Mel flashed in my mind. Her tear-streaked face and broken sobs. Her best friend, Grace, had been turned too. She was the reason Prince Ryn had been sentenced to four years staked and now he was out. A lick of anger curled inside me.

I shoved down the emotions and looked at the letter once more.

"He didn't even put a return address. How would we even know where to find him?"

Kohl didn't answer.

I set the letter on my desk to puzzle over later. My eyes caught Kohl's in the mirror. Heat flooded me at his longing gaze.

Our friendship meant everything to me, but try as I did to feel something more, I couldn't.

"I'm getting nowhere with the curse. How are the others doing?"

Kohl sighed. "Same. I haven't found anything new either."

"And Diego? Any more trouble with him?"

"Not as of this morning, but there's still plenty of time left in the day for him to do something stupid."

My eyebrow arched. "Let's hope that he doesn't."

We fell quiet. Somewhere downstairs, someone was laughing. The sound reminded me of my older sister, Mel. Pain punched me. Of course, it wasn't Mel. Mel was dead. Like the others. Conversation drifted to us. I couldn't make out the words, but the tone sounded casual and relaxed. Bitterness filled me. When was the last time I'd been able to relax and not have to deal with every problem?

As if reading my thoughts, Kohl squeezed my hand. "Are you okay, Kenzie?"

The gentleness in his voice cracked my stony façade. Holding back tears, I forced a smile for him. He wasn't fooled.

"I'm queen of a dying coven. Trying to stop the end of the world. None of this is okay, Kohl. I shouldn't be queen. It was supposed to be Mel."

Pain etched his forehead and before I could stop him, he pulled me into a tight embrace. I wrapped my arms around his solid frame and let his warmth blanket me. He smelled like waxy candles and minty aftershave. I looked up and met his soulful, hazel eyes. The intensity of his gaze sent a shiver up my spine and flooded me with renewed sorrow.

I couldn't give him what he wanted. My chest tightened. I couldn't be the queen my sister would have been, the one my coven needed, and I couldn't be the one for Kohl. Pushing away the guilt, I withdrew from his embrace and went to stand by the open window.

Heaviness hung in the air between us.

"I have to get back to reading. See you at lunch?" I softened the dismissal with a smile.

Kohl straightened and gave me a curt nod, no hint of disappointment or regret. I watched him leave, my emotions crashing together like tidal waves.

There was work to do, and no time for me to dwell on the past or my best friend's desires. Whatever happened to my coven was on me now.

8

VALERIA

I stood by the fire, facing my pack. Their haunted faces were illuminated by the dancing flames. My wolf sensed their uneasiness.

Aside from the people still on guard duty, we were all there. Even the humans, who I'd hoped would remain in their tent, unseen. Drew's dark eyes shot me daggers while his twin scanned the crowd with a narrowed gaze. I had the feeling if I ordered them to go, they would resist, and I didn't need my pack to witness any weakness from me.

Jay and Tati arrived at last. I bristled. I'd told him to return to camp. Where did he go? He met my eyes, face just as wary as the others.

The lack of confidence from him and Tati burned. They'd always been supportive of Elijah. Why couldn't they trust me just the same?

Ignoring my own doubts, I addressed them. "We were unable to save the human girl. She's buried outside of camp. There's been no sighting of any of Diego's pack or vampires, so we should be in the clear. However, we should remain on guard and stay within the confines of our territory."

I glanced at Drew and Becca, who stared at me, disbelief and confusion written on their faces. Worry prickled at me as I held their gazes. Would they speak up about Jen? Stir up trouble within my pack?

After a moment of silence, my concern settled. They wouldn't tell.

"Tomorrow, the humans will return to the city." My words grew louder, drowning out the crackling of the firewood.

Jay took a step forward. "I think I should go with them."

My head snapped to his. "What?"

He met my stare. "To find Elijah."

I clenched my fists. "Elijah doesn't want to be found, Jay. He told us not to come after him."

"You mean he told *you*. None of us saw him leave."

Heat spread up my neck. Was he... accusing me? Of hurting Elijah? Anger burned inside me. My wolf snarled.

"He didn't want to have to say goodbye to the pack," I snapped.

Jay's dark gaze swept over my face, his lips flattened. Even his mate, Tati didn't look convinced. Behind me, Cruz and Leah —two of my most faithful friends—moved closer to me to offer support.

"You will stay here with the pack. Where you belong, Jay." My voice was steel.

His big, broad shoulders tensed visibly, but he fell silent. I watched him, waiting to see if he would speak out of turn again. He didn't.

After dismissing everyone, I went to my own tent to get some rest. Sleep didn't come easy, but eventually it won over. Despite the harrowing events of the day, my dreams were pleasant.

Memories of Elijah and I exploring and chasing each other flashed before me. Jaime was there too, trying so desperately to impress his idol and future alpha, Elijah. The beautiful, brown eyes of my mate bore into mine and in my dream, his laughter rang around me. So genuine and endearing. I almost wept at the familiar sly smile and mischievous twinkle in his gaze. Elijah before the world broke him.

Just as he pulled me into a dance, his face dipping toward mine, I was yanked from the dream.

Danger, my wolf warned.

Footsteps thundered toward my tent. I shot up. My head spun and I stumbled to my feet, still disoriented from the memories and images. I turned, looking for Elijah, but reality caught up. Cold washed over me.

He's not here, my wolf reminded me with a whimper.

"Val, you need to see this." Tati's voice broke my thoughts.

Slipping into my boots, I unzipped my tent and stepped out. My beta's stricken face made my heart lurch. I didn't bother to correct her wrong address. Following her, I strode out of the tent toward the others.

A tall figure, more skeleton than flesh, walked through our camp. Its bony legs jerked from under a faded dress as it moved, long dark hair caked with dirt swished behind it.

My heart leapt to my throat. The witches. The witches were rising.

"What is it?" someone's question echoed in the distance.

More corpses followed, coming from the forest. All in different various stages of decomposition. The pungent smell of death spread in our camp and burned my throat.

Some of my wolves shifted, shedding their clothes. Their growls filled the air.

In unison, the gruesome bodies turned toward me. My inner wolf's hackles rose. Their decaying skin and parched, white bone moved slowly and oddly. Like puppets pulled by a string.

Nausea rolled in my gut.

The one in front stopped in front of me and pointed an arm, mostly bone, at me. "The forest is ours. Leave or you will die."

I gaped at her.

Growls emanated from my pack along with whispers of shock.

"This is our home. Who are you?"

She didn't answer me. Her eyeless sockets stared into my very soul.

Kill it. Sink your teeth into its neck and thrash it until it dies. Again.

I pushed my inner wolf back. My teeth were going nowhere near that decomposed body. Bile rose up at the thought. Despite my wolf's bravado, I could sense her fear underneath.

My wolves skirted the witches, watching and waiting.

"Alpha?" Jay's silver eyes narrowed on me.

Right. I had to make the call.

Kill, my wolf demanded.

"Destroy them," I answered.

Unleashing my inner wolf, I leapt into battle along with the others.

The sky was tainted with the smell of death. The woods trembled. My wolves surrounded me, and I let out a howl—a command.

Kill them. Kill them all.

My beta charged first, leading the others. I snarled at him. I was alpha.

The first kill was mine.

He dropped the twitching skull to the earth. My eyes swept the area and landed on the witch who'd threatened my pack. She'd moved forward, way too quickly for those brittle bones. Before I could launch myself at her, a gunshot rang out.

I whipped toward the brain rattling sound. The humans. Anger burned hot within me. I raced toward the girl who was now the bigger threat. I would tear out her throat before she could hurt my wolves. My human's alarm echoed in the back of my mind, but I ignored it.

Smoke and the scent of rotted bodies filled my lungs. I leapt over the dying fire and landed in front of the two humans. The end of the gun greeted me. Shouts and snarls rang out around us.

I jumped for the girl. She fired. My body jerked, anticipating the hit.

It never came.

The boy shoved her out of my path, and I collided with him instead. My teeth grazed his shoulder. He let out a cry.

"Get off of him!" His kin pointed her weapon at me once more.

I turned to find a crumpled body in the spot behind where I had stood. Bones and tattered clothing. Realization struck me as I backed up.

They weren't after my wolves... they were on our side.

A howl of pain caught my attention. I took off toward it. More and more bodies lumbered into our camp, coming from the trees. Ice filled my blood.

How? Why? There were so many witches—too many.

One came for me, his nails long and sharp. I bit his wrist and slammed him into the earth over and over until he stopped moving. Another yelp came from one of my wolves.

I moved toward the sound, clawing my way through the mass of undead bodies. Their slick bones brushed against my fur. Nails dug into my back. Pain blossomed along my spine.

Snarling, I lashed out against the onslaught.

I bit. I clawed. Ducked and dove.

Blood—my own blood—dripped from my head into my eyes. I shook it off. A witch caught me by the ear, sharp nails ripping into the sensitive part.

Rage boiled within me. I tore myself from her grip and launched myself at her throat. She collapsed under my weight. I yanked her head clean off the rotting neck and spat it on the ground.

When I looked up, dread washed over. More witches were coming. They crowded our camp and blocked my view of the tents. I watched as three of them pushed one of my wolves into the dying fire. They struck fast and relentless, nails cutting into him again and again. My paws moved me forward, but it was too late.

His last howl pierced a hole inside me.

My heart thundered. This wasn't working. My pack was dying, and the witches were... unkillable. Already I saw the ones who'd been struck down rise back up as if their puppet master had pulled on their strings. Even dead and without their magic, we couldn't take them all on. There were too many.

I had to end this.

I let my human take back control. *Stop this. Save the pack.*

Pain rushed through me as I transformed. Naked and trembling, I scanned the bloody scene before me. Where was the head witch now? Spotting her near Cruz's tent, I made my way over.

A fallen wolf made me stumble. Her pained eyes burned into my soul. My inner wolf howled.

Fury rose up inside of me.

"Stop this! Stop it now. We'll leave. Do you hear me? We're leaving!" My throat was raw.

The witch who'd spoken to me appeared at the front. "Leave the forest. Don't return."

My wolf growled. We both wanted to rip her apart, but I couldn't endanger my pack. I couldn't lose anyone else.

I turned to my wolves. "Retreat. Shift now and get all your things. Hurry."

Jay shifted first, his eyes narrowed. "Where are we going to go? The other packs won't let us stay in their camps for long."

Pain lanced through me. "Then we go to the city."

Everything stilled. The witches paused in unison as if a switch had been turned. Their sunken eye holes turned toward us, and their frail bodies swayed. Shame flooded me.

Bony corpses. That's all they were and yet... I couldn't stop them.

My eyes swept the damage, heart shrinking. Two. Two of my wolves dead and how many injured?

I took a shaky breath and turned to find myself staring into Drew's widened eyes. His gaze dipped down and snapped back up, a flush appearing on his face.

My eyes followed his, and I realized that once again I was naked. Only this time, I didn't care. My wolves were dead.

And that was on me.

My wolf had gone unnaturally silent, but I could sense her anguish. Our failure struck her even harder than it did me. This was our pack. We were supposed to protect them.

We failed. Her words rattled me.

Yeah. We failed.

Swallowing the lump in my throat and fighting the urge to strike the witches who continued to watch us, I went to get my stuff.

Once dressed, I helped the others tear down the tents and pack up our things. The witches stood guard, their creepy eyeless stares unnerving and infuriating. I wanted to knock their heads clean off. Becca aimed her gun on them while Drew helped with packing.

When he looked at me, I averted my gaze. I'd apologized to him numerous times for the injury I'd given him. Thankfully, the bite was too shallow to do much damage and Cruz had cleaned and bandaged it up nicely.

The air was thick with grief and anger. Numbness filled me as I moved along the camp. I spotted Cruz and Leah taking care of the injured. Would any of them be able to make it to the city? I refused to leave them behind.

"Alpha." Tati's voice made me pause.

I turned to her.

"What about our dead?" she asked, wiping blood from her chin.

"We bury them."

I moved toward one of the bodies and fought back the wave of sorrow. My wolves. I'd failed them. Hot tears burned in my eyes.

Where the hell were you when we needed you, Elijah?

Pushing away the rage of emotions, I carried the wolf to the edge of the camp. Jay and Tati brought the others. Whimpers and howls echoed around us.

Jay's eyes met mine. I shuddered at the accusing glare. Though he didn't say anything, I knew it was coming. I should have told him. Warned him and Tati of the danger, but I didn't. I thought it could wait, and I'd been wrong.

Not that their knowledge of it would have helped us anyway, but it was a betrayal of trust.

After the bodies were buried and I'd spoken a little prayer to Mother Nature, I turned to help the others finish the packing.

Jay stood in my path. Tati was beside him.

"I saw it, *Alpha*."

My eyes narrowed on the big beta. "Saw what, Jay?"

His jaw hardened. "That creature. Half human. Half vampire. And half wolf."

Jen. He'd seen her back in the clearing with Drew and Becca? Or had she risen again with the witches?

I scanned the camp but didn't see the monster.

"I was going to discuss it with you in the morning. So, we didn't scare the rest of the pack unnecessarily."

Jay issued a harsh laugh. "Yeah, how'd that turn out?"

My wolf growled at his tone.

"Jay," Tati warned, her eyes wide.

He ignored her. "Two are dead. Three seriously injured. Brian's wolf was blinded. You think Cruz can heal that?"

I stilled. His words rattled me to the core.

Silence fell over the camp. I didn't have to turn my head to see that everyone was watching us.

"Since when did we start keeping secrets from the pack? Huh? Elijah never—"

"Elijah is gone, Jay. He's gone. He's not coming back. And he did keep secrets. You think you knew him? That he was your best friend?"

My anger was unraveling, and I couldn't stop the words now. The poisonous, piercing words seeking release.

"You might have loved him, but he didn't love you. Any of you. And especially not you, Jay. Do you want to know what he really thought about you?"

Stop.

I ignored my wolf. It was too late. I couldn't stop.

Jay glared at me, his lip curling.

Don't.

"He thought you were a pathetic loser. An idiot jock, perfect to be his mindless soldier."

Someone gasped.

Jay reeled, eyes flashing silver to brown. He gave me a look of pure anguish and turned away, marching off in wounded silence.

Heat spread across my face, regret instantly flooding me.

Tati's silver eyes narrowed on me. My wolf could sense her wolf and the anger boiling under the surface. They wanted to strike me.

And I deserved it.

Eyes fell on me. Shame spread through me at their stares. Though I'd spoken a half truth, I knew it was wrong. Elijah did love Jay. He always had.

Why did I say that?

Human emotions. They make you weak.

My wolf was angry with me too. Jay and Tati were my betas, and despite their hesitation to follow me, they'd still done it. Been faithful to me.

I was a terrible, terrible alpha.

No response came from my wolf. I took her silence as agreement. Swallowing the lump in my throat, I forced the emotions back down.

"I promise, I'll do better," I spoke to no one.

Or maybe it was to Elijah. The broken boy who'd left me just as broken.

9

———

MCKENZIE

Night came quickly, and the day passed uneventfully. Still no progress with the spells. The werewolf, Elijah, remained as tight lipped and hell bent on revenge as ever. At least there were no more run-ins with Fane or Diego.

After dozing off for the umpteenth time, I gave up on my reading and set the heavy book on the nightstand. I blew out the candle and blinked against the darkness. My window still open, moonlight streamed in, highlighting the vanity against the wall and the stack of books piled there. Guilt filled me at the sight, but there was only so much my body could handle.

Delicious sleep overtook me as I snuggled into the cool sheets and soft pillow.

A knock on my door pulled me out of a dream. Fane's beautiful face evaporated into thin air. Dream? I splayed a hand on my chest, cheeks flooding with shame. Nightmare, I corrected myself. Because what kind of girl would I be to dream about him... like that?

Another knock sounded.

"I'm coming." My voice was hoarse.

Throwing off the covers and grabbing my silky robe, I padded barefoot to the door and flung it open.

The witch—Riley, maybe—blinked at me, mouth gaping.

"What is it?" I prodded her.

She quickly recovered and bowed. I fought the urge to roll my eyes in irritation. If she was waking me up, it better be worth it.

"There's been an incident, Queen. A witch. Drained."

I sucked in a breath. "When? Where?"

Riley flinched. "In the back alley of Coral Street. She was just now discovered when someone tried a tracking spell to find her. She's been missing all day."

I flung the door open wider, not caring that I stood there barefoot and in my nightgown.

"Drained you said? Was she turned?"

Her eyes averted from my disheveled form. "No, but it looks like she was... compelled."

Only the higher-class vampires could use compulsion. *Fane.*

My jaw clenched. "A royal? Did you catch them?"

"Carly, I told you not to wake her. The queen needs her rest." Kohl's voice cut in sharply.

He strode down the hall with a thunderous expression. The witch—Carly—flinched at his approach.

"Yes, but I thought she would want to know."

Kohl glared at her and swiveled toward me, his eyes dipping down and quickly snapping back to my face.

Flushing, I folded my arms across my chest to achieve at least some decency. Even with the robe on, it was hard to hide the girls.

"Did you catch the vampire?" I still sounded groggy.

"No. But I have a search party ready."

"That's not necessary. I can handle this."

Kohl's eyebrow shot up. His silent warning made me smile. How did he expect me to go back to sleep now?

"Who was it? Who made it through our ward and snuck out?"

The girl shuffled her feet and stared at the carpet. I looked to Kohl.

"Julia. She's been gone since morning. Never made it back to the coven."

Morning? What was she doing outside the coven all day? I glanced back at the blonde witch who continued staring at the ground. Why wake me up to tell me if she wasn't going to give us more answers?

"Let me get dressed, then we'll go."

"This can wait until morning, My Queen."

I turned and threw Kohl a look over my shoulder. "I can't sleep, anyway. Might as well take care of this now."

"I am more than capable of handling it—"

"I'm coming, Kohl."

With that, I shut my door and went to my closet. Questions raced in my mind as I pulled on some black leggings and boots along with a bra and dark T-shirt. Not my most 'queenly' outfit, but it was comfortable and easy to move in.

Going after one of my witches was a break of the agreement. Anger lit inside me. Why now, after all these years, were the vampires deciding to do this? Did they think to attack while we were vulnerable? My fists clenched. They picked the wrong queen to mess with.

I threw open the door to find Kohl waiting and the witch girl gone.

"I want you to reset the wards again and make sure no one else leaves tonight."

"And the wolf?"

Right. I'd forgotten about him. "Have a sleeping spell ready in case he wakes up while I'm gone. Post another guard at his door too... just in case."

Kohl frowned at me.

"What?"

"I'm not letting you go out alone, Kenzie."

I sighed. "Then come with me if you want, but there's no more time to waste. How many people for the search party?"

"Two. Counting us, four."

"Leave them here. You and I can handle this alone. You have a tracking spell started?"

He lifted his hand to show me the faded black mark on his palm—the spell already taking form.

I smiled at him. "Always ready aren't you, Kohl?"

He returned the smile. "Of course."

I took his offered arm and headed for the stairs. His long strides met mine and I appreciated his support. Kohl was a good guy. I didn't know what I would do if I'd lost him too. He was my pillar and rock. An anchor to my past and compass to my future.

His eyes found mine, making me turn away.

If we were supposed to be together, wouldn't there be something there? A pull or a tug? Or was I being totally stupid and naïve about it?

Pushing away the thoughts, I focused on the task at hand. Would we find other witches drained? Was this because I hadn't listened to Fane or answered their stupid letter?

Irritation welled inside me. I had enough on my plate with the curse and Diego. Now I had to worry about ancient enemies testing me?

"Did you see the body? Julia, I mean." I winced at my harshness.

Kohl tensed. "Yes. We brought her back to the coven so she can be buried."

"Did it look she'd been compelled?"

He opened his mouth and hesitated. "Possibly. It's possible too that she was... willing."

I snorted. "Willing? To get sucked and drained by a vamp?"

My words echoed in the hall, the edge in my tone surprising me. Since when did I become so cold and crass? Mel would never have spoken like that. My chest tightened. Mel would never have let a vampire attack one of our witches in the first place. Not after what had happened to Grace.

Kohl's eyes stared straight ahead. "I've heard some find the experience... pleasurable."

I shuddered. "Which part? The bite or the blood drinking?"

He turned his head toward me, his nearness sending a shiver of awareness through me.

"Maybe she asked to be turned."

I frowned. "Maybe, but she's not turned. She's dead. And I'm pretty sure she didn't ask for that. If she was compelled, we're going to have some problems."

He grunted. "What else is new?"

My lips twitched as I fought the urge to smile. Kohl was the Robin to my Batman, and I loved how well we worked together. How well we knew each other. He could handle my bad moods and I didn't have that with anyone else.

We stopped at the front door and instructed the others to reset the wards and stay in the coven. Maybe after hearing about the draining, the horny little witches would listen to me now.

You imagined him too...

I pushed that thought far from my mind. It was a dream—nightmare—and I refused to feel guilty about something I had no control over.

Moonlight bathed the street in its silvery glow. Warm, thick air swirled around me, carrying the smoky scent of campfire and lemony, sweet magnolias. It was still weird being in the city and not seeing any lights except our flashlight. No streetlights, headlights, or lights from the restaurants and shops that lined the squares.

Ghost town came to mind, but it wasn't. Not really. Unless we were the ghosts. My nose scrunched at the thought. If I didn't solve the curse, all of us would eventually be gone.

"You're quiet. Tired?" Kohl's voice broke through my thoughts.

I turned to meet his worried gaze. "I'm fine. Just thinking... about how things used to be."

He gave me a sad smile. "It's easier if you don't. Don't try to remember."

An ache grew inside me. I knew why he was saying it, but it felt wrong to forget. If roles were reversed, my parents and sisters wouldn't have forgotten me.

"I don't like this." Kohl's voice echoed in the alley.

"Yeah well wandering dark, creepy alleys at night isn't my idea of fun either."

His lips pursed. "You should have let me come alone."

I waved away his concern. "I needed the distraction, Kohl. After Diego's little demonstration and that alpha who wants to kill one of our witches."

Kohl's face hardened. "Diego needs to be taught a lesson."

A snort escaped me. "Sorry. It's just... Diego Garcia." I shook my head. "How in the hell did someone like him get put in charge? Wasn't he like a drug dealer loser back in school?"

"How should I know? I was too busy trying to pass all my AP classes. Doing everything my parents expected. Everything to get into college." His voice turned bitter.

I sobered at the memory. Kohl worked harder than anyone I'd ever known, and he would have done amazing things. If the world hadn't gone to hell. Now he was stuck as my sidekick. Did it bother him?

It bothered me.

I was supposed to have college, a time to be me on my own and immerse myself with the human culture. Though I'd always known eventually I would end up as a right hand to Mel. I would have obligations to fulfill for my queen, but I never expected to *be* queen. To take her place. It was so, so wrong.

"What if I can't stop the curse, Kohl? What if this is really the end of… everything?"

His eyes stared straight ahead, his emotions masked from me.

"Then we should enjoy the little time we have left. If we're going to be gone anyway, we might as well try to find some happiness here and now, right? Take risks now before it's too late."

I rubbed my arms. The fervent look in his eyes unnerved me. I didn't want to hear what was coming next. For him, I knew what that risk he was referring to meant. Me—us.

"Kenzie, I—"

"Witches. In my square?" a voice drawled, cutting Kohl off.

Fane.

My head snapped in the direction, eyes squinting to find the source. He remained in shadow. Beside me, Kohl leapt into action, chanting a defensive spell.

"Your square?"

He emerged from the darkness, Kohl's flashlight revealing his pale face. Beautiful. Elegant. Arrogant. It was hard not to stare, but my good sense kicked in, reminding me of the monster that he was.

"Fane."

His eyebrow lifted. "Prince Fane, please."

I scoffed.

"You killed a witch."

He only smiled. "I thought that would catch your attention."

Anger filled me at his coldness. Amusement sparked in his eyes. He was enjoying himself, the bastard.

"I'm here to collect repayment."

His smile widened. "You? The queen for a low witch? Who comes if I kill you?"

Kohl stepped in front of me, hands raised and ready. "You wouldn't get the chance."

Fane's eyes flicked to him. "Down boy, down. If it weren't for your coven tattoo, I'd mistake you for a wolf. The queen's fearless lapdog."

Kohl stiffened.

Fane angled toward him. "Does she know? Does she know how badly you want her? You'd do anything wouldn't you? To get into—"

My hand shot forward, a burst of magic pushing him back. "Shut up. We're not here to play games with you, Fane. I have better things to do."

He straightened his jacket and met my glare. "Better things like the spell? How is that going by the way? Have you found a way to save everyone yet?"

Irritation flared inside me. Fane and his questions. If it weren't for his brother and his retaliation, I'd shoot fire right up his ass.

"Maybe we can help."

I scoffed. "You can't help anyone."

His jaw hardened. "Perhaps I could if I had the right... motivation."

My lip curled. Everything was a game to him. He'd been a bastard before the fall and now...

He was probably loving the new order of things.

"You killed one of my witches."

"Well, I didn't receive a response to my brother's letter." He stopped right before us, fangs gleaming in the flashlight. "I warned you he wasn't the most patient prince."

"Are you saying he did this?" I frowned at him.

"Did what?"

"Don't test me, Fane. I'm not in the mood. Was it you? Did you compel her?"

He smirked. "Send your lapdog away and I'll tell you."

I shot him a cool look.

Kohl's face flushed with fury. "One more smart remark from you, Fane."

I could sense the magic curling in his palm, ready to be unleashed. Before he could shoot, I motioned him to the side.

Fane watched us with that irritating smirk.

"Go back to the main street, Kohl."

His eyes widened. "What? I'm not leaving you here alone with him."

"He has a name. And I promise I'll be on my best behavior," Fane drawled.

"It's fine, Kohl. I could snap his neck with a snap of my fingers." I spoke louder for his benefit.

"Catchy. You should use that slogan for your next royal campaign. That is if you're still alive to campaign."

I rolled my eyes. Did the vampire have a retort for everything?

"Kenzie, you can't trust him." Worry danced in Kohl's eyes.

"I know. But you can trust me. I can handle him. And you'll be right around the corner if I need you."

"But…"

"Go. Please, Kohl."

Fane snickered. "You heard your master. Run along."

Kohl's head snapped to him. "If you so much as breathe in her direction..."

Fane's harsh laugh cut him off. "Be a good boy and maybe she'll throw you a bone."

I touched Kohl's shoulder and nodded in reassurance. He hesitated and fixed Fane with another deadly glare before stalking off.

Before he'd even made it around the corner, Fane was by my side. Way too close for comfort.

I fought the urge to shudder and turned to face him, taking a step back. "What do you want, Fane?"

He smiled. "It's not about what I want, Kenzie."

My eyes narrowed. "You don't get to call me that."

His lips parted, feigning shock. "What do I get to call you? Darling? Gorgeous? Beautiful?"

I bristled. "Queen is fine."

"No. I don't think so."

"What? You don't think so?"

He nodded to the spot Kohl had been. "He gets to call you Kenzie. I want a special nickname for you too."

Heat rushed over me. What game was this vamp trying to play?

"That's twice you've broken the agreement. I want payment."

He circled me, long legs moving so gracefully I couldn't help but notice them. Everything he did was part of the show. I hated him for it. The world was ending, and he was having the time of his life.

"I mean it Fane. You will pay for what you did."

His head leaned toward me, all humor vanishing. My heart slammed against my ribs at his nearness. Blue eyes bore into me. I didn't want to be pulled in, but damn it, I was. Summoning all my strength, I shielded myself, making my face neutral.

A smug smile tugged at his lip. "Name your price."

"A life for a life."

My words reminded me of Elijah. Weren't those the same ones he'd spoken to me? Was that what the world was now? Just a big cycle of death, revenge, and more death?

"I'm not sure my brother would agree to those terms, but I'll be sure to tell him."

"This isn't a joke, Fane. You're in breach of our agreement."

He chuckled. "I did warn you my brother wouldn't be very happy with you ignoring him. If you want to discuss the terms of this so-called breach, then you'll have to meet with him."

His words made me boil. It was all manipulation to make me do what they wanted. I fought the urge to use my magic on him.

"I don't have to do anything, Fane. I'm leaving."

"If you were going to go, you would have already gone, *cariad*."

I frowned. "What did you call me?"

Ignoring my question, he straightened and backed away. I felt like a weight had been lifted from my chest. I could breathe again.

"Fane."

He closed his eyes and feigned a shudder. "As much as I love hearing my name on those beautiful lips, I have to remind you, it's prince. Prince Fane."

My face flamed. I glanced at the direction Kohl had gone. Could he hear us?

Fane followed my gaze and chuckled darkly. "Please. You don't care about him. Not like he cares for you."

How could he even know that?

I whipped to him. "Shut up. You don't know anything about us."

The smug smile was back. "I know you've been pouring

over those dusty, old books, hoping for answers. I know you wanted to escape Savannah and see the world, experience college. You never wanted to be queen, did you?"

His words rattled me. I gaped at him, not knowing how to respond. How did he know? How? It was creepy. Unnerving. A vampire stalking me?

"How did you get past the wards?" I blurted the question.

"I have my ways."

My mind raced. Did I have a traitor in the coven? Was that how he'd gotten in? Was someone... actually sleeping with him? It wasn't that big of a stretch. He was gorgeous, and maybe for a weak, desperate witch that allure was too much to refuse.

That was a problem.

10

VALERIA

I stood and waited as everyone gathered their packs and crowded around me. Their eyes were glued to me and my wolf could sense their wariness. Though they didn't voice it, I could see the doubt written on their faces.

My own doubt rolled inside me. Was I leading them to their deaths or to a worse fate? I cringed at the thought. What other option did we have but to go?

Pushing away the questions, I faced them and squared my shoulders. "I know you don't like this and trust me, I don't like it either, but we have no choice. The witches won't let us stay here and the barrier keeps us from going farther into the forest. The only place left is the city. Back to where we came from."

I paused and waited for complaints. Some shook their heads and scowled while others huddled together, eyes wide in distress.

"We can stay in the clubhouse there. We don't have to go into the houses."

"How do we know it's safe there? That the humans won't be there?" Jay interrupted.

I frowned at him. "We'll check it out first. Make sure it's safe."

"There's no one there. We came through it when we left the city," Drew spoke up.

Jay glared at him. "How can we trust you? It could be a trap."

I stepped between them. "There's nowhere else to go. Like I said, we'll check it out first before we make camp."

Wisely, he shut up and averted his gaze. The rest of the wolves followed his lead.

I adjusted my pack and lifted my chin. "Time to go. Fall back, Jay. You and Tati can bring up the rear."

"Yes, Alpha," he answered in a clipped tone.

Guilt needled me. There was still hurt in his voice, but he was too proud to bring it back up. Tati, on the other hand, still looked like she wanted to tear me apart.

At least they'd be in the back, so I didn't have to face them. Motioning Drew and Becca to follow, I led everyone through the forest.

The witches watched as we left and the injustice of it burned inside me. I wasn't going to give up that easily. Once we were safe and settled, I'd find a witch who could tell me what this resurrection was about and then I could come up with something that would destroy them.

Make them pay for hurting my pack.

They will pay. My wolf agreed.

Morning was coming soon and the thought of sleeping in our old neighborhood made me nauseous. I didn't think I could bring myself to walk in my old house where they'd died one after another. There were too many horrific memories.

Would Elijah come? He would sense us as soon as we came into range. My wolf practically leapt at the thought. What would he say about the wolves we'd lost? I glanced around at the injured ones Cruz had healed. Some were carried on makeshift cots and would need more time to heal and some... I wasn't sure would make it.

Dismissing the dark thoughts, I continued through the woods. Our footsteps bounced off the trees, the snaps and crunch of the underbrush beneath us made the animals scurry out of our path.

Flashlights bounced around and whispers flew back and forth as we went. Drew and Becca exchanged hushed words beside me, thankfully not trying to draw me into their conversation.

My mind raced with worried thoughts and possible solutions. Before long, we made it to the lonely road that led toward the city. A gas station stood in the distance. The scent of pine and yarrow faded as we left the woods behind.

Ahead, shadows stood stark against the night sky. Houses. My heart twisted. Our old neighborhood. Everyone grew silent as we passed through the large sign: Shadow Oak Subdivision.

Steeling myself, I strode forward, ignoring my racing heart. Inside, my wolf whimpered. The memories of the past were too vivid. Houses stretched before us on the looping streets and cul-de-sacs. There were more houses left than people in our pack and that realization rattled me.

We were the last of the Shadow Wolves.

Overgrown grass and weeds replaced the once manicured park. My eyes fell on the playground and sorrow gripped me. All the kids who had played there before were gone now. Before all the depressing thoughts could overwhelm me, I turned away.

My gaze swept the area for any signs of intruders. I sent two scouts ahead to make sure it was safe to approach. Humans had broken through our defenses in the earlier months. Stolen our food and shot Felix dead. A chill crept up my spine as the image of his unseeing eyes and bloody wounds flashed in my mind.

Elijah caught the human responsible, just a boy, barely older than my brother had been. That boy was Elijah's first kill, and I remembered it so clearly. The shock on his young face, Elijah's shifting, and the wolf's merciless revenge.

Someone sniffled behind me, pulling me out of the dark memories. I glanced back at my pack. Mixed reactions of fear, sorrow, and anger showed on their faces. The scouts returned and gave me the okay.

Sucking in a breath, I mustered all the strength I had left and continued walking.

Drew and Becca followed me in silence with grim expressions of their own. I stopped at the corner and stared at the sign. Early morning light illuminated the words written on it: River Run Circle.

Our old street. Two abandoned bicycles in one of the yards caught my eye. My chest tightened. I could still remember Tessa and Hunter, the little boy and girl who lived there. They'd been among the first to die from the mysterious sickness.

My wolf tensed inside me. We could all feel it—the heaviness and darkness of the place. It wasn't home anymore. Without the people we'd lost, it was just empty buildings, hollow and bare like our battered hearts.

I stopped at the corner. A tall, brick house stood with overgrown grass. The shutters were splattered with dried blood. Something had happened to the humans who'd pushed us out.

Mom's old car was parked in the driveway, windows smashed.

Numbness filled me. It felt like another life. I scoffed. It was another life ago. A happy one. The others milled around behind me, reminding me I wasn't alone.

Forcing the grief away, I squared my shoulders and headed for the clubhouse. The others followed.

Jay met my strides. "We shouldn't be here."

I didn't look at him. "It's our home."

A snort sounded from him, making my head turn.

"No, it's not. Not anymore."

Ignoring him, I continued along the sidewalk. The hushed voices of the pack filled my ears. No one was happy to be back.

My heart hammered against my ribs. Did I make a mistake?

No, I was doing what I had to do.

Then why did I feel like I was screwing up—again?

I stepped into the large, brick building and waited for everyone to enter. Some slunk into the seats while others remained on foot, throwing nervous glances around.

For the most part, the clubhouse looked untouched. Nothing hinted at the tragedies that had played out in the last six months. Clusters of chairs and sofas crowded the area along with the glass coffee tables. In the back were the bathrooms and the small gym. A pool table stood against the wall and images of the weekend parties Elijah used to host flashed in my mind.

There were too many memories of the clubhouse. Even I could barely tolerate it, but we had no other choice.

Voices grew around me.

I held up a hand to silence them. "I know you don't want to be here. You think I do? But this is the only place we have. Bitching and moaning about it isn't going to change reality."

Eyes studied me.

"We will stay here until we can figure out a way to defeat those witches and take back our forest."

They murmured their agreement.

"Our alpha is right. What does it matter where we live, anyway? We're all cursed. Going to die eventually. Might as well die here where we came from," Leah spoke up.

I winced at the bitterness in her tone.

"You don't know that. The witches might find a way to stop it," another argued.

Angry voices echoed. Those who still believed in the queen and those who didn't voiced their opinions.

Moving to the middle of the room, I silenced them all.

"Whatever happens, we will remain strong. We will get through this together."

My eyes met Jay's. His gaze was steel and the guilt of what I'd said to him earlier rushed over me.

I would have to apologize sooner or later. More than ever we needed to show a united front.

"Now—"

The sound of an engine cut me off. Everyone fell silent. Jay, not waiting for my order, disappeared out the door, with Tati following.

Wolves. Red Wolves. My wolf confirmed my fear.

Diego.

I looked to Drew and Becca. "Hide. Now."

They didn't hesitate.

Sunlight streamed in through the windows as the humans ran for the supply closet. My wolves shuffled nervously and looked to me. A surge of protectiveness filled me. They were so vulnerable and after our fight with the witches and no sleep, they needed rest—not another fight.

I headed for the door and motioned for the others to fan out in the room. The stronger ones stood in front of the injured, eyes flashing silver.

Throwing the door open, I pushed down my weariness and fear.

Jay and Tati glanced at me.

"If he wants the humans?" Jay asked.

"There are no humans here."

His nostrils flared, but he didn't argue.

They came from the city, the back-gate entrance to our neighborhood. My heart skipped as an old truck pulled up. It was a battered one they'd probably stolen from somewhere. Only the outdated cars still in decent shape could run without technology.

Diego sat in the front passenger seat with the window down. His eyes landed on me.

"I'm going to go meet him. You two stay here with the others. Do not give up the humans."

Jay and Tati nodded.

I walked toward the rusted truck, my own wolf's warning ringing in my ears.

The Red Wolves were known for their violence, the cliché name they'd chosen portrayed their penchant for blood, but they'd never been a big enough threat to my pack.

My heart thundered as I stood waiting.

Protect the pack, my wolf urged.

Diego and his mate, Sylvie, jumped down first, three more members of their pack trailing them.

An easy smile spread on Diego's face, but there was a sharpness in his dark eyes. Just like I remembered him. Quick to scheme, and expert at reading a room. Sylvie stood by his side, looking thinner than I'd last seen her. Her blue-green eyes stared straight ahead, no emotion visible on her face. I didn't know much about her, but with a mate like Diego, I couldn't dismiss her strength.

They approached me, their wolves fanning out.

"Valeria." Diego spoke first.

I turned to him. "Why are you here, Diego?"

His smile didn't falter. "Just welcoming you back home. We got rid of the humans."

One of his wolves chuckled. My stomach churned. The splattered blood. I didn't want to know how he'd done it.

He continued to watch me, eyebrow arched in expectation.

"Thanks," I muttered.

"Of course. We wolves have to stick together. I'm glad to see you finally took my advice and moved back. Though I'm surprised it took you so long."

I didn't respond.

My mind raced with questions. What was he really doing? Did he think we owed him? Fire stirred in my belly. We were not his Red Wolves and if he thought he could order my pack around, he would find I wasn't some weak alpha.

"Elijah here?"

I bristled. "Elijah is busy. You can talk to me."

His lips pulled back in a smirk. "Of course. I just wanted to see if he'd left the witches yet."

My eyebrows lifted. "Witches?"

Diego watched me with narrowed eyes. Waiting to see what I would do?

I drew myself up. "What would Elijah be doing with witches?"

"Isn't that why you're here? To get him? The queen is holding him prisoner."

My heart dropped. Prisoner? Inside, my wolf snarled, ready to tear off after this queen.

I pushed the emotions away, hating that Diego could read me so easily.

"You've seen him?" Jay's voice caught my ear.

I shot him a cool look. Instead of listening to my order, he was walking up to us.

He stared at Diego and ignored me. "You've seen Elijah?"

My wolf bristled at my beta's defiance. Later, he would pay for it.

Diego's gaze slid to him. "Yes. Last I saw, he needed a doctor."

His words cut through me like a knife. My wolf howled, urging me to go.

Our mate is in trouble.

I forced her back down, trying to remain in control. Running after him without a plan was stupid. My wolf whined. Her pitiful cry made my skin flush. Wolves were strong creatures, but one without their mate could turn volatile, a slave to their own emotions.

Diego's eyes scanned the clubhouse and playground behind us. Looking for the humans? I stiffened, ready for any threat.

This was still my pack. I was still the alpha and he would respect that.

"Why did Elijah leave?"

His question made my hackles rise. It was none of his business. If he thought our pack was an easy target with only one alpha, my wolf would show him he was wrong.

My wolf snarled her agreement.

The burly alpha studied me, his inner wolf neutral.

"What do you want, Diego?"

His taunts had gone on long enough. It was time for him to leave.

"Something is happening in the city. It's the humans. They won't stop until they're back in control. Until every one of us is dead."

"We'll all be dead soon enough with the curse," I muttered.

"Sooner if we let them wriggle their way back on top."

"So, what is it you want, Diego? Why are you here? What happens in the city isn't my concern."

He flashed me a smile that didn't reach his eyes. "It will be. They won't be content with ruining what we have in the city. They'll be here too. For you."

My lip curled. "And what is it we have in the city?"

His chest jutted out. "Power. Control. The humans serve us. Like it should be."

I fought the urge to shudder under his cold gaze. There was

a wolf that had all but shed his humanity completely, but even wolves could be empathetic. Not him. He was all ice.

"Slavery? Is that what we've resorted back to?" I shook my head.

"Would you rather they hunt us like animals? We can't trust any humans unless they have a collar around their throat."

Nausea rolled in my gut. Slave collars. It's what the vampires used to keep their victims under their compulsion. How could Diego stoop to using them? It was barbaric—even for a wolf.

"You want me to join you, is that it? You came to ask me for support?"

"I didn't think I'd have to ask." He frowned. "I thought I already had your support."

My heart raced. Dangerous. This wolf was dangerous, and my inner wolf and I could both sense it.

"I won't risk the lives of my pack to help you with your vendetta against the humans, Diego. We've seen enough death."

His feral smile returned. He didn't look anything like the drug-dealing senior I remembered. There was a darkness that hadn't been there before, or maybe it had, and I never noticed.

"You'll see more if the humans get their way, Valeria. You know that."

I turned away, keeping my chin raised. I would not be bullied into submission.

"When Elijah returns—"

His harsh laugh cut me off. "He's not coming back, Valeria. He told me he left you."

Anger rolled in my gut. "He would never betray his pack."

Diego leaned toward my ear. "He already has."

My wolf rose to the surface, a deep growl escaping me.

His eyes narrowed, but he didn't back up. He towered over me.

"Diego." One of his wolves interrupted us.

She marched toward us, her gaze flickering to me and back to him. "There are humans here. Two. I can smell them."

Drew and Becca. My pulse quickened. I couldn't let him take them.

Jay glanced at me, but wisely, he said nothing.

"I see the humans have already come." Diego's brown eyes drilled into mine.

I didn't respond.

"My guess is it's those two that got away with that girl," another wolf added.

Jen. A fresh wave of anger stirred inside me. So, his pack was involved in the poor girl's torture. How could someone like Jen be a threat to him?

Diego watched me—studied me and I couldn't hide the disgust on my face.

"I don't think she would have survived the turn. Not with her injuries." Sylvie spoke up and glanced away.

My eyes darted to her. "What did you to her?"

I inwardly cursed at myself as the question escaped.

Diego smirked, his eyes lighting up at my confession. "Everything. Anything we wanted. Payback for what her friends did to us."

The cruelty in his voice made me shudder. Maybe he'd been a monster all along and I'd never seen it, but I could see it now.

Sylvie rubbed her arms, her eyes on her alpha. Worry swam in their blue depths and I couldn't help but feel sorry for her. She saw him for what he'd become too, but she was bonded to him and a wolf's bond was unbreakable.

Noticing my stare, she turned to me and scowled.

"Where are the others, Valeria?" Diego's voice hardened.

"What I do is my business, Diego. I think it's time for you to leave." I lifted my chin.

He blew out a breath. "I'm disappointed, Valeria. I always thought you were the stronger alpha over Elijah."

I glared at him. My wolf growled.

Diego shrugged and motioned his pack to retreat. His eyes shot to me. "We are not your enemies. But I will take down any threat to my pack and all wolves."

"So will I."

He stared at me and I met his gaze with a steely look of my own.

After a tense minute, he finally turned away and led the others back. I watched him retreat, my heart still pounding in my ears.

He'll be back, my wolf warned.

Once I was sure they were really leaving and not playing some trick, I turned on Jay.

"You were told to stay with the others."

He tensed, anger flashing on his face. "If my alpha is in trouble, it's my duty to help."

My eyes narrowed. I wasn't sure if he meant me or Elijah, but I was pretty sure he was being vague on purpose.

"Elijah needs us." His face was like stone.

I bristled. "We can't just walk into the coven and break him out."

Jay grunted. "Why not?"

My wolf snarled.

I leapt toward him, striking him hard and fast. He winced as my fist connected with his jaw. Wisely, he took it and didn't try to defend himself.

Taking a deep breath, I tried to calm my rage. "Do not question me again, Jay. You are my beta and you will listen."

His lip curled. "Yes, Alpha." He said the last word as if it pained him.

Voices murmured behind us. Everyone poured out of the clubhouse to gawk, eyes wide. Heat spread across my face.

"I want guards posted at the city entrance and back entrance. The rest of the pack can get some sleep and then we'll do a sweep and recount of all our resources."

They moved at my orders. Ignoring their questioning glances, I marched inside to tell Drew and Becca it was safe. I'd let them stay one more night to make sure Diego and his pack weren't waiting for them then they could go home, and I could figure out what to do about Elijah.

My wolf whimpered for him.

Hopefully, he hadn't done anything reckless yet like make himself an enemy of the witch queen. Though I suspected it was too late to wish for that.

I sighed. Once again doubts filled me. What was I supposed to do about Diego and the witches? Was there nowhere safe for my pack anymore?

11

MCKENZIE

A warm breeze tickled my skin, and the moonlight cast shadows against the city statues and pebbled street. Fane watched me without blinking and all my senses were on high alert. His confession still rang through me. Watching me from inside the coven? How?

"Who was it?" I frowned at him. "Who let you in?"

"Jealous?" His lips pulled back, revealing his fangs.

I shuddered. "God, no."

Amusement danced in his eyes, but he didn't speak.

"Have you been following me?" I demanded.

"Maybe? What can I say, I'm a romantic."

"That's not romantic. That's creepy. Stay the hell away from me."

His smile widened. I fought the urge to blast him with my magic and wipe the smugness right off his face, but I had a feeling he would enjoy it more than I would. Sicko.

"Why are you doing this? Why now? What about our agreement?"

He shrugged a shoulder. "Void, wouldn't you say? Seeing as

every single person who signed the original and annual reevalu-ations is dead."

My lip curled at his coldness. "That doesn't make it void. Under that oath, I have the right to punish you for breaking your word."

His eyebrow rose. "Punish me? How... kinky."

Annoyance spread through me. There was no talking to him. He was impossible. Utterly, completely impossible.

"Be serious, Fane. For one second of your life. Do you want a war right now? Is that what you and your brother want?"

He shook his head. "Hardly. A war is too easy. We'd wipe out your coven in one night."

"I doubt that."

"We just want to help. Break the barrier. Be free to leave Savannah."

"Leave Savannah? All of you?"

"Try not to sound so excited at the prospect."

"How do I know this isn't just some trick you're playing?"

He shot me a feigned wounded look. "Me? Play tricks on you? Never. We just want to help."

I folded my arms across my chest. "I don't believe that."

His lip quirked, the smug smile back. "Believe it or not, but it's true. We would benefit from this as well, and surely you can see this is in the best interest of... well, everybody."

Breaking the barrier would mean I could find ingredients for spells I'd saved but couldn't try. It would mean I could look for other witches outside of the city that could help. But I didn't trust his motives were pure. What game was he playing?

Sighing, I met his gaze. "So, what do I have to do, Fane?"

"Meet with my brother. Join him for a tea or a coffee. Wine. Whatever you prefer."

I growled in frustration. This was so not what I needed right now. Wasn't dealing with the werewolves bad enough, but now I had to seek out the vampire prince?

"My Queen," Kohl cut in.

I turned at his voice.

"The ward alarm is going off. We're needed back at the coven."

Cold dread filled my insides. "What is it? The wolf?"

Fane's head cocked. "A werewolf? Aren't you just full of surprises, *cariad*?"

Kohl scowled at him.

"Think about the offer. Not that you really have a choice. Every day my brother doesn't get the response he requests, a witch will be drained."

My magic stirred within me. "Is that a threat, Fane?"

He chuckled, eyes narrowing. "It's Prince Fane. And no, that was a promise."

Before I could get in the last word, he was gone. The air whooshed where he'd stood and blew my hair back. I scanned the area and growled in frustration.

"Let's go." I nodded for Kohl to start walking back to the coven.

We walked in silence, Fane's words replaying in my mind. I didn't want to get my hopes up, but if what he said wasn't a trick... it could mean everything. Finally, a breakthrough, a chance, a real chance to stop the curse.

Kohl disarmed the ward as I waited behind him on the giant porch. My body protested the idea of summoning more magic to deal with the wolf. Why couldn't everyone just wait until morning before pissing me off?

"I can take care of the wolf, Kenzie. You should get some sleep." Kohl's words startled me out of my thoughts.

I shook my head in disagreement as he finished his work and took a step back. His eyes found mine and his lips twisted in concern.

"Let me cast. Save your energy," he pleaded.

Before I could respond, the door burst open and a witch bowed. Behind him, voices chanted, and we pushed our way through.

"What happened?" I demanded.

"The sleeping spell wore off, and he tried to attack. He got Mario in the shoulder, but everyone else is okay."

"And where is the wolf now?"

"They're trying to find him. He can't have gotten past the wards. He's got to be somewhere inside the coven."

I groaned and shared a look with Kohl. The last thing I wanted to do was play hide and seek with the werewolf.

"I'll cast," he offered.

Repressing a sigh, I nodded to him and held his hand as he summoned magic. Pain etched his features as he used the energy to locate the alpha. The fading mark on his hand filled back in and glowed. Everyone watched in silence.

I frowned at them. "Why couldn't any of you cast a locating spell?"

Their eyes darted away from me.

"We tried," one answered in indignation.

Kohl squeezed my hand, a reminder not to go off on them. I bit back the insults on my tongue. Mel wouldn't have spoken harshly to the witches. But she was a natural leader and teacher. I didn't know how she put up with their incompetence.

"He's at the back door. In the kitchen." Kohl opened his eyes.

"Alright. Let's get him." I waved him forward.

I turned to the others. "Reset the ward and make sure no one leaves, and no one gets in."

My eyes swept their faces. With the dim candlelight, it was too hard to make out distinct features. Which one of them was the traitor?

I'd have to deal with that later. Pushing down my irritation, I followed Kohl to the back.

Two witches stood in the massive kitchen, their backs to the door as we entered. They turned at our approach and gave me a quick bow. Deepa and Blake, two of my best witches.

So, they had performed their own tracking spell? Irritation stirred inside me at the other witches for not telling us. We had to be more careful with casting. We needed to save our magic.

Moonlight streamed in from the giant window above the sink, illuminating Deepa and Blake's silhouettes. I followed their outstretched hands to the cornered wolf. A pair of silver eyes narrowed on me.

He was in wolf form which meant he was in no mood to talk it out.

"We've strengthened the ward, but we need someone else to cast the sleeping spell."

The wolf growled.

"I can do it," Kohl answered.

My head snapped to him. "You just cast, Kohl. I can do a simple sleeping spell."

He frowned at me.

I raised my hand to start the chant. Elijah shifted before I could cast it. He stood in the shadow, face, and body hidden in the darkness.

"You can't keep me here forever." His voice was deep.

"One more night then. Tomorrow, we're letting you go. You have my word."

Kohl turned to me sharply but didn't argue.

"He bit Mario," Deepa spoke up.

I turned to her. "How deep?"

She shook her head. "Not deep enough to turn him."

"Good. Then it will heal."

Elijah took a step toward us. The pale moonlight lit up his muscular body. Muscular and naked body.

My eyes flew back to his face.

"I'm not going back to my pack until I find the witch responsible for—"

"Your sister's death. Yes, we know," Kohl cut him off.

"Don't you have a duty to your wolves to protect them? Shouldn't you be there with them instead of here pissing me off? And do you have a mate? Do they know you're here?"

He stilled. "She's better off without me."

I stared at him, weariness filling my every limb. The last thing I needed was to get involved in the wolf's relationship issues. First of all, there was literally no time for me to play therapist and second of all, I couldn't care less about his girlfriend problems.

He moved closer to us and before he could say more, my magic shot out and engulfed him. Anger flashed across his face before sleep overtook him. He fell face first onto the ground with a loud *thud*.

"Ouch." Blake flinched.

Kohl glanced at me. "My Queen, I wish you had let him get dressed before you did that."

Blake snorted. "Does this mean I have to help carry his naked ass all the way upstairs?"

"We can lock him in that closet. Have someone bring down a blanket and pillow, I guess."

"Are we really letting him leave, My Queen?" Kohl's questions brought my head around.

I met his gaze. "I meant it. After we hex him of course."

The witches nodded in agreement. Heat rushed through me. We needed to be saving our power. Not wasting it on stupid murderous wolves.

"Move him to the closet and bring him a blanket and pillow. We'll lock him in and do the hex tomorrow."

"We're going to need extra witches to perform the hex," Deepa said.

I sighed. "Yeah. We'll figure out who tomorrow."

They bowed as I turned on my heel. Kohl stayed behind to help move the wolf and see to my instructions. My head spun as I climbed the stairs to my room. Fane's threat echoed in my ears and his face flashed in my vision. I shuddered at the thought of him having access to my coven—to me. I didn't like where things were heading, and my gut told me this was just the beginning. Things were in motion now and I doubted we would be happy with the outcome.

Trying to dismiss the dark thoughts and the day's events, I undressed and slipped into bed. My dreams were filled with happier memories and Fane's cold, blue eyes. They were there watching me in the past and though somewhere in the back of my subconscious, I knew I was just dreaming, I couldn't help but wonder... had he been there all along, and I'd never known it?

A disturbing thought, but not as disturbing as the fantasies my warped mind created. Fane and I together. His lips on mine and his fingers roaming, his touch scorching and—I woke with a start, heart racing. His smirking face vanished from my mind. I sat up and rubbed my face, cheeks still on fire from the dreams —no, nightmares.

"Never going to happen." My voice bounced off the walls. I blushed, feeling silly for the outburst.

There was no way he could see me, I knew that, and yet I

couldn't shake the feeling of being watched. Unable to sleep after that, I sat up and waited for daylight.

When the first early rays of sunlight appeared, I rubbed my tired eyes and dragged myself out of bed to pull on a pair of jeans and shirt. After a light breakfast and giant cup of tea, I met Kohl in the kitchen along with the other witches.

Silently, Blake and Deepa followed Kohl and I. Danny and Willow, the other two of my five best witches, were there, chosen by Kohl to help us with the hex.

A tremor ran through me as Blake opened the closet. Elijah looked up from the floor, He was dressed in the jeans they'd left him, but shirtless. His face was thunderous and already his brown eyes were shifting to silver.

Kohl frowned. "We gave you a shirt."

Elijah drew himself to full height—an impressive one—and glared at him. "It's too small."

Willow let out a giggle. I whipped toward her and she shut up quickly. Deepa shook her head at her.

What the hell did she think this was? We were about to perform a hex and she was tittering like a stupid flirt.

I turned back to face the wolf. "It doesn't matter. It's time for you to go."

His dark eyes narrowed on me and slid to the others. He didn't budge. Of course, his inner wolf was probably warning him, and he wasn't an idiot. There were six of us and he knew I wasn't letting him loose out of the goodness of my heart.

"The sleeping spell." I nodded to Deepa.

Her fingers flew as she chanted and threw her magic at the wolf. His head snapped back, colliding against the wall as the spell took over.

"Alright. Let's move him out."

Kohl didn't waste any time. The others followed his lead. I

watched as they carried him out and set him on the kitchen floor. Deepa kept the wolf asleep as we prepared the hex.

Blake lit the black candle carved with Elijah's name and handed me the long black string. I bent to tie it around his hands.

"What about his wolf? Will the hex work on his wolf too?" Willow asked.

"It should. He and his wolf are one," Kohl answered for me.

She flushed and looked away. Though she didn't admit it, I assumed it was her first time performing a hex on anyone. Most of the witches in our coven were inexperienced. The elders left the majority of our education up to our parents and families and not everyone had gifted witches in their family tree.

Kohl took a knife and carved a large S, our coven symbol, into another black candle and lit it.

"Hold hands and repeat after me," I instructed them.

We stood in a circle around the werewolf, hand in hand.

"With the power of the Coven, we bind you." My voice rose.

They repeated the chant.

"Elijah, Alpha of the Shadow Wolves, enemy of witches. You will not hurt us, not as man and not as wolf. Should you raise your hand against us, you will fall. Death will find you. Be careful of what you do, or the magic will make this true."

I waited for them to repeat my words before I started it over. After the third time, I gave Blake the nod to extinguish the candle at the same time as Kohl blew out the other.

Magic swirled in the air, whipping around us and through us. The werewolf twitched on the ground as the hex took effect. A black swirl appeared on each of his hands before disappearing.

"Put him back in the room to rest. Once he's up and well, see him out," I commanded the others.

Part of me felt guilty for marking the alpha, but he'd left me no choice. I couldn't leave my witches unprotected which was another reason I decided to give in to Fane's request. I would call my top witches together to tell them so we could come up with a plan.

I would have to face the prince of darkness, the heartless heir—Prince Ryn.

12
─────

VALERIA

The morning was gray and rainy. As if mother nature mourned our circumstances too. I'd been there along with the others to do the sweep inside the houses and felt the heavy pull of grief. All the resources had been stripped save for a couple of flashlights and some spare clothes.

If the humans had been scared off, where did all our stuff go? Anger stirred within me at the thought of Diego's pack hoarding our things.

We'd slept the rest of the day and night in shifts just to make sure Diego didn't return for Drew and Becca. I'd barely gotten more than a few hours.

I held my coffee tin in my hands and drank down the watery, grainy liquid. Instant coffee was better than nothing but paled in comparison to the real thing.

Sighing, I set the cup down and went outside on the covered porch to stretch my legs. Others milled about, some smoking and others nursing their own cups of powdery caffeine.

In just six months we'd gone from normal teens to weathered war vets. It was both impressive and really sad. None of us would have ever imagined to be living through the end of the world.

My head snapped up as Drew and Becca headed toward me.

They ignored the suspicious looks my pack shot them as they walked up.

I waited for them to speak first.

Drew flashed me a tentative smile. Becca just stared at me. She still gripped her gun as if it were a life preserver. My wolf growled with warning.

"Hey. I wanted to say goodbye before we left. And thank you for... everything."

I shook my head at Drew's words. "You don't have to thank me."

He glanced at his sister who arched a brow at him. I looked from her to him. What was it now?

"There's something else. Before you say no, just hear me out."

"Drew—"

He held a hand up and his dark eyes pleaded with me. "Please. We need a safe place. Out here, we could make our own camp. Over there in the field. We wouldn't have to be at the houses."

I looked to where he pointed. The old soccer fields.

"I don't think that's a good idea. Look, I'm not blaming you for what happened, but humans are the reason we had to leave this place in the first place."

His hopeful smile faded.

"I can't ask my pack to share a home with people... people who—"

"We had nothing to do with whatever happened here." Drew cut me off.

I sighed. "I know, but it's just... it would be a bad idea.

Humans and werewolves together."

"But we would stay on that side. Wouldn't come near."

Becca scoffed beside him, eyes rolling. "Give it up, Drew. I told you it's a bad idea."

His head whipped toward her. "So what? We just give up and let Diego sell us to the vampires?"

I gaped at him. "Vampires?"

He met my gaze. "As slaves. That's why they were trying to attack Jen. Some of them even have slave collars."

A chill crawled up my spine. Slave collars. The image it brought was horrific. Diego had confessed to using them too. How could the queen allow it? Wasn't anyone willing to stand up to the wolf? For the most part, vampires and wolves went their separate ways. Not really enemies, but not really allies either and now Diego was working with them?

"I... I'm sorry," I finally answered.

Becca snorted.

Drew frowned at her and turned back to me, face softening. "It's bad. It's really, really bad, Valeria."

His pained look made my heart twist. I looked away, not able to stomach it. How was I supposed to help them? What he asked was impossible.

"I'm sorry, but—"

"Come with me. Just one day in the city and see it for yourself." A fervor shone in his eyes.

"I can't just leave my pack."

"You said your alpha was in the city? I'll help you look for him. Let me show you our camp and—"

"Drew." Becca's voice was edged with warning.

He glanced at her and back to me. "Please."

"Our alpha doesn't want to be tracked. He'll return when he's ready. I'm not going to risk myself by going into the city for no reason if it's as dangerous as you say it is."

Drew issued a harsh laugh. "But you'll send us back there? To die?"

My lips pursed. "It can't be that bad."

"It is."

I sighed. Part of me wanted to go. To scope out the city for threat and maybe...

Find our mate.

At least make sure he was okay. Diego's words echoed in my mind. If what he said was true, I couldn't just do nothing. If the witches had him, I needed to get him—before it was too late.

"Alright. I'll go," I consented. "But this doesn't mean I'm letting you move your camp here."

Drew nodded. "I know. Thank you."

"It's not that I don't want to help but... I have to think about my pack."

He kept nodding. "Of course. I know."

I just had to tell Jay and Tati. The idea of explaining my decision to them made my stomach churn, but I couldn't leave without telling them what I was up to.

Excusing myself I went to hunt down my betas. I found them inside the clubhouse, finishing their breakfast. Their eyes shot to me as soon as I approached. Everyone fell quiet. Ignoring the heavy tension and curious stares, I strode up to them with purpose.

"Good morning."

"Morning," they returned, eyes still narrowed on me.

My chest tightened. I hated how things had become between us and I knew that it was my fault, but I couldn't take back what I'd said, and I didn't know how to make things better.

"The humans left yet?" Jay asked.

"They're leaving now and I'm going with them."

Everyone watched us but didn't say anything.

"I'm going to look for Elijah. To see if he's really with the witches like Diego said he was."

Jay's face hardened. "And if he is?"

I met his stare. "Then we'll get him back. We'll have to come up with a plan first, but we'll do it."

"You're not worried this is a trap? That the humans will take you captive?" Tati asked.

I scoffed. "I'll be fine. But if it is a trap, then you two will be in charge. Don't come after me."

Jay shared a look with Tati but didn't argue any further. After giving them instructions to keep an eye on everyone, I grabbed my rain jacket and hunting knife before meeting up with the twins. My wolf's apprehension filled me. The thought of finding Elijah was the only thing convincing her that this was a good idea.

In silence, I followed them out of the neighborhood. Thoughts raced in my mind as we headed for the city.

What would we find there?

It didn't take long until we made it to the outskirts of Savannah. Sweat beaded my forehead, the summer humidity thicker after the rain had stopped. The smell of campfires filled the empty streets. My chest tightened. Seeing the city for the first time since the curse made me pause. All the buildings looked the same, almost as if the spell hadn't happened, but the abandoned cars and broken storefronts were proof enough of the world we were living in now.

"We have to move quickly." Becca interrupted my thoughts.

Drew nodded to her and looked to me. "Our camp is on the other side of the city. An old movie theater."

I scanned the square, my eyes snagging on the direction the

Savannah witch coven would be. My wolf stirred, desperate to forget the humans and chase after Elijah. Pushing her down, I followed the others across the street.

They led me past empty restaurants and stores and down alleys. We made it to the older section of Savannah without any problems. The older, historical buildings and cracked, cobbled streets looked unchanged. Large, oak trees covered with Spanish moss sprawled here and there, offering shade. We ran along the trolley and railroad tracks and entered the old, city park. Vines and weeds sprang up along the old statues and lampposts.

Wasting no time, Becca and Drew led me down a side street, motioning for me to be quiet.

"This is where all the humans are. Those who haven't been captured by Diego or the vampires," Drew explained.

"There should be guards posted. Where is everyone?" Becca frowned.

She loaded her gun and scanned the area.

Humans, my wolf warned. I looked around, squinting against the sun to spot what she'd sensed.

"Stay close with us." Drew leaned closer to me.

My wolf bristled at his nearness.

Three armed humans appeared ahead of us, their expressions too far away to read.

Becca sighed in relief and moved forward.

Drew stood by me and gave me an encouraging smile. I watched as Becca led the others to us.

Two burly guys and one petite girl, all carrying guns, and judging by their harsh faces, they weren't exactly thrilled to see me.

Careful, my wolf warned.

"Where's Ben?" Becca demanded.

They exchanged glances.

Drew sucked in a breath. "What? What happened?"

One of the boys sighed. "Ben is dead. He was turned by a vamp. We had to put him down."

My eyes widened at the confession. Drew swore, running a hand through his short hair.

"Jason is in charge now," the other boy added.

Becca scoffed. "Jason? That twat can't even shoot a gun."

"That right, Becca?" a deeper voice called.

We turned to find a giant of a guy striding toward us. Small, blue eyes peered at us from under a dirty, baseball cap. The sleeves of his camo T-shirt were cut off to reveal muscular arms, the envy of any football quarterback.

Becca's lip curled. Drew stiffened beside me and my wolf stood on guard. Jason's eyes landed on me, lingering on my chest a little too long.

He grunted. "Who's this?"

Drew took a step closer to me. "We should talk inside."

Jason turned his head and spit. Becca shook her head in disgust and spun on her heel. Drew motioned me after her.

My heart pounded as the other humans brought up the rear. The thought that Jay had been right, and I was walking into a trap crossed my mind and made me shudder.

Loose gravel crunched beneath our boots as we walked. I twisted my neck, trying to take it all in and commit it to memory. Just in case it turned out to be a trap. But my gut instinct was to trust Drew. I didn't know why, but I had faith in his sincerity.

They led me to an old movie theater where another guy stood guard, holding a shotgun. Letters were missing from the sign above it and the building was badly in need of a new paint job.

"How did Ben get turned?" Drew asked as we entered the building.

Jason shrugged. "Ambushed."

"Here in the camp?"

The big guy shook his head. "No. In the alley."

He turned to me. "What's she doing here? She human? Her eyes look funny."

I fought the urge to roll my 'funny' eyes. "*She* is right here and can talk for herself."

He frowned at me. Clearly, he didn't like a woman who could speak her mind.

"I'm Valeria. And I'm Alpha of the Shadow Wolves."

His nose crinkled in distaste. "Werewolf?"

I dropped my arms by my side, ready to spring into action if needed.

"She's our friend. She helped us with... Jen." Drew stepped between us.

Jason's eyes narrowed. "Then, where is she? Huh? Where is Jen?"

"There was... she—"

"Jen's dead. She got bit. Valeria, tried to help her. But she didn't survive the change," Becca cut him off.

I glanced at her. Wasn't she going to tell him about the woods? About the body coming back to life?

Still frowning, he looked at us all and scratched the stubble on his chin. Others crowded around, whispers growing.

I could see it in their eyes. They didn't trust me. I could hardly blame them after what happened to Jen.

My wolf snarled in warning.

"Well, what is she doing here?" Jason demanded.

Drew frowned at him. "I asked her to come. To see what it's like in the city." His gaze slid to me. "To convince her to let us make camp near her pack. Farther outside the city."

Jason scoffed. "Why would we do that? We're fine here."

Drew shot him a glare. "Fine? Jen was taken—"

"That's because she left the compound. That's on her," Jason cut him off.

"They're not going to stop coming after us," Drew insisted.

Jason rolled his eyes. "And moving outside the city isn't going to stop them either. Why would we go to a wolf's camp?" His eyes met mine.

"I never agreed to let you camp with us." I glanced at Drew.

He gave me a pained look. "It would be better for everyone if we joined together. You need us."

My wolf growled.

"I can't risk my pack."

Jason snorted. "The alliance isn't going to work, Drew. Even Ben knew that. Just give it up."

Drew whipped toward him. "So what, we just surrender ourselves to Diego?"

"What about the witches? Won't they help you?" I interrupted.

Someone gave a harsh laugh.

Jason sneered at me. "The witches? They're the ones who helped Diego take over the city."

A sliver of fear ran through me. Elijah was with the witches. Was he okay?

"I'm sure they wouldn't hurt your friend." Drew grabbed my hand and squeezed it.

My heart warmed at the contact. He wasn't part of my pack, but I'd started thinking of him as one of us.

He's not one of us. He's human, my wolf reminded me.

Regardless, I couldn't just do nothing while Diego hunted them, could I? My mind raced trying to come up with a solution.

Drew sighed. "We're going to run out of food at some point and then we'll be forced to leave camp. If we don't make an alliance, we're dead."

Everyone fell silent at his gloomy prediction.

Guilt prickled at me. Jen's monstrous transformation flashed in my mind, making me shudder. Would that happen to Drew? To Becca?

"Come with me to see the witch queen. Maybe she can help." I looked to Drew.

He nodded. "Standing together is our only option."

His twin shook her head, but if she disagreed, she didn't voice it.

"How are you going to meet the queen without Diego catching you? She's on the other side of the city," someone pointed out.

Drew looked at me. "There's a group of rogue witches on the other block. They haven't exactly gone out of their way to help us, but they steer clear of Diego and the vampires too. Maybe we could go see them first?"

Rogue witches. My wolf howled with fury. The images of the attack were still fresh in our mind.

"Let's go," I agreed.

I wanted to speak to them and find out more about what had happened in the forest.

"Take a gun, Drew," Becca instructed. "I'll meet you at the back."

He waved to her in acknowledgment and motioned for me to follow. I glanced around at the others sitting around, their eyes narrowed in distrust.

They looked tired and dirty.

Scared, my wolf added.

Drew led me farther into the old movie theater. The sunlight didn't reach the back and there was a stale smell of popcorn, mildew, and pee. I covered my nose as I walked across the old carpeted floor.

He turned on a flashlight and took me into one of the screen rooms. The white glow of his flashlight revealed blankets and pillows thrown around the chairs. Is this where they slept?

I watched as he rummaged inside a backpack sitting on one of the reclining seats.

"Your friend. You said he was your alpha?" He glanced at me.

"Yes."

"So... like your mate?"

I flushed. "Well we haven't completed the bonding ceremony with our wolves. He's... just a friend."

My wolf growled at me. *Mate.*

"Why did he leave?"

"He needed time... personal reasons."

Drew frowned. "Sounds like you're better off without him then."

My wolf snarled, wanting to tear into him.

"He said he needed time, that's all. The spell... it took everyone in his family except his sister. She was killed in the city. By a witch. He needed time to grieve."

He set down his flashlight, the light illuminating around us. "I'm sorry. We've all lost someone."

I nodded. Drew pulled out a gun, checked the safety, and shoved it into the top of his jeans. I watched as he zipped his backpack up.

As much as Elijah's desertion still stung me, it didn't feel right to tarnish his image in the eyes of this newcomer. He was still alpha.

And our mate.

My wolf's words made me cringe. It was the promise I'd grown up with that Elijah and I were going to be together. I was expected to accept it and follow tradition, but the truth was, I'd never fully accepted it. I loved Elijah. He was my best friend, but I hated the idea of being bonded with someone against my will. Not that he would ever force me, but our wolves were fated to be together whether our human sides wanted it or not.

"Valeria?" Drew's voice brought me back.

I met his gaze and blinked in surprise at his nearness. My wolf's hackles rose. She didn't like it.

"Sorry. What did you say?"

A small smile spread on his face. "I said his loss is my gain. I'm glad you're here."

I lashed out and shoved him against the theater wall, my wolf emerging before I could stop it.

His eyes widened in surprise and then something else flickered there. Desire. Heat spread across my skin as I stood nose to nose with him.

"I'm sorry... I—"

He removed my hand from his chest and pulled me closer. Shock filled me. My inner wolf pushed at my restraints, eager to rip him apart.

I shoved her emotions down. I wanted him to kiss me.

"Drew." It was Becca's voice that broke our moment.

He dropped his hands and groaned. "Sorry."

I stepped back. "It's okay. We better go."

"Drew!" Her voice grew louder.

He sighed and grabbed his flashlight from the floor.

I followed him out, touching a finger to my lips and wondering what it would have felt like to be kissed by him.

My first kiss.

He's not our mate. My wolf was indignant.

Right. I barely knew Drew. The shame of what I'd almost done washed over me. She was right—he wasn't Elijah, but Elijah left. I rubbed a hand over my face. What was I doing? What was he doing? I'd seen how our new life pushed people together way too quickly. With the curse looming over everyone and brutal day-to-day survival the others needed something good to hold on to even if it wasn't real.

But I was supposed to be the sensible one. The alpha.

I pulled my shoulders back and took a steadying breath. I could do this—be strong. I had to.

13

MCKENZIE

"Are you sure about this, Kenzie?" Kohl's measured tone didn't match the worry I read in his furrowed brow.

I turned to face him. "No, but what other choice is there? If he can help me break the barrier then I have to go."

He blew out a breath and shook his head. "I don't trust his motives. Why is he offering to help us now? Why didn't he come forward when he first woke up?"

"All good questions. Which I'll be sure to ask him when we get there."

Kohl's lips pursed. "What if this is a trap?"

I walked over and grabbed his hands. "I'll be fine, Kohl. He'd be stupid to try anything. You and the others will be right there if I need you."

"I just don't see why he wants an audience with you alone."

Yeah, I didn't see why either and I had my own doubts, but I wasn't going to voice them. Kohl didn't need any more reason to worry about me.

"You're the one who told me I should go."

He scowled. "Yeah, with me."

"And you'll be there. If I start screaming for you, then you'll know it was a trap. And if he kills me then—"

"Don't say that. He's not going to kill you. I'll kill him first."

His hands tightened around mine and his eyes grew stormy. A jolt went through me at his reaction. I averted my eyes.

"I was joking... kind of."

"Not funny."

I sighed. "Sorry. Look, I'm only telling *you* this, but I'm scared too. But we don't have any other options. Let's hear him out and see what he has to say. If it is trap, then we'll take care of him."

Kohl's face softened. "Alright. I'm on your side. You know that, Kenzie."

I did. Kohl was so painfully loyal at times, and I wasn't so sure I always deserved it. He waited for me to take the lead. I pushed away my doubts and headed for the stairs to gather the others.

The sun was starting to lower as Kohl stopped our rust bucket of a car in front of the towering gates. Blake and Deepa fell silent in the backseat.

"Are you sure this is the right place?" Kohl's brow furrowed.

I shrugged. "This is the address Fane gave me."

"It doesn't look like anyone's lived there in forever. Everyone have their charms spelled?"

The others nodded in response. Our bracelets were spelled to keep us from being compelled. It was temporary, but all of us were strong enough casters to respell when the time came. After what happened to Mel's best friend, many witches wore the charms for protection. Apparently Julia wasn't one of them. I shuddered at the memory of her drained body. Her death wasn't the first in our coven since the curse, but it was the first one caused by a vampire.

We passed through the giant, open, rusted gates, and drove up the long winding driveway. The manor rose above the trees, looking every bit as haunted as I imagined. Dark shutters hung crookedly against the vine covered windows. Dead grass spread across the yard, dotted with creepy, crumbling statues.

Once parked at the entrance, we piled out of the car and looked around.

I held my breath as the front door opened for us. A fierce looking vampire stood guard, his body built like a professional wrestler. His narrowed dark eyes followed me as we passed by. I didn't like the way his lips twisted into a cruel smile. As if we were doing exactly what they wanted... as if it was a trap like Kohl feared.

My witches closed in around me, our magic thrumming to life.

It was more palace than haunted mansion. My head whipped as I took it all in. I felt as if I'd stepped back into the past. Into a world of ballgowns and elegance.

Decadent, gold trimming bordered the striped wallpaper. Rich colors of red and black adorned the room. Despite the age of the building, everything was vivid and looked like it was sparkling new. Even the shiny, gold-plated mirrors and marble statues, so obviously antiques, looked like they hadn't aged at all.

Everything was frozen in time—cursed. Like the vampire prince himself. Except he wasn't anymore. Who had woken him? I shivered at the thought of coming face to face with the heartless heir.

We were led farther in, and I was surprised to find even more lush décor. Giant oil paintings framed in gold, intricate tapestries, and a blood red rug. Full bloomed roses filled the various vases, adding life to the room.

It was beautiful and frankly impressive though I hated to admit it. How could a place this beautiful be home to someone so dark?

"The prince is waiting for you." A feminine voice interrupted my thoughts.

I nodded to the blonde vampire who appeared in the doorway. "I'm ready."

But I wasn't. My heart pounded too fast. Sweat gathered on my palms and it was all I could do not to bolt. I shoved away the fear. I was the queen. I had my magic. What could he do?

Well, he could bite me. Turn me. Drain me.

My lip curled at the thought. I wouldn't let him get that chance. I could stake him before he could get close enough for a bite.

"The rest of you can wait here," she added with a sneer.

Kohl's eyes met mine. I nodded at him in reassurance.

He opened his mouth to speak, but snapped it shut. We'd already had the argument a hundred times over. I would call him if I needed him. Which I wouldn't.

I was more than capable of dealing with this myself.

Without a final glance back, I followed the blonde down the hall. My footsteps echoed around me, drowning out the sound of my heart. Candle wax and cinnamon filled the air. Strange. It smelled like someone had baked something fresh. The soft glow of the candles created shadows along the endless hall. Paintings of ancient figures stared down at me. Their eyes held anger and contempt. I held my head up high. I would not be intimidated by some old pictures.

When we made it to the end, I stopped. A giant, gold frame stood over the doorway. The candles burning from the candelabras bolted on either side of the closed door illuminated a stern yet beautiful face.

Warm, gold-brown eyes burned into my very soul. He looked nothing like his brother—complete opposite, actually. Honey, gold skin with dirty, blonde curls combed back to highlight a strong, handsome face. My eyes snagged on his proud chin and full lips. Even with his eyebrows furrowed so harshly, he was mesmerizing.

A shiver ran down my spine. Prince Ryn?

Noticing my hesitation, the vampire stopped and walked back to me. "Sexy, isn't he?"

My eyes widened at the girlish infatuation in her voice. Sexy? Well, yeah. I couldn't deny the proof in front of me, but this was Ryn we were talking about. The heartless heir. Prince of darkness.

He had no right to look like that.

Before I could muster an appropriate reaction, the doors burst open. My escort flung herself to the floor in an exaggerated bow.

I barely registered her response. I was too busy staring at the gorgeous god who had just stormed in.

His eyes met mine and my heart skipped. The picture didn't do him justice. He was almost too beautiful to look at, as stupidly cliché as that sounded.

A dark eyebrow arched at me. "Queen McKenzie." His voice was softer than I'd expected. Not full of smugness like his brother. In fact, it sounded almost... kind?

I blinked. *Get it together, girl.* This was just sad. He wasn't *that* hot.

"Prince Ryn." I finally found my voice and thank God it was strong, holding no hint of my initial reaction.

He glanced at the prostrate vampire between us. "Thank you, Lilly. You can leave us now."

She scurried to her feet and bowed once more before backing away in a fit of nervous fluttering.

I watched her go, my heart speeding up. His eyes were on me now and I needed a minute to prepare myself before facing him once more.

"Come in. Would you care to sit?" he asked.

Pulling back my shoulders, I turned and nodded at him. "Thank you."

Ignoring the thundering of my heart, I followed his lead past the doors. My eyes widened. This room was just as elegant as all the others.

His hand swept the fancy furniture. "Sit anywhere you like."

I sank into one of the upholstered chairs and folded one ankle over the other. He stood and watched me, his face unreadable.

His golden curls were combed back like in the picture, but one stray lock kept dipping down his forehead. Noticing my gaze, he brushed it back with a finger, a slight frown on his face as it sprang free again.

"Would you care for a drink or something to eat? Viktor made cinnamon rolls."

My mouth hung open. Viktor? Cinnamon rolls? If it weren't for the sweat beading my forehead and the very real, very hard seat underneath me, I'd think I was in a dream. In what reality did the prince of darkness offer me breakfast pastries?

I was expecting the fierce vampire in the painting. Not... this.

"I... uh. No thanks." I tried to shake off the unease.

A smile spread on his face, one dimple appearing. My head reeled back. Was this some kind of trick? Why was he being so nice? To disarm my guard?

His smile faltered. "I'm sorry if I've offended you. I don't have company often."

Pushing away my fear, I straightened in my chair. "No, I bet not. With your reputation."

He flinched. Was that genuine remorse I saw flickering in his eyes?

"Being the Prince of Darkness and all."

His jaw hardened at my address. "Yes. I've heard the rumors."

I frowned. "Rumors? Are you seriously trying to deny what you've done?"

Amber eyes narrowed on me. His lips flattened into a thin line.

"Did you or didn't you kill those humans?"

He glanced away. "Does it even matter now?"

"It does to me."

His eyes snapped to mine. "Did you know them?"

His question took me by surprise. The anguish and regret I saw on his face made me pause. Did he actually care?

"No, but my sister did. And Grace. Do you remember Grace? She was my sister's best friend."

Silence stretched between us. He didn't answer, but he looked sad. Heat spread up my neck at his reaction. After all he'd done, it didn't seem fair that he could apologize and move on from it.

"Does your sister seek restitution?"

Restitution? Nobody talked like that anymore.

My face hardened. "She doesn't seek anything. She's dead. The curse took her."

Ryn winced, and turned away, leaving me sitting in silence and sorrow.

"I'm sorry." His voice was so soft and broken, I almost wondered if it belonged to him at all.

This couldn't be the vampire prince I grew up listening to stories about. The one who did these cruel things without feeling. Could the curse have changed him for the better? It was a ridiculous thought, but how else could I explain his change of heart?

I leapt to my feet. "You're sorry? What good does that do? They're dead."

I drew on the memories of Mel as she sobbed over her best friend, Grace. She'd been compelled and turned by Ryn two years before the spell. He'd broken the ancient agreement, and in response the coven had pushed for his punishment. Four years of confinement—in his coffin. It wasn't enough.

He took the seat in front of me and sighed. "I do remember Grace. Two years of being frozen, all I could do was think about her and all the others I turned or killed."

"Who woke you up? You still had two years left of punishment."

"I don't know."

I snorted. *Yeah, right.*

"Why did you do it?" The questions escaped me. My anger made me bolder. Or stupider.

His eyes bore into mine. "Grace? She asked me to."

Shock filled me, but I recovered quickly. "Liar."

"She did. She was already dying. Already bitten."

"By you." My voice rose.

Ryn shook his head. "No. I found her like that. I tried... it was too late to take her back to the coven. Giving her my blood was the only way to save her and it's what she wanted."

I blinked back the hot tears threatening to spill. "Then why didn't she tell us? Why didn't she ever come back?"

"She wanted revenge. She was compelled and couldn't remember the vampire who bit her, so she spent all her time searching."

"Who did it?"

He looked away. "It doesn't matter now. Most of the vampires were taken with the curse."

I watched him, waiting for further explanation, but it never came. This wasn't some trick to make me lower my guard. His pain was genuine, and it frightened me.

"You drained one of my witches. That's a breach of our agreement. That and your brother showing up on my doorstep. That's twice you've breached it."

His brow furrowed. "I didn't drain any witches. I haven't fed since... the first day I came back."

I folded my arms across my chest. "Who did it then? Fane? I expect you or him to pay for that crime."

He sucked in his lower lip, revealing his fangs. I fought the urge to skitter back.

"Are you sure it wasn't one of the low life vampires in the city? There's too many of them for me to keep watch of."

"She was compelled. That says royalty or at least a higher-class vampire."

Anger flashed in his eyes before he looked away. "Let me handle it. I'll find out who it was and punish them."

"No, I don't think so. You hand them over to us for punishment. That's how it works, Ryn."

He arched a brow at my informal address and smirked. "Alright."

"Alright?"

"You are right. We've broken the agreement and owe you recompense."

Confusion swept over me. He was agreeing to my terms. Why so easily? I shifted in my seat and changed the subject.

"Fane said you could help. With opening the barrier?"

He met my eyes. I forced myself to hold his smoldering gaze despite my reflexes urging me to look away.

"Yes. I want to help."

A harsh laugh escaped me. "Help? You want to help me? Why now? Why not six months ago when all this started?"

Folding his hands together, he sat forward. His scent enveloped me. It was musky, warm, and way too inviting. My body prickled with awareness in a similar way it did with magic. Heat washed over me, and immediately I knew I was in danger. He was too close. Too alluring.

I didn't like it. Except, I did, and that's what scared me. What in the hell was wrong with me? Sure, he was gorgeous. Like otherworldly gorgeous, but I was the freaking witch queen, and he had admitted to turning Grace and killing others.

"Six months ago... I was hardly at a place to help anyone. Besides, I didn't discover how to break the barrier until a month ago."

My eyes widened. He'd already found a way to break the barrier?

"What? How? How did you discover this?"

His lips pursed. "You won't like this, but it was with a witch's help."

I reeled. "One of my witches?"

He shook his head. "No. She was a rogue witch."

Was.

"What happened to her?"

He sighed. "She... turned twenty. A week ago."

Dread curled in my gut. *The curse.* It was deadly specific, and no one survived it.

"I'm sorry."

He nodded along as if he expected me to say that. My head was spinning with this revelation. Despite the doubt, hope flared inside me. If I could break the barrier...

"Her name was Allison. She was a friend of my brother's." His words snapped me to attention.

"A friend of Fane?" My nose crinkled.

"My brother's charm always seems to have that effect."

I scoffed. "Charm? He's disgusting."

Ryn cocked his head at me. "I see he's had an effect on you as well."

Schooling my features, I turned my attention back to the barriers. Questions raced in my mind. So many questions.

"She figured out a way to break the barrier?" I prompted.

"I believe so. Her grimoire is here. I can show you."

My eyes widened. "Yes. I need to see it."

He smiled. It was a glorious, infectious smile, but my stomach clenched with dread. Was it a trap? Was this how he'd charmed his way with the humans before he drained them?

Don't fall for it. Don't fall for it.

But I was already on my feet. I glanced back at the way I'd come and debated calling for Kohl and the others. Would it make me look weak?

"Queen McKenzie?" Ryn called to me.

I fought down my fear and nodded at him. "Show me."

14

VALERIA

I met Drew and Becca outside the theater room. Becca's eyes darted from her brother to my flushed face and narrowed with suspicion.

"Got my gun. We should bring an extra one for Valeria." Drew spoke first.

Becca's eyebrows shot up her forehead. "Um no, Drew. Let's not give the werewolf a weapon."

My wolf growled in my mind.

Drew frowned at her. "Valeria is on our side. She's going to help us."

Becca's cool gaze slid to me. I pushed my wolf's anger down, insisting the girl was no threat to us.

"It's okay. I have a knife. I don't need a gun."

Drew opened his mouth to argue but stopped himself at my stare. Becca turned on her heel and led us past the other screen rooms. My mind raced as I watched the scattered humans huddled in the darkness. Where were these fighters Drew claimed they had? Was it just a bluff? After hearing him talk about achieving peace without violence, I was beginning to think he'd said those things only as a means to sway me.

Lies, my wolf retorted.

But could I blame him? As I pictured their weary faces, I couldn't help but pity them. I knew what it was like to live in fear... as prey.

We are their prey. Humans hunt us.

I ignored my wolf's reminder. Not all humans were our enemies. If the covenant worked like Drew hoped it would, maybe there was a chance we could all coexist. At least until we died off from the curse. I pushed the thought away. No good came from dwelling on a circumstance we couldn't change, and after what we'd endured, I wasn't afraid to die.

You lie.

My lips pursed at her taunt.

Becca opened the doors, sunlight streaming in as we stepped out.

"Thank you for coming." Drew's voice caught my ear.

I turned to him, his nearness startling.

"Here. To our camp. You... you're not like the others."

Bristling, I opened my mouth to respond.

He shook his head. "I don't mean it in a bad way. It's a good thing. You... you're a good person." He flushed and looked away.

I blinked in surprise. Was he... flirting with me? Wasn't that what you were supposed to do before kissing? Heat spread across my face as I remembered our near lip contact.

My wolf snarled at the memory.

His eyes met mine and the intensity of his stare made my heart skip.

I stilled.

"Someone is coming," Becca interrupted.

My wolf rose to the surface.

Drew and I turned to face the street. Footsteps sounded in the distance. Angry shouts and gunfire rang out. My heart slammed against my ribs.

Wolves. Red wolves.

Becca shoved us back inside and slammed the door. Jason and the others gathered around us.

"They're here," she rasped.

Someone cried. Others swore.

Jason strode forward, gun in hand. "We'll shoot them when they come."

Drew shook his head at him. "Shoot them? That's your solution? No! Not all of us have guns, Jason and they outnumber us. We need to get everyone out of here."

Argument ensued among the humans. My wolf grew restless as they went back and forth. They needed a plan and they needed it fast.

"We get everyone to the witch's camp. Now," Drew insisted.

He started moving toward the front entrance, motioning everyone to follow. Becca and I were the first to go.

"You're not in charge," Jason hissed.

His words went unnoticed as everyone scrambled to catch up.

A scream came from the other side and a gun fired. My blood turned to ice. They'd already made it to the front door.

Panicked cries echoed around us. Chaos erupted. People dove into the screen rooms and some ran back toward the back door. Bodies slammed against me, separating me from Drew and Becca.

My heart raced as I scanned the theater. Flashlights jerked all around, highlighting terrified faces. Where was Drew? Becca?

More screams drew my attention. Why was Diego attacking and not capturing the humans instead? I pressed myself against the edge of the wall and crouched out of line of the bullets. I fumbled in the dark, heading for the safety of the concession stand.

Why did they choose a theater of all places? There wasn't much shelter and before long Diego's pack would overrun their camp.

Something was burning. I turned to see flames licking the floor near the front entrance. Dread coiled in my gut.

Was he was trying to smoke them out?

More flames appeared along the carpet. They lit up the theater in a hellish glow. Screams echoed around me, striking my nerves.

Get out. My wolf urged me.

I couldn't leave without Drew and Becca.

The crowd poured out of the screen rooms in a wave of panic, their shouts bounced off the walls. Smoke followed them. My heart sank. More fire.

En masse, they raced for the back exit. But what would they find out there? It was a trap.

"Valeria!" Drew's voice called from behind me.

I stood and ran to him.

"We have to get out of here," he insisted.

Becca was by his side, gripping two guns and staring at the rising flames.

"Is there another way out? We have to get everyone out, but not that way. Diego's pack is waiting out there."

Drew swore and glanced at the horde of people running for the exit.

"They have both the exits blocked," Becca answered.

"Is there any other way?" I asked.

"There should be a fire escape in one of the rooms."

Becca shook her head. "The one we tried was blocked which means they probably all are."

Fear rushed through me. We were trapped.

"We'll just have to get through with the others. Maybe he'll be distracted..." Drew trailed off.

"We'll be walking right into a trap," Becca argued.

"There's no other way?" I asked again.

Dread coiled in my gut. I didn't want to surrender to Diego, but we couldn't stay in the building.

Get out, my wolf agreed.

"Let's try another fire exit. Maybe they missed one," Becca suggested.

"It's too late. We'll get stuck with the fire," I shouted over the noise.

Outside, the wolves were howling. Gunshots rang out and for a second, I was back with Elijah and my pack racing out of the city as the mobs swept through.

But this time it wasn't the humans attacking. The wolves were exacting their revenge, and I knew Diego wouldn't stop until he had them all—either dead or alive.

"Then we try to escape Diego. Later. And take as many as we can with us," Drew agreed.

Smoke filled our eyes as we headed for the exit along with the last of the humans. Had they all made it out?

Sunlight welcomed us as we streamed out. I blinked, my eyes watery from the smoke. Coughs echoed around me.

"Valeria." Diego's voice made me flinch.

His eyes narrowed on me. "What are you doing here?"

I lifted my chin. "What are *you*?"

"You're siding with the humans over your own pack? Against us?"

I snarled at him. "You are not my pack."

He strode forward. "Wake up, Valeria. There is only one

pack now. It's us against them." He glanced at Drew and back to me. "Don't be stupid. Make the right choice."

My fists clenched as I fought the urge to unleash my wolf on him. She desperately wanted to be loosed, but I couldn't afford her recklessness right now.

"They were going to help me get Elijah. Get him back from the witches."

Diego frowned at me. "You went to the humans for help? Why didn't you ask me?"

"Why didn't you offer?" I scowled at him.

Everyone fell quiet. Tension ran high as the humans huddled together, surrounded by Diego's wolves.

"You know I would have helped you if you asked, Valeria. Now your pack is alpha-less. I guess it's a good thing I'm here to help them."

My wolf pushed, begging to be set free. To tear into Diego.

"My pack would never submit to you. You're a monster. You should be ashamed to call yourself a wolf. Turning on another wolf?"

Diego's lips pulled back in a tight smile. "Isn't that what you've done, Valeria? Turning on me? I was never your enemy. Until now."

I tensed. I didn't want to fight him, but my wolf was ready. We couldn't back out of this challenge. Before I could shift, something happened.

One by one, the wolves staggered back, pushed by an invisible force. Magic? I whipped around to find the source.

Shouts echoed in the street. Fire leapt higher from the theater roof, filling the air with the smell of smoke and burning wood. Flames jumped for the line of werewolves. My eyes widened as they fell on one's arm. He yelped in pain, shifting to wolf.

"Run!" someone shouted as a break appeared between the other shifting wolves.

Everyone tore through at once. I raced along with Drew and Becca. My heart drummed loudly in my ears as my wolf urged me forward.

Were the witches helping? Where were they?

My boots pounded against the stones as we fled the area. Drew ran ahead of me, leading the others down the street. Howls and screams sounded behind us. I shuddered.

We made it, but what about the others?

I turned to see Diego watching us. Fear ran up my spine. I would take him on if I had to, but to my surprise, he held his wolves back. I returned his glare before turning back and leading the others away. My head pounded as we made it out of the smoke.

Dread unfurled inside me. It couldn't be that easy. They would come after us again.

I picked up my pace, helping Drew and Becca lead the others through a side street. We didn't stop until an invisible barrier knocked us back mid-step.

"Why aren't they letting us in?" a girl asked, wide-eyed. She glanced back at the direction we'd come and flinched.

Becca slammed a fist into the air, frowning as it connected with something unseen.

"Lower the ward!" she growled.

Two guys appeared in the doorway of an old townhouse. They flung their arms toward us and chanted something. The barrier dissolved and we ran forward. My heart was still racing as they reset their ward and turned to us.

"The others. Diego's pack has them. We have to get them." Drew spoke first.

I shook my head at him. His desperation, I could understand, but I doubted the witches appreciated his command.

They exchanged looks and motioned us inside.

Drew's brow furrowed. "Did you hear me? He has the others. We—"

"Just shut up, Drew," his sister snapped.

She followed the others after the witches, leaving him standing in the street alone. My chest tightened at the lost expression on his face.

I pulled his arm, urging him to follow. My wolf bristled at the touch.

His big, brown eyes met mine and I could barely stand the sorrow I saw in his pained gaze.

"Come on. Maybe the witches can help," I urged, though I suspected they'd already done as much as they were willing. We stumbled after the others.

Candle wax and burning sage assaulted my nose as we entered the old townhouse. Sunlight poured in from the open window in the small kitchen. Becca and the rest of the humans stood together, taking up most of the room. The two witches were nowhere to be seen.

"They said we can stay for the night. Once the wolves are out of the area, they want us gone," Becca informed us.

I growled in frustration. My chance to speak to the rogue witches about the woods and they'd disappeared before I could ask them anything.

One of the girls, who couldn't be much older than thirteen was sobbing. An older girl hugged her tightly, and the scene pulled at my heart. Anger replaced my sorrow. How could Diego do this to them? And the threat he made to me—I couldn't forget that.

He had to be stopped.

Drew sighed. "What about the others?"

Becca shook her head at him. "They're not going to help us, Drew. We're on our own. You know that."

His jaw hardened. "We have to go to the queen. She's the only one powerful enough to stop Diego."

Becca grunted. "What's going to make her do it now? She could have stopped him any time."

"Where else can we go?" The defeat in his voice stung me.

"You can come back with me. To my camp. For now. Then we'll talk to the queen about this... alliance."

Everyone stared at me. Drew's eyes widened, a spark returning in his gaze.

"You'll unite your pack with us?" he asked.

I sighed. "We'll talk to the queen and get Elijah freed first. Then we'll go from there."

Becca scoffed. "Yeah. We'll see. I'm going to see if the wolves have left yet."

Without waiting for a response, she stormed back outside and slammed the door. The others sank into the chairs around the small kitchen table.

I walked up to stand beside Drew. "Your sister is... fierce."

His face fell. "She pretends to be."

"But she's not afraid to shoot, to kill."

He shuddered. "I know. She wasn't always like that. She was anti-gun believe it or not."

My eyes widened. "I don't believe it."

His lips twisted in a bitter smile. "When Ruby died, something snapped inside of her. It's like a part of her died too. She... couldn't kill the vampire to save her girlfriend. Now, she's killed"—he blew out a breath—"I don't even know how many vampires. And wolves."

Ruby? Was that the name he'd mentioned before when she hit him?

I didn't know what to say to all that, so I just nodded as if I understood. The grief of losing a loved one and the need for justice were things I could relate to, but constantly living in a cycle of violence? I didn't ever want to get used to that. Did that make me a weak alpha?

Drew sighed heavily, snapping me out of my thoughts. "I wish she didn't have to. I know she thinks I'm a coward for not killing. But... I feel like if I lose that part of myself, I'll lose my humanity. There has to be a way for us to make things better. Without killing."

The passion in his voice startled me. I shared the same sentiments, but were we wrong? After everything that had happened, were we only fooling ourselves in believing we could have peace again?

"The alliance will change things. Change everything."

I looked away and bit my lip. "How do you know?"

He splayed his hand over mine, warmth spreading through me. My wolf growled. I pushed her back before she made me lash out at his touch.

His eyes met mine. "It has to, Valeria. It just has to."

I looked around at the small group. Only five. Five counting Becca and Drew, but Diego wasn't going to give them up like that.

He will come for them, my wolf agreed.

Yeah and when he did, I'd be ready.

For now, they'd have to return to my camp, but I couldn't keep them there forever. Drew was right—we needed the queen.

15
___

MCKENZIE

Prince Ryn leaned over the glowing grimoire, the light from the huge, floating book and the surrounding candles highlighting his striking features. Honey eyes, strong jawline, and full lips.

I swallowed hard, averting my eyes from his handsome face. Even his furrowed brow was sexy and that was just ridiculous.

The spell book was open, golden script crowded the cream pages and the magic I sensed guarding it made me pause. How did a rogue witch get enough power to ward it so permanently?

"I've tried to move it, but it won't budge. Maybe you can?" Ryn asked.

A heavy sigh escaped me. "No. It's warded well. She didn't want it removed. I could try copying the words. Do you know which page has the spell to break the barrier?"

Ryn pointed at the grimoire. "This is what she was working on, but I can't tell if it's complete. I'm not a witch." He gave me a rueful smile.

My gaze returned to the flourishing, gold words and inked symbols. *Arimar.* The language of souls. "It's... beautiful."

"Isn't it? I like to come up and look at it sometimes. Not that I understand what any of it means..." Ryn trailed off, his face flushing.

I looked away from him and moved closer to inspect the words. Try as I might, I couldn't find a single fault in her written instructions. Who was this witch that she knew more than I did? A rogue witch wouldn't have access to the old spell books or supplies.

"Is it about the barrier?" The prince's hopeful voice broke my concentration.

"No. Actually it's a spell for... raising the dead."

His eyebrows lifted. "What?" He came around and stood beside me, his body dwarfing me.

My skin prickled with awareness as he leaned closer. He smelled like warm spices and the burning candles around us. There was also a hint of cinnamon lingering on him. The cinnamon rolls? His eyes met mine, and I flushed.

"Maybe she was trying to reverse the curse." He looked back at the grimoire.

Happy to have somewhere to focus besides his lips, I turned and reread the spell.

"No. This is only for witches. Maybe she was trying to bring back someone she knew."

My heart twisted at the thought. I'd tried that too, but wherever our loved ones went when the curse took them, it wasn't the spirit world.

"Well, you can make more sense of it than I ever could. She told me she was working on the barrier spell."

Disappointment wormed inside of me. Was it just a lie or had she really discovered a way to break the barrier spell?

"It will take me some time to go through her spells and notes. I'll copy down everything important."

"Of course. Take as much time as you need." His eyes bore

into me and though he moved back to a respectable distance, his presence was still overpowering. Overwhelming.

"Call the others in here. Please." I blushed at the realization I was ordering him—the prince of darkness, and in his own palace too.

His eyebrow arched and an amused smile spread on his face. "It's been a long time since I've had the pleasure of entertaining a queen."

"Well, you were in a box for two years."

The smile vanished and his eyes darkened at my words. "Yes. I haven't forgotten. My imprisonment. I thought I was going to go mad in there. The silence and utter darkness. Though I admit it's nothing compared to what I did to those humans." He looked away.

I stood, gaping at him. His regret seemed genuine, but what if it was a trick?

"Why did you do it?" My words came harsher than I meant.

Ryn looked up at me with a pained expression. "Bloodlust. My father used the humans as a tool to teach me self-control. I failed."

With that, he left the room. I turned back to the grimoire and flipped through the pages, but my mind was still racing, trying to make sense of what he'd admitted.

Kohl, Deepa, and Blake were ushered into the room by a vampire I didn't recognize. Prince Ryn didn't reappear, and though I could admit I was a little disappointed at his absence, I knew it was probably for the better.

I didn't need any distractions.

"How do they have a grimoire?" Deepa broke the silence.

She circled the floating book with a frown. Blake waved his hand in front of it, testing the magic that surrounded it.

Kohl came up to me. Worry swam in his eyes. "Are you

okay? They wouldn't let me check on you. You were gone for a while."

I smiled at him. "I'm fine."

He studied my face but didn't question me further. Guilt prickled me. For some reason, I couldn't bring myself to tell him what Ryn had confessed, and that unnerved me. Kohl was my best friend. There were few secrets we kept from each other. So why wasn't I telling him?

"I haven't found anything about breaking the barrier. It's going to take a while to go through it and it's warded. We can't move it."

"We could copy it," Kohl suggested.

"I have a feeling it's warded against that too, but try it."

His face scrunched up in concentration as he waved a hand above the grimoire. He shook his head with a sigh. "Yup. Can't copy it."

"Do you think it's worth trying to copy it the old-fashioned way? Paper and pen?" Deepa asked.

Blake scoffed. "That would take forever."

She frowned at him. "We wouldn't have to do it all. Just the sections we need."

"No, this spell is strong. Permanent. Unless we break the ward around it, we're not going to be able to copy it or move it."

I stifled a groan. "Guess that means we're going to be here a while."

An hour later and we were nowhere closer to breaking the dead witch's spell. I didn't know how she'd been able to perform something so strong and permanent. And by herself? It should have been impossible. There had to be a part we were missing.

Watching as Kohl tried for the umpteenth time to break the ward, I needed a break.

"Do you think they have any real food around here?" Blake muttered.

"Or water." Deepa added with a wistful look.

"I'll find out. Ask Ryn to bring us something."

Kohl frowned. "You don't have to do that, My Queen. Send Blake."

Blake scowled. "Thanks."

"It's fine. I need to talk to Prince Ryn, anyway. About the witch they drained," I added quickly.

"Julia." Deepa's dark brows furrowed.

I nodded. "Yes. Julia."

"I'll come with you then," Kohl offered.

"That's not necessary, Kohl. Stay here and help the others. I'll be back shortly." The words tumbled out of me.

He blinked at me in confusion but didn't argue. I turned away before I had to explain myself. The truth was, I couldn't explain my behavior nor the strange pull I felt toward Prince Ryn. Morbid curiosity? Why else would I want to spend more time around him than I needed to?

My pulse quickened as I left the others and retraced my steps through the dimly lit hall. Questions plagued me as I readied myself to face the vampire prince again.

A shadow moved ahead. I stopped in my tracks, squinting against the darkness.

"Hello? Ryn?"

It moved toward me, too quickly to make out. Fear crawled up my spine as I summoned my magic to shield me.

"Queen McKenzie. No one told me you arrived." Fane's silky voice reached my ears.

My body tensed.

"I'm not here to see you, Fane." I huffed.

He emerged from against the wall, looking far too confident and too appealing. His vivid, blue eyes lit up as he stepped toward me. The candles along the wall highlighted his sharp features.

A smug smile spread on his face. "So, you've agreed to help us? With the barrier? I didn't realize you cared so much about us bloodsuckers."

My eyes narrowed. "I don't. I care about my coven. I'm trying to save them, remember?"

There was that amused smirk again. It made me burn from the inside out.

"Trying to save them when they're rooting for your failure?"

"What are you talking about?"

His blue eyes danced away. "Rumors have a habit of spreading. Even my recluse of a brother has heard what they say about you."

I snapped my lips shut, refusing to give him the pleasure of any reaction. Curiosity bubbled inside me, but I wouldn't do it. I wouldn't ask.

As if reading my thoughts, he continued. "They say you can't do it. Break the barrier. Break the curse. That you're the weakest queen the coven has ever produced."

Red spots dotted my vision. Who said that? Why hadn't Kohl told me? Did he think it too?

"Oh, and that you're kind of a bitch."

I gasped.

Ungrateful assholes. I never wanted to be their stupid queen.

I tossed my hair back and glared at him. "Well, they're wrong."

His smile grew. "Obviously. If they saw what I saw..."

My eyes snapped to his, heat spreading up my neck. Was he... complimenting me? I shook off the uneasiness and licked my lips. His gaze followed my movement.

I stiffened. What was going on? How had I let the conversation get so out of my control? Ignoring the fluttering in my stomach, I lifted my chin and turned away. Space—I needed space from him. A place to clear my mind and unwind all the emotions that rolled inside me.

He moved first, giving me what I needed. Though his eyes still watched me.

"I'd be careful if I were you. My brother... isn't as strong as he used to be. Never quite learned to control his bloodlust. I'd hate to find you dead and drained like that... what was her name?"

Anger sparked at his coldness.

"Julia. And please, don't waste your worry on me. I don't need it." I shot my magic to the candles. The hallway glowed brighter as the fire burned with intensity.

Fane glanced at them and back to me. His face grew serious. "Even the strongest flame can be extinguished, *cariad*."

Before I could ask him what his words meant, he was gone. Air whooshed around me and down the hall, making the candles flicker.

Coldness seeped into my skin. I scanned the emptiness, expecting to see a spirit. Was the dead witch still there? Could she have somehow found a way to preserve her spirit from the curse and if so, would she help us?

"Hello?" My voice bounced back to me, sounding eerie.

Shaking off the feeling, I started moving again. If she hadn't helped us while living, I doubted she'd be any more willing to do so in death.

Fane's words echoed in my mind. *The weakest queen...*

Pushing away the thought, I straightened and marched down the corridor. They wouldn't be saying that once I broke the barrier spell.

I found Ryn in the same room I'd met him in. He was sitting in an armchair with a book in his lap. His head turned in my direction and I nearly stopped at the intensity of his gaze.

"Finished already?" he asked.

"No. I... we were hoping you had some food."

Setting the book down, he stood and stretched, a smile on his face. I couldn't help but notice what a paradox he was with his massive body that screamed warrior and yet a sweet, almost boyish grin.

"Of course. I've already anticipated you would stay for dinner. I have the dining room set for us."

I blinked at him. Did he sound... excited? One day in his presence and I was questioning everything I ever knew about him.

"What about the others?" I finally found my voice.

He smiled brightly. "I sent in a tray for them so they could continue their work."

My eyebrow rose. "How thoughtful."

His smile faded. "I'm sorry, was that something I should have discussed with you first? I just thought you'd want to dine like a royal..."

I waved off his concern. "It's fine."

"Will you be eating with me then? Or?" He ran a hand through his hair, messing up the curls. "I'm not sure what you mean by fine."

My face flamed. *Tell him no. Tell him no.*

"Yes. That's fine. I'll eat with you."

The brilliant smile returned, that irritatingly, adorable dimple appearing once more.

Regret slammed into me, but I couldn't take it back now. Why had I agreed to dinner? Dinner. I was having dinner with the bloody vampire heir.

Stupid. Stupid. Stupid.

"Are you ready now then?" His question broke my thoughts.

"Okay."

Ryn led the way into a massive dining room that would

easily fit two of my coven dining rooms. I gaped at the lavish décor feeling sorely underdressed in my jeans and blouse.

"Wow. You eat here all by yourself?"

Sadness flickered on his face. "We all used to eat here. My father, stepmother, Fane, and me. Sometimes a friend or two."

I spun around in surprise. "Stepmother? You and Fane aren't brothers?"

He shrugged a shoulder. "We have the same father. Different mothers, but I call him brother."

How had I not known that? I frowned, trying to remember the history I'd been taught, but found my mind coming up blank. There were so many pieces I didn't know.

Ryn came around to pull out a chair for me, much to my surprise. Guilt needled me at the thought of the others still working without me. I should have been there helping them. Not sitting at the massive table with the vampire prince.

But I didn't leave. I sat and listened to Ryn's stories as somewhere in the distance classical music began to play. A servant brought us food fit for a king. Well-seasoned steak and vegetables. Antique silver goblets filled with red wine. An assortment of chocolate. How in the hell had their cook been able to whip all that up so quickly?

What did vampires need with all the lavish treats, anyway? Wasn't blood their main source of nutrients?

"Are you thinking what I'm thinking?" Ryn's voice brought my head up.

I gaped at him, unsure of what to say.

He spread his arms, indicating the table before us. "How crazy this is? You and me. Here. On a date."

My eyes bulged. "Date?"

A small smile spread on his face. "Food, candles, and music. Not that I'm any expert, but I'd say this has all the makings of a spectacular date."

I straightened my back and stared down at my plate, heat spreading up my neck.

"I'm sorry, Kenzie. I didn't mean to offend you. It... was a joke. In bad taste, I guess."

Kenzie? I sucked in a breath. How did he know my nickname?

"Only my best friend calls me that."

He cocked his head at me. "My apologies. I didn't mean to offend you. I thought the nickname suited you."

My eyebrow arched. "How do you know what suits me? You don't know me."

Silence filled the room.

His lips spread in a small smile. "Of course. I'm sorry."

I bit back my own smile. *Damn.* Why did he have to be so... sweet? *Remember what he did to Grace. To the others.* But he'd admitted he was the one to save her, doing what she requested. The humans though... their blood was on his hands. I couldn't forget that.

Noticing his stare was still fixed on me, I tossed my head back. "It's fine."

I took a sip of the water, hoping the cool liquid would cool me down. The room had grown ten times warmer.

"But if it was a date... how is it? For you, I mean?"

I took another sip. His eyes watched me, making me blush even more.

"I... I don't know how to answer that?"

His face fell, and I immediately regretted my response. Ryn was nothing like I'd pictured. He was nothing like his arrogant brother, but I couldn't get swept into their games. I had my coven to think of.

"What are you thinking?" His low voice sent another shiver up my spine.

I refused to meet his gaze. If I didn't look maybe I could be strong.

"Kenzie."

My heart raced.

"What's wrong?"

The genuine care I heard in his voice made me wince. It was real. Whatever it was. It was real for him just as much as it was for me.

But it was wrong. Wrong. Wrong. So wrong.

I licked my lips and took a breath. His eyes dipped, following my movement. My face flamed.

"I... I have to go."

A wounded look flashed on his face. "Did I do something? Say something wrong?"

Ugh. Why? Why did he have to be so... different from what I'd expected? This couldn't be the same vampire who had earned the nickname *heartless*.

It just couldn't be.

"No. You were fine, but I should go. Figure out the grimoire and stuff."

My mouth was running away, and the more he stared at me the more idiotic rambling spewed out.

"It's because I called it a date, isn't?" He frowned. "I shouldn't have said that."

"No. It's fine. It's just that it's getting late and I should go back to check on the others. It's all good." I winced at how high and squeaky I was sounding.

I shot to my feet and fought the urge to squirm under his unnerving stare. My skin flushed. Damn these vampires and their otherworldly beauty. It was hard not to be transfixed.

Unlike his cocky brother, Ryn didn't seem to notice my turmoil. He stood and walked toward me, concern written on his face.

My gaze dipped to his lips. What would they feel like against mine? My eyes snapped up, heat spreading up my neck.

He stepped closer, making my heart fly. I backed up instinctively and cursed at myself for allowing him the higher ground.

My back pressed against the stone wall. I shivered at the cold contact. Ryn's eyes drifted to my exposed neck, his nostrils flaring.

Shit.

16

VALERIA

Morning light streamed in the small window of the old townhouse. I rubbed my sore back and cracked my neck, trying to get out the knots from sleeping on the hard, kitchen floor. The thin blanket the rogue witches had left was hardly enough cushion. Though I appreciated their help, I didn't understand why they wouldn't let us sleep in an extra room.

The witches, my wolf warned.

I stood and glanced at the others. Drew and Becca were already up, but the others were still curled on the floor.

"They're coming." I broke the silence.

Drew and Becca gaped at me. The same two witches reappeared from the staircase, whatever invisible barrier they'd built now gone. My wolf lurked near the surface, silent and ready.

Though these weren't the same rogues who attacked our camp, we couldn't help but remember the damage caused by the witches. The death. The destruction.

My wolf growled.

I drew myself up and took a step toward them. "I'm Valeria. Alpha of the Shadow Wolves."

They glanced at each other. I waited for them to introduce themselves, but they just stared at me in silence.

The shorter one nudged his companion and made a gesture with his hand. My wolf tensed, expecting a spell. The other witch nodded and signed something back. Realization hit me. He wasn't casting. It was sign language.

"I'm Mark. And my boyfriend is Reed." The taller one motioned toward the other.

I nodded at them in acknowledgment.

"Thank you for helping us. I know it was probably a risk for you."

Mark grunted. Reed continued to stare at me.

Drew came to stand beside me. "Yes, thank you. Is there anything we can do for you?"

Mark signed the question to his boyfriend. Reed made a gesture that I suspected meant for us to leave.

"No. Just leave. It should be safe to go now. The wolves haven't found us here and there's only a few of us. We don't want any more trouble."

"Wait. Before we go, there's something I have to ask you. Do you know anything about the rogue witches buried in the woods outside of the city?"

The two witches exchanged glances.

Mark frowned at me. "A lot of rogues practice their spells in the forest. Or used to anyway. But our group isn't one of them."

"Do you know what would have caused the bodies to... come back to life?"

His eyebrows shot up. "A resurrection?"

I nodded. "They threatened to kill us if we didn't leave the woods. We were forced to come to the city."

He turned to his partner and signed something. Reed's eyes widened. His fingers flew and I looked to Mark to translate.

"He's asking if you've seen any witches out there recently? Alive witches who have been casting. Only someone with a lot of power could perform that kind of magic."

"No. No one."

A skeptical look flashed on Mark's face as he turned to Reed. I watched as they communicated, curious to know what they were saying.

Mark faced me. "When it's safe, we will send someone to investigate."

Disappointment filled me. I wanted to ask if they knew a way to return the witches to their graves but wasn't sure they would help me with that.

"We can perform a protection spell for you. It's temporary, but should be long enough for you to make it to the other side of the city"

"Thank you." Drew gave them a grateful smile.

His eyes lit up with calculation and I knew what was on the tip of his tongue.

"We're going to seek the queen. To form an allegiance. To stop Diego. You won't have to live in hiding anymore."

A stormy look crossed Mark's face. "We want nothing to do with the *queen*."

Drew's brow furrowed. Maybe he didn't understand the rivalry between the rogues and the Savannah coven. Even I didn't fully comprehend their refusal to acknowledge the queen's power.

"But she could help. Help you. Help all of us," Drew continued.

Mark's nostrils flared. "We don't need her help. The queen and her witches think they have a claim on all the magic, but they're wrong. Every witch should be equal."

Drew gaped at him.

Reed shot his partner a questioning look, but Mark just shook his head at him and turned to us.

"Now. For the protection spell."

After they waved their hands over us, they left. I couldn't blame them for not wanting anything else to do with us. They were probably scared of Diego's retaliation for what they'd already done.

It was a bold move on their part, but at least they had magic to protect themselves.

"Looks clear. We should head out." Becca threw a pointed look at her brother.

He loaded water bottles into a bag Mark and Reed had left us. Anger rolled inside me at the thought of Diego and his wolves pawing through the few belongings the humans had. His pack didn't need any more resources.

More and more, the alliance Drew insisted we needed made sense. We couldn't keep surviving like we had been. We needed to be smarter. Stronger.

"Ready?" Drew's question snapped me back.

I nodded and followed them to the door. Becca—still carrying her beloved guns—went first with Drew and I bringing up the rear.

"Are you sure you know the way back to my camp?" I asked her from the back.

She glanced over her shoulder at me. "Yes."

My wolf snarled. How could she remember the way so easily? I frowned, wondering if I was making a mistake by bringing them home. But what else was I supposed to do? I couldn't let Diego hurt any more humans.

The sun was bright as we scurried from building to building, scanning the area for any danger. My wolf was on high alert, though she was desperate to break away and tear off after Elijah instead of escorting the humans to safety.

We ducked behind an abandoned catering bus. The back doors were open, and the shelves emptied of whatever had been there. It was a sobering image that portrayed our new life so well.

For a second, I felt as if we were in some elaborate apocalypse video game or TV show. Any minute and the zombies would show up. Except this wasn't pretend and there were no zombies. The danger was real, and our enemies were everywhere. I shuddered.

There was no restart or ending to this. At least not a happy one.

We made it to the outskirts—surprisingly—without any trouble.

My wolf was nearly beside herself as we left the city. I didn't like being so close to Elijah and not knowing if he was okay either, but the humans needed a safe place to hide.

He will find them easily, my wolf argued.

I ignored her and took the lead as the back entrance to the subdivision appeared. They'd tied the gate closed with a string of Christmas lights, but where were the guards? My fists clenched as I strode forward. Had Diego come while I was gone? Heart racing, I listened for any sound.

Shadow wolves, my wolf confirmed.

Two members of my pack, Nick and Adele, walked up to the gate, eyes widening on the humans behind me.

"Open it," I instructed.

They hurried to obey.

"Any trouble while I was gone?" I asked them.

Adele shook her head. "No, Alpha."

Her gaze darted to Drew and the others. "Did you find... is Elijah... did you see him?"

The gate squeaked open. I ushered the others forward and motioned for Nick to tie the gate back up.

"Not yet," I finally answered. "But I will."

Without explaining further, I pushed by them and took the humans farther in. I stared straight ahead afraid to look around at the old streets and houses. Getting caught up in the memories would only bring pain and anger.

"This is nice," one of the human girls murmured to the others.

Becca whirled on her. "Yeah, how nice you get to camp out in the suburbs while the others are probably sitting in some basement right now with a slave collar, enduring god knows what." Her face hardened. "Or dead. They could be dead already."

The girl flinched at the harsh words and looked away, falling silent.

"Becca." Drew frowned at his twin.

She arched a brow at him in challenge, but he didn't refute her.

Nausea rolled in my stomach at the images Becca painted. How could Diego think this was okay? The revenge I understood, but what he was doing went far beyond that.

"Are we going to be safe here?" The other girl spoke up and glanced around.

No one answered her. It was a question we'd all been asking since our parents were taken. Was anywhere safe when the world was cursed?

My wolves emerged from all around us. Their eyes narrowed in obvious suspicion.

"Where's Jay?" I asked, ignoring their questioning looks.

He appeared at the head of the crowd before anyone could answer. Tati stood by his side, her mouth hanging open when she spotted our guests.

Jay's eyes shot to me. "Alpha."

"The humans are staying here. Diego destroyed their camp and took most of them prisoner. I don't want any problems. I'll be heading back into the city as soon as I see them settled. Elijah still needs me."

No one spoke, though my wolf could sense the pack's surprise and anger at my decision.

What else was new? I could never do anything right in their eyes. Even Cruz and Leah exchanged worried looks.

"Jay. Tati." I called them to me.

I turned to the group. "Leah, can you set them up in a spare tent or somewhere they'll have some privacy?"

"Yes, Alpha." She motioned the humans to follow her.

Becca trailed them, but Drew lingered behind with an uncertain look on his face.

"You can go help them. I'll catch up in a moment." I gave him a reassuring smile.

He nodded and turned away from me.

"Are you sure about this, Alpha?" Jay's tone was clipped.

I turned toward him, letting my wolf surface enough to warn him.

"They stay for now. I'm taking the twins to see the witch coven. We're going to get Elijah back and talk to the queen about an alliance."

His eyebrows lifted to his forehead. "An alliance? With the witches? How do you know the queen will help?"

I didn't.

A couple of angry murmurs echoed around us. I couldn't really blame them. Elijah was convinced a witch killed Rachel and he'd declared them our enemies. The truth was none of us really knew who'd been responsible for her death. She ran away from the pack and it was Elijah who'd found her before her final breath.

"We have to try. We need them. Diego is too powerful. He tried to come after me and claimed he would take this pack for his own. We have to stop him. If that means allying with the witches and the humans—"

"The humans?" Jay fumed. His dark eyes flashed to silver.

"The humans who stole our home and killed Felix and hurt others?" His voice rose.

"No. Those who were responsible for that have already been dealt with. These humans are innocent, Jay."

He scoffed.

"Diego's gone too far. I won't let him come after our pack or the humans. The queen has to help us and maybe she can deal with those dead witches in the forest too. We can return to the woods if we want."

Jay folded his broad arms across his chest, scowling at me. "What would Elijah choose?"

I bristled. "I'm alpha too."

Even as I spoke the words, I hated how I sounded. Like a jealous child, demanding attention.

"I'll go with you to get Elijah."

My wolf snarled at Jay's boldness. He'd gone too far. My hand whipped out, fingers gripping the front of his T-shirt.

I leaned into him. "You will stay here and guard the camp."

Anger flashed in his eyes, but he didn't fight me. Tati grabbed his wrist and squeezed, a silent warning to get him to back down.

He glanced at her, face softening and turned back to me. "Yes, Alpha."

I released him and stormed away. The eyes of my pack followed me as I left, but I refused to meet their stares.

Guilt needled me as I replayed the scenario. I was doing what I was supposed to—keep the pack safe and maintain my dominance—but why did I feel like I was doing such a crap job of it?

My wolf remained silent which only set me even further into a bad mood.

Before the day got too late, I changed, grabbed water, and went to find Drew and Becca to accompany me. The others stayed behind in a spare tent outside the clubhouse.

They seemed unsure of my wolves despite my reassurance, but I refused to travel the city with them again. The protection spell was probably worn off and I didn't want them to slow us down.

In silence, the twins and I made our way into Savannah, cautious not to draw attention to ourselves.

We darted through the town square and crossed the street as the sun began lowering. The coven house—like the rogue witch's place—was warded. My wolf could sense the strangeness of it as we stepped onto the brick steps of the front porch.

The old mansion looked freshly painted with wine red siding and black shutters. A giant chandelier hung down in front of the front doors. Gaudy. Tacky. Their coven was screaming for attention and I couldn't help but smirk. Without electricity the fancy light fixture was useless.

They don't need lights. They have fire, my wolf reminded me.

I pushed away the image of the flames attacking Diego's pack and knocked on the door. Becca gripped her gun and Drew stood beside her, face serious.

The door opened and a pale skinned witch appeared. He frowned at us. "Yes. What do you want?"

"I'm here to speak to your queen. You have one of our wolves here and I want him back."

The witch blinked at me, mouth gaping like a fish.

Kill him, my wolf urged.

I pushed the urge down, warning my wolf this wasn't the time to get violent. I still had to make my way past more of the coven. We did not want to start a fight.

"The queen is busy," he answered.

He started to close the door, but I shoved my boot in the gap and pushed forward.

"Then I'll wait. This is important."

His eyebrows knitted together, and he raised his hand toward me.

My wolf snarled. *Magic.*

"What is it, Alex?" a voice interrupted.

Another witch appeared, her eyes widening when she saw us.

"Please, we just want to talk to the queen. We need her help," Drew spoke up.

I flushed, realizing his approach was probably the wiser one.

The witches glanced at each other and looked behind us to the streets. With the sun setting, the city was growing darker.

"Alright. Come in. Just—"

The guy witch whipped toward her. "Willow, what are you doing? We're not supposed to let anyone in or out."

She frowned at him and shoved him out of the way to let us enter. I didn't hesitate. Becca and Drew followed.

"I'm sure the queen would agree to let them in. It's getting dark and they're harmless."

My wolf's hackles rose at her estimate.

I looked around at the dimly lit sitting room and sniffed. It smelled like candle wax and some strange spice I couldn't put my finger on. Drew and Becca wandered around, talking in hushed voices. It was warm and stuffy, and the candlelight cast shadows of the antique furniture giving the coven an eerie feel.

The door shut behind us with an ominous thud and my wolf tensed within me.

"You said you're here for your friend? Elijah?" the girl asked.

"Yes. Is he here? Is he okay?"

Her lips quirked into a smirk. "He's fine. Resting... you'll have to wait until the queen is available. I'm not sure she'd allow me to take you to him."

Make her take us there now.

Ignoring my wolf, I frowned at the girl. "Why not? If you've hurt him..."

Her eyes widened. "No. No. He's okay. I just don't want to get into trouble."

"Then you probably shouldn't have let them in," her friend muttered.

My wolf was restless, pushing to be released so she could hunt down our mate. I shoved her back down and glanced at the others.

"I just want to make sure he's okay," I pleaded with the girl.

She bit her lip and glanced at the giant staircase.

"Is he up there?"

Instead of answering me, she hurried to where Drew and Becca stood puzzling at a strange symbol stitched onto a sofa. The other witch eyed me, fingers flexing. Annoyance flickered in me.

Why couldn't he join the others and give me a chance to make a run for it?

I was about to ask where the bathroom was when his companion called him over to the others. He frowned at me and walked over to them.

Before anyone could stop me, I tore off after Elijah.

Yes. Find our mate.

"Valeria!" Drew's voice called behind me.

But I didn't stop. The witches were scrambling after me and I could feel a shift in the air which meant—

Duck.

I obeyed my wolf's command and bent just as an invisible force flew over my head. My legs pushed me forward and suddenly I was at the top of the landing.

My heart pounded as I looked around. Where was he?

There.

I followed my senses down the hall and to a closed door. The witches were right behind me. I flung the door open and leapt inside. My breath quickened as I shut myself in.

"Elijah," I gasped.

He looked up, his eyes burning through me. His wolf would have alerted him as soon as I stepped into the manor, so he knew I was coming.

A purplish bruise marred his cheek. My wolf snarled. *Who dared to touch our mate?*

"Val." His deep voice sent a shiver up my spine.

He stood in the center of the room looking just as handsome as ever in the low candlelight. My legs felt like jelly as I stumbled toward him. Tears threatened to break loose, but I blinked them back, refusing to look weak in front of him.

The pungent odor of candle wax filled the room, but I could still smell the woods on Elijah. Woods, smoke, and the subtle hint of his sweat mixed with soap. The scent was overpowering and completely his. My wolf urged me closer.

"Elijah." My voice was steadier than I felt.

He drew a deep breath, his chest rising and falling. "What are you doing here, Val?"

I bristled at his question. Was he seriously asking me that? My eyes narrowed on him.

"I don't abandon my pack, Elijah."

He flinched.

The door flung open and the witches stood in the doorway.

"We're just talking." I scowled at them.

"You shouldn't be here," the guy hissed.

Elijah tensed. "I'm not your prisoner anymore. Remember?" His voice was steel.

"Sorry," the redhead girl blurted and closed the door.

We could hear them arguing, but their words faded down the hall.

Emotions stormed through me. I wanted to scream at him for leaving, wanted to wrap my arms around him and never let him go. But most of all, I wanted him to be happy I was there. Didn't he miss me at all?

His stony face hid any emotion. I tried to ignore the pain. This wasn't the same boy I knew, and I was stupid for forgetting that. Elijah, the one I'd loved, was gone. In his place was this hard, broken creature.

"You shouldn't have come, Val."

I reeled. My wolf whimpered inside me. Her sorrow mixed with mine. He didn't want us.

He balled his fists and covered his face. "Please. Just go. Go back to the pack."

Anger ripped through me. My vision grew spotted. Go? After everything we'd been through and he was sending me away? I was there to rescue him, and he was rejecting me.

"No." The word came out harsh.

His head shot up, his dark eyes meeting mine. "They need you."

I scoffed. "They need you too, Elijah. But that didn't stop you from leaving."

Despite my wolf's insistence, I kept her restrained. Hurt or not, she wanted to go to Elijah, but I wasn't done being mad at him.

"I needed you. You said you were coming back. You promised—"

His eyes flashed silver. "I never promised that, Val."

I glared right back at him. "You promised to be by my side until the end. You made that promise in front of our pack, our parents, the same as I did. When we had our first shifting."

A humorless laugh escaped him. "Yeah, I promised. Wake up, Val. This *is* the end. Our parents and elders are gone. The pack is nothing more than a bunch of weak, stupid kids now."

I leapt at him with a snarl and shoved him back. "We're still a pack. This is still our pack. You don't get to turn your back on them. On me. You're a selfish coward, Elijah."

Heat rushed through me. Even my wolf was angered by his words. We were not weak—I was not weak.

"If you don't want to come willingly, I will drag your ass out of here and you can explain to them yourself because I'm not covering for you this time."

His eyebrows shot up and a smirk lit his face. For a second, a flash of mischief flickered in his eyes, a reminder of the boy he used to be.

"How are you going to do that?" he taunted, arms folded across his chest.

"I'm serious, Elijah. Don't make me."

A grin split his stupid face. "Don't make you what? How exactly do you think you're going to make me come with you?"

Irritation flared inside me. He wasn't going to make this easy.

"I'm not leaving here without you."

Elijah's smile disappeared. "Don't do this, Val. I'm not going back to the pack."

"I'll do what I have to. It's your choice. Come with me like the alpha you're supposed to be or be a spineless coward and I'll drag you there myself."

His nostrils flared. "If I go with you and tell them I'm leaving for good, you'll let me?"

I winced at his words. Leaving for good. How could he do this to us?

Tell him about the Red Wolves.

I didn't want to tell him about Diego's threat. It would make me look weak in his eyes. I could handle the alpha on my own. I didn't need Elijah.

Pushing away the pain at his words, I nodded. "Sure."

How could I let him leave us like we were nothing to him? Like I was nothing. My wolf was already howling at the thought of him leaving.

Our mate.

He wasn't our mate yet, I reminded her. Though if we did perform the bonding ceremony, we'd be tied forever. That was the one way to make him stay, but I couldn't use it. Why would I want to be bonded to someone who didn't want me?

17

MCKENZIE

Ryn's intense eyes held me captive, and though I should have pushed him back, I couldn't bring myself to stop him as he leaned forward.

I summoned the magic around us as quickly as I could and used it as a shield to protect myself. Fane's words echoed in my mind. *He never learned to control his bloodlust.*

"You have something on your cheek." Ryn's voice was deep and rough.

It sent a thrill up my spine.

He brushed a cold finger against my skin. I flinched, God help me, I flinched.

My eyes widened as he brought his finger to his mouth and sucked. "Chocolate." His gaze bore into me.

I flushed. *What is happening right now?*

"Were you hoping for blood?" I lifted my chin.

His eyes darkened. A throaty sound escaped him, making my cheeks flame even more. What the hell was I doing?

"He said you were losing control. Your brother."

Anger flashed on his face and then it was gone. He stepped back, the air growing chillier without his presence.

"Fane always loves a good scandal, but I assure you, I'm in complete control." His eyebrow arched as if expecting me to argue.

There was something elegant and beautiful about him, but also fierce. I didn't respond, words too difficult at that moment. As much as I hated to admit it, Ryn had an effect on me and it was freaking terrifying.

"Have you done it? Chosen your queen?" the words rushed out of me.

What? Why would you ask that?

Unfazed, he shrugged a shoulder. "Why would I? So pointless. Pick a queen to rule the end of the world with me?"

"Then how can you claim to be king? If you don't follow tradition?"

He turned back to me. "I don't. I don't claim to be king."

I gaped at him. "But... then your brother. You'd give him the throne?"

"Why not? He wants it more than I do. Always has."

Horror ran through me. Fane as king would be a nightmare.

His nose scrunched up at my reaction. "You disapprove?"

I snorted. "Of course. Fane as king? You have to see the problem with that. You can't be that blind."

He turned his back on me. Worry crawled up my spine. He wasn't serious, was he?

"Ryn?"

His head swiveled to me, his piercing eyes making my heart skip. I fought the urge to squirm under his scrutiny.

What was wrong with me? It wasn't like I'd never seen a vampire before.

"Kenzie?" His voice was low.

I stiffened. *Get out. Just get out of there.*

I sucked in a breath for strength and summoned more magic to me, hoping it would soothe me.

That was a mistake.

As soon as it filled my senses, my emotions thickened, and I couldn't deny them—desire and longing.

Oh hell no. Nope. Not happening.

Before he could take another step toward me, I turned on my heel and ran.

Ran away like a little bitch. My face was crimson. Thank God none of my witches were there to see me in such a state. What would they think of their queen now? What would Kohl think?

Guilt struck me like an arrow. Kohl. Nice, cute, loyal Kohl. Why couldn't I fall for him?

Because he wasn't Fane or Ryn.

I slapped myself. *No. Don't do that. We're not doing that.* Queen of the witches falling for a vampire? Not just any bloodsucker, but the next vampire King? That love story had tragic written all over it.

When I returned to the grimoire, I apologized for my absence and explained where I'd been. That I'd had a lot to discuss with Ryn on behalf of the coven. There were plenty of reasons, but I'd never admit to the real ones—that I was curious, intrigued, and drawn to the heartless heir.

It wasn't something I could even admit to myself.

The others had found the written spell for the barrier and lucky for us, it was completed. The ingredient list checked off in ink.

"I don't understand. If she had this done and had all the

ingredients. Why didn't she use it?" Deepa voiced the question we all were thinking.

"She would have needed a lot of witches to pull off this spell. Maybe she couldn't find enough to help her." Blake shrugged.

"What I want to know is how a rogue witch came to have so much knowledge and access to these ingredients." Kohl pointed at the check marked list with a frown. "An enchanted key, a strand of hair from a dead queen?"

Dread coiled deep in my gut. I wondered the same. Blanca, the previous queen, had been buried in the coven cemetery in the city, but it was warded—warded by the elder witches centuries ago. How could one rogue witch have gotten in?

"Looks like we have a mole situation on our hands." Blake's lip curled.

My thoughts drifted back to Fane's creepy insinuation that he'd been stalking me. Was someone in our coven working with Fane to finish what the rogue witch had started? Then why had the prince dragged me into it?

The words the vampire had spoken replayed in my mind. *They say you're the weakest witch the coven ever produced.*

Anger lit hot and bright within me. If someone were sneaking around with the vampires and hiding things from me, I would find the culprit. *Show them who was weak.*

"We'll deal with this when we get back. For now, we're going to have to get some rest and hunt down where she stashed these ingredients."

Deepa and Blake exchanged glances. Kohl frowned at me. "You want to stay here... for the night?"

I sighed. "No. Of course I don't, but we can't leave now when we're so close to cracking this."

Rubbing my tired eyes, I led them from the room to see to

sleeping arrangements. My heart raced at the thought of staying the night in the prince's home.

~

"I don't like this." Kohl scowled.

Deepa and Blake disappeared into separate spare rooms. The mansion was big enough to house my entire coven and then some.

I turned to Kohl. "You think I do?"

He glanced around the hall. "Why is this necessary again?"

I frowned. "Because Kohl, I need more time to look at her grimoire to figure out this barrier stuff."

Kohl shook his head. "It's a trap. I can feel it."

An inelegant snort escaped me. "Please, Kohl. You can feel it?"

"Well, I don't trust them. We should respell our charms. Just to be safe."

I didn't answer. It wasn't that I disagreed with him, I just didn't want to have to defend my decision—not to him. He, of all people, knew there was no other choice.

We were doing the best we could. What else was I to do but choose the least shitty option?

"I'm staying with you. There's no way I'm letting you sleep alone here."

My eyebrow raised at his command. He flushed, no doubt remembering himself.

"I mean if you want me to. I would feel much better if we were in the same room."

"Fine. But you'll have to sleep on the couch."

He followed me into the room and glanced away, cheeks red. "Of course. I didn't mean... I wasn't..."

I turned my back on him, willing him to drop it. If we were

going to be sharing a room, there was no reason to start acting awkward now. It would be a long night. Thankfully, the weirdness faded, and we fell into a comfortable silence.

Hiding the skimpy slip of silk Ryn had left for me before Kohl could see it, I slept in my own clothes and lay in the giant bed. My face heated. Had he really expected me to wear that? It was clearly made for a girl much skinnier than me.

I pushed away the thought and struck up a conversation with Kohl about the grimoire and barrier spell. Eventually his well thought out answers turned to sleepy grunts, and I left him alone.

At some point, I fell asleep. When I woke, my heart was racing. I sat up and blinked against the darkness. The candle was out, and the heavy clouds obscured the moon. My eyes scanned the room. The feeling of being watched made the hairs on my neck bristle.

"Kohl?"

No answer.

I leapt to my feet and ran to the couch. He was there. Still sleeping. My shoulders sagged in relief as I walked over to him and gave his shoulder a shake.

"Kohl."

He didn't stir. Why wasn't he waking up?

Fear shot through my veins. "Kohl!"

I shook him harder. Something was wrong. I bent down to listen to his heart. The steady thump was a welcome sound. Alive, then, but why couldn't I wake him?

After trying to jostle him once more and tickling his face, I knew it was pointless. A lick of anger curled inside me. Who was responsible for his deep sleep? Was it compulsion? A spell? How had they gotten past our own protection spell?

If they wanted my help with the barrier, they'd made a big mistake in messing with Kohl. Slipping into my shoes, I threw my hand over Kohl's body and chanted a quick spell. It was temporary, but at least it would keep him safe while I dealt with Fane.

The hall was pitch black and cold. Unnaturally cold for summer with no air conditioning. I rubbed my arms and blinked against the heavy blanket of black. How was I going to find my way now? I didn't want to summon magic. Not if I needed to defend myself against the vampires, but I couldn't very well stumble around all night.

"Fane," I called.

My voice echoed down the hall, sounding otherworldly as it bounced off the walls. I fought the urge to call on the magic that was stirring in the air. Not yet.

"Fane, get your ass out here. I know you're listening."

But was he? Was he even in the mansion still? My lip curled. Someone had done something to Kohl.

"When I pictured you shouting my name, this isn't exactly what I had in mind." Fane's voice made me jump.

My head whipped around, searching for him.

"You guys on a candle budget or something? Can we get some light?"

"Can't you do your little magic trick?"

I bristled. "It's not a trick. And why can't you just light some candles?"

Something rustled and a click sounded. One by one, flames appeared in candles mounted on the wall. The hallway was bathed in a warm, golden glow.

Fane's blue eyes drilled into me and I almost wished I hadn't insisted on the light. He fit so perfectly with the castle's haunting, dark beauty.

"So, you prefer lights on, huh?" He smirked.

I flushed at his insinuation. "What did you do to Kohl?"

"What makes you think I did anything to him?"

"He's under some kind of sleep compulsion."

His eyebrows shot up. "Is he? How strange."

"Don't play with me, Fane."

He chuckled. "As endearing as your refusal to use my proper title is, I'm afraid I must remind you that unless you and I are... to put it delicately, rutting the brains out of each other, it's Prince Fane."

My face flamed. "You're disgusting."

"And yet here you are seeking my presence."

I clenched my fists. "No, asshole. I'm here to tell you to snap Kohl out of whatever hold you put him in."

"Why do you assume it's me? There is another royal here."

"Ryn wouldn't do that."

Fane's eyes narrowed. "Ryn now is it? Is that who you've been rutting with?"

I shot him a glare. "No. Shut up. And nobody says rutting anymore."

He shrugged. "The words may change, but the act itself hasn't. Is it that other guy then? Tell me, does that puppy dog fulfill all your needs?"

"What?"

He nodded toward the room. "Your manservant."

Anger rolled through me. "Kohl is not my manservant. He's my friend."

"Friends with benefits?"

I made a face. "He's just a friend. What do you care, Fane?"

His eyes pinned me. "Curiosity?"

"Fix him. Now."

He chuckled. "It's just a sleep compulsion, *cariad*. It will wear off in thirty minutes or so. Just enough time for me to show you something."

"I'm not going anywhere with you."

Fane circled me, eyes dipping down my body. I called my magic to me to guard myself from whatever he was planning.

"Come with me, or stay and forever wonder what it was I wanted to show you."

I grunted. "Get over yourself. Why would I care about anything you wanted to show me?"

He shrugged a shoulder and started to turn. "Suit yourself."

My heart sped up as he walked away. What if it had to with the rogue witch and the barrier?

Or it could be a trap. Like this doesn't happen in every horror movie. Don't go.

But I could handle Fane.

"Wait," I blurted.

He stilled and turned around slowly. Wordlessly he waved me forward and idiot that I was, I followed.

My eyes narrowed on him. "Did you compel me?"

He laughed. The harsh sound echoed off the walls. His smile wasn't like Ryn's. It was smug and cold. So why did I still find it so alluring?

"I didn't need to, *cariad*."

I paused. "Why do you keep calling me that? What does it mean?"

Instead of answering, he picked up his pace and led me through a set of doors and corridors. Voices drifted in the distance, but I couldn't make out what they were saying.

Worry filled me as we made another turn. Any hope of finding my way back on my own was shot. My magic thrummed around me, giving me strength.

Fane pulled a key from his pocket and unlocked the massive door ahead of us. Fear crawled on my skin as I blinked against the dimly lit room. It looked like some kind of ancient parlor room with lounge chairs and side tables strewn about. Large shadows moved in the back.

18
———

MCKENZIE

Fane strolled farther in. "Ah. Looks like they're awake."

A wave of nausea rolled through me as I trailed him. "What is this Fane?"

"Don't worry. They're just humans. Not witches."

My heart lurched at the sight. There were five of them. All with slave collars around their necks. Their eyes were glazed under compulsion and their mouths hung open. As badly as I wanted to, I couldn't look away from them.

They were dressed in stark, white clothes. I couldn't see any sign of violence, but I doubted he kept them there just to look at them.

I could feel Fane's eyes on me. Pushing down my apprehension, I turned to face him. "This is horrific."

He laughed.

Anger stirred in my gut. It was barbaric and disgusting. How could he think I wanted to see this?

"Release them, Fane."

His arms folded across his chest. "Why would I do that?"

"Because I told you."

His laugh deepened, and I hated how it sent a shiver of awareness through me. What the hell was my problem? The vampire was sick. Sadistic, even.

"You think these are innocents? Look a little closer, McKenzie. Don't you recognize any of them?"

His words caught me off guard. I glanced around, body growing numb. I did recognize them.

They were the humans who'd led the mobs in the beginning. The ones who'd killed some of my own witches in cold blood. Images of the shootings and violence flashed in my mind.

What they'd done was unforgivable. Worse than what Fane did to them but keeping them like this... it still felt wrong.

Guilt stung me. I'd been the one to help Diego capture them. Nausea rolled in my gut.

"You can't keep them like this, Fane."

He scoffed. "Why not? This is the only way to tame monsters."

I shuddered.

"Does Ryn know about this?"

Fane's face darkened. "You mean Prince Ryn. Only his closest acquaintances call him sans proper title."

I ignored his clipped tone. "Does he know what you've done?"

"The prince of darkness? He's done far worse things than this, darling."

He circled me, eyes sharp and demanding. "Oh, I see. You think I'm the monster, and what? That my brother is prince charming?"

His harsh laughter echoed off the stone. "Did he tell you about them? Ask him about Isabel. I promise you won't like the ending to that story."

I swallowed, trying to steel myself. Fane's words were like little arrows flying and finding their mark deep into my chest.

"I don't care what your brother has done. And I don't care what you've done. You want to keep the humans here as slaves, fine. Just stay away from me and my coven. And stay the hell out of my territory."

Fane's smile widened. "How else will we be able to see each other? I can't seem to get your attention any other way."

My skin flushed with anger. "My attention? You thought I wanted to see this?"

I flinched as his finger came nearer to my face. "Of course. It's all for you, *cariad*. Don't tell me you haven't felt the pull. I know you have."

"What the hell, Fane? I don't have time to play your stupid mind games. Leave me alone."

His face lowered, inches above mine. My heart stilled. Piercing blue eyes pinned me to the spot, and I shuddered. His perfect lips quirked at the movement.

Damn him.

"You're sick."

"And yet you still want me? Doesn't that make you just as sick?"

He clucked his tongue and gave me a patronizing smile. "What would your coven think?"

"Don't talk about my coven. I know you're the one who killed that girl—Julia. In payment, I'll see you staked. For eternity. How does that sound?"

All humor fled from his face. "It's cute you think you have that much power."

I bristled but recovered quickly. "Oh, that's right. I'm talking to the wrong brother. You're just... what exactly? The court clown? The city slut?"

His eyes narrowed. "Careful, you wouldn't want me to have to cut out that pretty tongue of yours. Not when we could find so many other good uses for it."

My hands balled into fists. The bastard knew all the right buttons to push.

"You will pay for what you've done, Fane. I'll make sure of it."

Fane leaned in toward me, his scent overpowering.

"And you? Will you pay for what you've done?"

Heat rushed over me. "I haven't done anything."

A cold smile spread on his face. "If you say so."

With all the swagger of a king himself, he turned away from me and disappeared into the shadows. I watched him go, furious at myself for letting him goad me.

There was no doubt, my threat meant nothing to him. Well, I'd just have to make myself extra clear. The next time I found a drained body in Savannah, I'd stake him myself.

I took one last glance at the humans. Fane's words rang through me. It was my fault they'd become enslaved, but they'd started the fight first. I'd only done what I'd done to survive. There was no right or wrong at the end of the world.

There was only survival.

Stumbling my way back to my room, I tried to bridle my emotions. What was I thinking letting Fane fluster me?

A nervous chuckle escaped me. It was this house. It had to be. Maybe despite his denial, they had compelled me. Even as I thought it, I knew it was untrue. It was all me. Stupid, pathetic me.

Somehow—magically—I made it to my room and threw open the door. Kohl was standing on the other side and collided with me as I entered.

The glow of the candle revealed his hard face. Relief flashed across it.

"Kenzie! Where were you? I woke up and you were gone. I was just about to hunt down Ryn."

My pulse was still racing, and heat spread across my face as I thought of a response. I couldn't tell him.

"Are you okay? What happened?" His hand gripped my wrist.

The concern pouring off him made me shrink further into myself. I was a horrible queen and a horrible friend. Pushing away the emotions, I gave him a big smile.

"What? Nothing. Just went to snoop on the grimoire." The lie came easily.

His eyes searched my face. "Why didn't you wake me up first?"

I licked my lips and sighed. "I tried. They had you in some kind of sleep compulsion. I went to tell them to break it."

"And then you... went to the grimoire?"

Stilling myself, I nodded. "They said you would wake up on your own, so I took a quick peek at the book when they thought I was gone. But it was useless, anyway. There's no more info."

Kohl's eyes narrowed in suspicion, but he didn't question me any further. We returned to our separate beds and while his gentle snoring told me he'd fallen back to sleep, I couldn't stop replaying the images of the enslaved humans and Fane's cold eyes. Eventually, even those faded away as I slept.

We left early in the morning before the vampires woke up. A message came from our coven urging our return, and as much as I wanted to stay and figure out the barrier spell, I didn't trust myself around Ryn and Fane.

My mind was relentless, replaying the scenarios over and over much to my shame. Thankfully, the others took my silence for worry and scheming over the grimoire. Breaking the barrier —that's what I should have been focusing on. Not on the two vampire princes.

Once we made it back to the coven, I was able to push the

thoughts away enough to think more clearly. And of course, there were more problems waiting for me.

"It was dark, so we didn't want to send them away. You know with Diego out." Willow wrung her hands together as she spoke.

"You did the right thing." Deepa gave her a reassuring smile.

Willow flushed at her approval.

"He destroyed the human's camp and took more prisoners," Danny added.

Anger rushed through me. "Did he act alone or were the vampires and rogue witches involved in this too?"

Willow shook her head. "The humans said a couple of rogue witches helped them escape. The humans want to talk to you. About an alliance."

My eyebrow arched. "An alliance? With us?"

That was surprising. Were they desperate enough to make a pact with us?

"Should we bring them down so you can speak to them, Queen?" another witch, Alex, asked.

I exchanged a look with Kohl. There was so much to do now, I didn't want to have to worry about Diego and his minions. With Ryn on our side, that solved the problem with the city vampires aiding the werewolves, and if the rogue witches were rising against Diego, we might actually be able to deal with him quickly and effortlessly.

"Yes."

"And the wolves?"

I nodded and motioned for them to hurry. Elijah would have had plenty of time to rest after the hex, so there was no reason for him to still be in my coven, though I was interested in meeting his mate. If they could rally the other wolf packs then maybe, we could stop Diego without using too much of our magic.

"Do you want us to stay, Queen? Or may we be excused?" Deepa broke my thoughts.

I waved her and Blake to leave and turned to Kohl.

"What do you think? An alliance?"

He frowned. "I don't think a written pact is going to stop Diego. A covenant maybe, but not an informal alliance."

Covenant. Was it really coming down to that? Not so long ago, we were worrying about college entry exams and now here we were trying to keep Savannah from devolving into bloody chaos.

"How would we make him sign a blood oath?"

Kohl shrugged. "If the vampires side with us and the other wolf packs, he'd have no choice and once it was sealed, he couldn't go back on it." His hazel eyes lit up. "And not only would it be a blood covenant, but it's about to be a blood moon."

His words rang through me. The lunar eclipse. How could I have forgotten it was coming? Though the red moon was a natural phenomenon, it was more than that. It did something to magic, strengthening it. The impossible became possible.

A thought struck me, making me gasp.

Kohl shot me a worried look.

"The barrier. Maybe she was waiting for the eclipse before performing the spell."

"Maybe," he answered.

"Do you think... after what happened with the curse, the eclipse will still happen?"

"I don't see why not." His face scrunched up as he scratched his chin, clearly lost in thought.

There wasn't time to discuss it any more before Willow returned, leading two humans and the werewolves.

I drew myself to my full height and motioned for them to sit in any of the chairs or couch. Elijah remained standing, dark eyes narrowed on me and the girl standing beside him looked like she wanted to bite my head off as well.

My lips twitched into a smirk. "You must be Elijah's mate."

She flinched. Weird. Maybe they were having relationship issues.

"I'm Valeria. Alpha of the Shadow Wolves. I'm sure they told you why we're here."

"About this... alliance?"

She nodded, her brown eyes boring into me. It was obvious she wouldn't be taking no for an answer.

I glanced at the humans. They also remained standing though their eyes darted back and forth, shining with uncertainty. Behind me, my witches gathered.

"Call everyone down, Kohl. We're going to have a meeting."

He hurried up the stairs to obey. In no time, all the witches were there.

I looked around the crowded room and a wave of nostalgia hit me. As future handmaiden of the future queen, I'd been required to sit in for many coven meetings. Seeing us all there without the elders, with werewolves and humans who otherwise would never have been allowed in... it was too surreal.

For a minute I just stood there imagining it was all a dream, or that we were in some strange alternate reality and back in the 'real' world, Mel was preparing for her coronation and I was getting ready for college.

But this wasn't a dream and Mel, like the others, was dead. Completely, irreversibly dead and gone. I couldn't even call up her spirit. The reminder filled me with grief.

"Kenzie?" Kohl's voice interrupted my thoughts.

I turned to him. "Yeah?"

His eyes searched mine. "Are you having doubts about this covenant?"

The covenant. For me, it was only a means to shut Diego up and keep him tied up so I could focus on the more important things like the barrier and the curse.

"Do you think this will work?" Kohl pressed.

Conversation drifted around us, but I could feel their stares on my back.

"A blood moon covenant is a powerful thing."

Kohl nodded. "The magic will be strong."

"The perfect time for me to crack the barrier spell too."

His eyes narrowed. "Please tell me you're not doing that alone. That's way too much magic for you to handle by yourself."

I gave him a flat look. "I'm not an idiot. I'm just going to set it up and then once the covenant is signed, we'll open the barrier together. It has to happen on the lunar eclipse. All of it."

He gave me a thoughtful 'hmm' and turned back to face the others. Everyone fell quiet as I scanned their faces—their hopeful, anxious faces.

Fane's words came back to me. *The weakest queen...*

Somewhere in the room, there could be our mole. Our traitor. I already had Kohl listening and watching. We couldn't let the covenant or barrier spell news reach Diego. Not until we were ready. His little reign of terror was coming to an end and with him busy, I could focus on what was most important—the curse.

19

VALERIA

I stood by Elijah and the twins, watching as the witches crowded around us. My wolf didn't like their nearness nor their curious stares. Though she was content to be reunited with Elijah and his wolf.

"I thought it would be a lot harder to convince her," Drew murmured to me.

Becca grunted.

I turned to Drew and nodded. "So did I."

He smiled. "Thank you for your help, Valeria."

Elijah's head whipped toward us, cool gaze sweeping over Drew and Becca.

I tensed. The memory of Drew's near kiss made me flush, and I looked away before Elijah caught it.

The witch queen sighed. "It will have to be a blood covenant. Are you all willing to do your part to uphold this? Diego won't give up his control so easily. Not when he thinks himself in the right."

A chill passed through me. "I'm willing."

I didn't meet Elijah's grim face. I didn't need to look at him to see the disapproval or the uncertainty. This was the right thing, I could feel it, but I hated that he wasn't on our side—my side.

"And you?" she turned to Drew and Becca.

Drew stood tall, jaw clenched. "We are."

Her eyes swept the room. "Even with your pack and the humans, it's not enough. We need the vampires."

My heart jolted at her words. Vampires? How would we ever get them on our side?

"If they support the covenant, Diego won't have any choice but to accept it."

Elijah scoffed. "So, we're letting the vampires take control? That's a brilliant plan."

Her eyes narrowed on him. "Don't put words in my mouth."

My wolf growled at her tone.

"Prince Ryn has already agreed to help take down the barrier. If he truly means to help us, then signing his name to this covenant shouldn't be a problem for him."

Someone gasped in the back. Her words rattled me just the same.

Prince Ryn was awake? When? How?

Before the curse, vampires and werewolves lived apart and had little do with each other. We weren't exactly enemies, but we'd never been allies before. Not until Diego.

"Are we sure we can trust him? I thought Diego was working with the vampires." I voiced my concern.

Queen McKenzie looked to me. "He has the loyalty of the rogue city vampires, but Prince Ryn has assured me to put an end to that."

"And the barrier? Prince Ryn knows how to open it?" a witch asked.

I didn't hear her response, my mind too caught up with the

question. If the barrier was open did that mean others might come? Or we could go?

I turned to Elijah. He stared at the queen, his face a mask of coolness, but I had the suspicion her words affected him more than anyone else. With the barrier down, this was his chance to run away again. This time forever.

My wolf howled at the thought.

Elijah's gaze snapped to me. His inner wolf reaching for mine. For a second, it felt as if we were the only ones in the room. Heat flooded me and it was all I could do to keep my wolf under control. The thought of losing her mate was stirring her up.

Judging by the strained, pained look on Elijah's face, his wolf was going just as crazy. My heart thundered inside me and before I realized what I was doing, I was shifting closer to him.

Though he didn't touch me, his nearness soothed my wolf's emotions. We stood nearly elbow to elbow, so close I could feel the warmth radiating from him and smell the strong scent of smoke, sweat, and a hint of soap.

Drew followed my movement, his eyes flicking to Elijah and back to me. I shifted uneasily under his gaze. How could I explain myself to him when I could barely understand my feelings myself? I did care about Drew, liked him even, but... Elijah.

Our mate.

I sighed. It was complicated. Pushing aside the thoughts, I stepped away from my alpha and closer to the queen.

"We'll need more wolves on our side. I'll go to the other pack leaders."

She exchanged glances with Kohl.

"What? What is it?" I asked.

Lifting her chin, she met my gaze. "Some of the pack leaders... are missing. Or dead. I'm not sure."

"You're not sure?"

Her eyes narrowed. "I'm not queen of the wolves. I only know the rumors I've heard."

The haughtiness in her tone made me bristle. Rumors she'd heard and had done nothing about.

"Of course. What are some wolf lives to you?" Elijah was glaring at her.

Annoyance flickered on her face. "It's not my job to babysit the wolves too."

My fists clenched. "You knew this was happening, and you didn't try to stop it. When you had the power to? That's on you. You don't get to brush it off like it's nothing. Like we're nothing."

She flinched but was quick to recover. The steely look she gave me said it all—she would not take responsibility for this. She refused to be blamed, refused to acknowledge her own faults and emotions.

Coward, my wolf spoke.

That seemed too nice of a way to put it.

"I will go with you. To check on the other packs." Drew broke the awkward silence.

Elijah's head snapped toward him, lip quirked in a smile. It wasn't a real smile, no. It was predatory, cold, and arrogant.

"And why would you do that? Do you think the other wolves are going to just let a human waltz into their camps? After what you guys have done?"

Drew didn't break eye contact as Elijah hammered him with questions. I shifted, placing myself between them now. Elijah tracked my movement, his face growing stormier.

Don't, my wolf warned.

I paused. Going to Drew would seem like betrayal to Elijah's wolf and the last thing I wanted was him to shift and attack the human.

"I had nothing to do with that. I want to come. To show

them that not all of us hate wolves." Drew's eyes shot to me, and his face softened.

Elijah stilled. His inner wolf was at the ready, pushing to be released. Fear crawled up my spine. I trusted Elijah, knew he could handle the jealousy in human form, but if he let his wolf loose... I didn't want to think about what would happen.

"Elijah." I placed a hand on his arm.

He visibly relaxed and turned to me, eyes flashing from silver to brown.

"I'm coming too." His words punched me.

Bad, bad idea. My wolf was howling with joy. He wasn't leaving us anymore.

I gaped at him. "I don't... what about our pack?"

"Jay and Tati can handle it."

My eyes flickered to Drew, who stood watching us. This was not the right move. Drew and Elijah needed space from each other not a shared mission. How was I supposed to handle them both together?

"I'll be there too," Becca spoke up.

Drew frowned at her. "You don't need to go, Becca. It's safer for you here."

She laughed harshly. "Safe? There's no such thing as safe anymore, Drew. I'm coming." Her chin lifted as she turned to face Elijah.

I groaned inwardly. This was going to be a disaster.

"Anyone else?" the queen asked.

I looked to her. "One of the witches should come too."

Her eyes narrowed. "If they want. I won't force them."

One of the witches agreed to accompany us and hope stirred inside me. With all of us together we actually had a chance of pulling it off.

"What about the rogue witches? They might be willing to help?" Drew's question rose above the voices.

Queen McKenzie looked at him. "I'll talk to them. You guys just worry about getting the pack leaders and a rep from the human camp to be here tomorrow night for the blood moon. We'll sign the covenant together."

Elijah frowned. "Don't you need Diego's name? How are you going to get him to do it?"

She fell quiet for a second. "What's the one thing he cares about more than anything else?"

"Sylvie," Elijah answered.

My inner wolf bristled. I bit my lip, feeling the same apprehension. Hurting Sylvie to get to Diego wasn't something I relished doing. It felt wrong. Something he would do. We were better than that, weren't we?

"Elijah." I frowned.

His eyes darted to me and back to the witch. "Trust me. For a wolf, our mate is everything. He'd agree to anything. Anything to protect her."

My face flamed at his words. The bond. How could he speak about it like that when he abandoned me and our pack? Why wasn't I everything to him?

You cannot fight the bond. When it is time, there will be no stopping it.

I pushed my wolf's words away. That was trouble for another day.

McKenzie nodded. "So, we take her and do what exactly? Hold her here until he signs the covenant?"

"That could work." The tall witch beside her spoke.

His face was hard like stone, and his hazel eyes were sharp as he looked around the room.

Everyone spoke at the same time, some of the voices filled with excitement and others worry. Drew and Becca exchanged hopeful looks.

Elijah touched my arm. My body jolted at the contact. It

was a light touch, but because of our bond, it felt as if I'd been branded.

He pulled me aside to the corner of the room. "Val, what are you doing? Are we sure going against Diego is the best plan?"

"I'm doing what's best for our pack. He threatened to take it from me."

His eyes flashed silver. "Did he hurt you?"

Shaking my head, I pushed down my emotions. "No, but I told you, he burned their camp, Elijah. He's been taking them prisoners and giving them to the vampires."

Elijah shook his head. "But have you forgotten what these witches have done?" Pain flashed in his eyes. "What they did to Rachel?"

My chest tightened. I glanced away as the memories surfaced. How could I ever forget? She was burned alive while in her wolf form...

"You don't know who was responsible, Elijah. It could have been anyone. We might never know."

His eyebrows knitted together, the stormy expression on his face making my heart slam against my ribs. I fought the urge to squirm under his glare.

"Her killer could be here right now. And I can't..." his words ended in a choke.

The pain evident in his voice made my heart twist. I reached out and pulled his face closer to mine, wishing I could erase all the hurt.

Tears pricked my eyes as I made him meet my gaze. "You have to stop this, Elijah. Please. What happened to Rachel was horrific. Awful. I wouldn't stop you from tearing apart her killer, you know that, but this path you've chosen... it's breaking you. Can't you see that it's breaking you?"

My wolf whimpered within me.

A shattered expression flashed on his face and it felt as if my heart was cracking along with his. Why couldn't he just let it go? Before his emotions consumed him completely.

"She deserves justice." His face hardened.

"She does, but how? We've searched for her killer. We've found nothing."

"I'm not giving up."

I fell quiet. How could I make him realize the futility of his mission? Was it wrong for me to try to stop him? Rachel was my friend and I loved her too, but I'd given hope of ever finding out what really happened. Chasing a ghost when our pack needed us... I just couldn't do it anymore.

"Maybe the queen can help? She could use magic to track the killer?"

Elijah scoffed. "If she was going to do that, she would have offered already."

My lips pursed. "We'll talk to her again."

"They hexed me, Val."

I reeled at his words. My wolf growled.

"What? They... hexed you?"

Anger sparked inside me. I turned on my heel and marched toward the queen. The witch next to her stepped forward, eyes narrowing on me as he blocked my access to her.

All heads whipped toward me.

"Remove the hex." My voice was steel.

The queen's eyebrow arched at me. Her eyes darted around the room and back to me. "Excuse me?"

"Take the hex off of him."

A short, haughty laugh escaped her. "That's not happening. Look, I didn't want to have to do it in the first place, but your mate didn't leave me a choice. He bit one of my witches. I could have killed him. Thankfully, the bite didn't turn him. The hex was the only way to keep him from hurting my coven again."

My wolf urged me to attack, but logic told me to stand down. It was already done and there was nothing I could do to stop it.

"The hex will only hurt him if he tries to hurt one of us," she added.

I looked at him. This meant he couldn't have his revenge. Instead his anger would build up inside of him. My heart twisted at the thought. Was there any chance of saving him now?

With nothing else to say, she turned away and motioned the witches to follow her. I glanced back to find Elijah and Drew eyeing each other warily. Becca stood by her brother, lip curling at my alpha.

I hurried over to them. Since meeting for the first time, tensions had become high and I didn't trust my alpha alone with them.

Elijah stiffened as he met Drew's stare. I flushed.

They stood facing off, sizing each other up. Elijah was an expert at keeping his wolf leashed, but my wolf could sense our mate's anger and jealousy. It was hot and boiling under that calm façade.

Becca's eyes narrowed on Elijah, her hand ready on her gun. She wouldn't think twice before shooting him, alpha or not.

The thought of leading all three of them to find the other alphas made me nervous. Maybe someone would change their mind and stay behind. Despite my doubt of having them all together, I was happy to have Elijah back.

Our mate.

20

MCKENZIE

Thanks to Kohl, the preparations for the covenant went quickly and smoothly. With the wolves and humans heading back to their camp, we were able to discuss the possibility of a traitor in our midst. It was a problem we'd have to deal with, but first we needed to get the barrier down and the covenant signed.

"Are you sure you don't want me to just go? I can look at the grimoire myself."

I turned at Kohl's voice.

"No. I'm taking Deepa and Blake. I need you here, Kohl. To get the covenant ready for the blood moon. Let us handle the barrier. This has to happen as quickly as possible."

His lips pursed. "The scroll is ready. You've signed it. We just need the other signatures."

"Yes, and I want you to make sure no one leaves here to spill all our secrets to Diego. Keep an eye on everyone and protect that covenant."

Guilt needled me. That wasn't the only reason I wanted him to stay. I was going back into the lion's den and the others were easy to fool and command, but not Kohl. He knew me too well. He would see my... reaction to Ryn. I couldn't hide that from him and since I couldn't trust myself not to react, I had to keep Kohl far away.

He stared hard at me, his hazel eyes looking greener in the sunlight. I forced an easy smile on my face, trying to dissuade his fears and suspicion.

"If I need you, I'll call you." I pointed at the charmed bracelet around my wrist.

"I'll be too far to help. I don't like this."

I snorted. That seemed to be his motto lately, and I couldn't blame him. None of the choices we were left with were easy.

"I'll be fine. Just imagine once we break that barrier." I let the excitement slip into my voice.

His face softened and his lips parted into a small smile. "Yeah. This is really happening."

"With the covenant signed, Diego won't be a problem anymore and if we can get more ingredients, more witches, we could actually do this, Kohl. We can stop the curse."

"And then?" The hopefulness in his voice cut me like a knife.

And then? Was he seriously already trying to plan for after?

I snapped my mouth shut and averted my gaze. "Then... we'll restore everything. Rebuild society."

The words felt odd to me. Rebuild society? It was a huge, monumental, task and I didn't feel capable of it.

"And us?"

My cheeks flamed. I knew what he was asking, but I didn't have an answer. *Please don't make me say it.*

"We'll run the coven. Same as now." I turned my back to him, my fingers curling and uncurling.

Silence stretched between us and I glanced back to find him still staring. Still waiting. Still hoping.

Damn it, Kohl.

A knock on my door broke the tension

"Queen McKenzie?" a voice called.

I sighed in relief and flew to the door to open it.

The witch bowed quickly and looked from me to Kohl. "Kohl."

"What is it?" I asked.

Her eyes were wide, and she was breathing hard as if she'd just run all the way up to me. Maybe she had.

"It's... a carriage. A carriage is here for you."

I blinked at her in confusion. "What the hell are you talking about?"

She flushed. "Prince Ryn. He's here. In a carriage. A real carriage. With horses and everything."

How many times was she going to say carriage?

Kohl's face turned sour. "That's unnecessary."

Heat spread up my neck. Why would he come for me when he knew we were returning? And had he really come himself instead of sending someone else? I ignored my fluttering heart and followed the witch out, Kohl close on my heels.

I turned to him. "I'll be okay, Kohl. I'll be back tomorrow night as soon as we have the barrier open."

He bit his lip. "This is all happening so fast. What if... what if the barrier doesn't open?"

"Then I'll get back here as soon as I can to help with the covenant. Make sure Diego signs it and then," I shrugged, "we'll figure out the rest."

Tossing my bag into the open carriage, I looked up to see Ryn watching me from the driver's bench in front. My pulse quickened at the sight of him. His curls were combed back, revealing his handsome face. Warm, gold eyes stared into mine and his lips were quirked into a hesitant smile. I flushed as his eyes dipped to my mouth. My face grew warm and it had nothing to do with the late summer air.

Kohl gave me a hand into the back of the carriage, and I slid to the far side.

"I was never really a horse girl, but this…" I glanced around, "is actually really nice."

Deepa glanced at me, eyebrow arched, and I shoved down my emotions. She and Blake scurried in after me with their own bags.

I'd lived in Savannah my whole life and had never been on a carriage ride. We always made fun of the tourists who over-paid for it and now here I was, the Queen of Savannah, being led through town by the vampire prince.

"If anything happens to her…"

Ryn nodded at Kohl's warning. "You have my word, she'll be safe."

Kohl scowled. "A promise from the heartless heir means nothing."

A shadow crossed over Ryn's face, his jaw clenching, but he didn't reply.

"Kohl." I gave him a pointed look.

Stand down.

With a final wave to him, we were off. His worried face faded as we grew farther away. I scanned the area for any sign of Diego or his wolves. Was he too busy with his new prisoners? Or was he watching us, waiting for me to leave before he came after my witches next?

The gentle clip clop of the two horses echoed against the pebbled streets. I'd wondered where the trained animals had disappeared to. Besides the old cars or bicycles we had found, horses were our best source of transport. Funny how we'd regressed. Out of all of us, the vampires were probably the most adjusted to life without technology. They'd lived through it before.

"It's been a long time since I've been through this park." Ryn broke the awkward silence.

My head turned to see where he indicated. Towering oaks stretched above us, the branches sprawled out like arms reaching for the other trees. It was too early for the leaves to change and the weather was still warm, but visions of the past returned to me.

"It's beautiful in the fall." I smiled at the memories.

Ryn's eyes watched me and I flushed. The sparks that I didn't feel with Kohl, I felt with Ryn. The unfairness of it made my skin prickle. I tried to shake off the emotions. This wasn't a date. Ryn was the next vampire king, and I was queen of the coven. We had far more important things to worry about and the last thing I needed was a stupid, impossible crush. Not to mention Deepa and Blake sat beside me and would no doubt report back to Kohl everything I did.

The rest of the ride, Ryn shared stories from his past. Stories of a Savannah I'd only ever glimpsed from history books. Most of his memories featured Fane too, and it was hard to reconcile the spirited, good-natured brother in his tales with the cold vampire he was now.

I discovered a newfound hate for their father, the previous king, who was ten times the monster Fane or even Diego could ever be. Ryn and Fane were better off with him gone. They were free, and I liked Ryn as he was now. I liked him too much.

The sound of crisp pages turning echoed in the room and candle wax and dried herbs filled my nostrils. For a moment I was transported to the past. The study in my parents' house where we were tutored in spell craft came back in vivid detail.

Dark green walls and hanging plants. Red velvety couch and gold framed portraits of our family. Grammy's enchanted candlesticks, the pristine bookshelves, and the antique wooden table we had learned spell after spell on.

Mel always loved the smell of the old books and shriveled mint leaves. It had an almost magical effect on her, turning my serious, regal sister into a giddy child again. A twinge of pain stabbed me at the memories.

I hated those lessons—hated being trapped indoors to endure them—but what I would give to go back now.

"This should be all the ingredients." I nodded to Ryn.

Much to my surprise, he confessed that Fane, not him, had been the one to find the witch's secret supply. Though I questioned Fane's motives for helping us, I was grateful not to have to hunt down all the items.

Ryn stepped back from the grimoire. "Do you think this will work then?"

"I hope so. With the blood moon coming, we will have to act quickly. Magic will be at its peak. Deepa, Blake, and I will set it up tomorrow, and then once the moon is out, we'll perform the spell. Then we'll return to the coven. To sign the covenant."

"Yes, and I'll return with you. Make sure the vampires heed me."

The images of them with the human slaves flashed in my mind. *And Julia.* Kohl had seen to her burial, but I should have been the one to say some words over her grave. To reassure my coven that I would make the vampires pay. There was so much blood on their hands and yet here I was making deals with them.

What if they tried to enslave us next? The memory of the

glazed eyes of the compelled humans Fane had shown me made me shudder.

"Are you okay, Kenzie?" His concerned voice startled me.

I shook my head. "Did you know? Did you know what your brother did to those humans? The ones who led the mobs?"

Ryn's face hardened. "Yes."

Anger unfurled inside me. "How can you let him do that?"

"Would you rather he kill them? Turn them?" He frowned.

"I would rather he let them go."

Ryn shook his head. "That would be dangerous. After the things they did…"

"You weren't even there!"

"No, but Fane told me. If we set them free, they'll only hunt us again."

"No. Not with this covenant. We'll all be taking the oath. To coexist. Without the violence and slavery."

He stared at me. "Then I'll make him release them. I promise. If that's what you want."

I blinked. What I want? What did he care what I wanted, and couldn't he see how messed up Fane was?

"Kenzie. I know you've heard the stories of my past, but I'm not that same guy. I swear. I don't want to go back to the darkness." His voice was thick with emotion.

My own emotions rose up to meet his. I looked into his eyes. Big mistake.

The passion I saw there made my knees weaken. It was all I could do not to lean into him.

"What are you doing to me?" I hated the vulnerability I heard in my voice.

His gaze heated. "You feel it too?"

I turned away, unable to endure his stare.

"I don't know what I feel."

"I think you do."

My pulse quickened. What was this game he was playing? It was dangerous, it was so dangerous, but my heart—traitor that it was—wanted this.

Wanted us. It wasn't just lust. There was something there. Something real and powerful and completely, totally, undeniably impossible.

"We can't." I barely got the words out.

I didn't look at him, but I willed him to understand. To listen to reason. If he could be logical about it, then I could too. One of us had to stop this before…

"Why?"

His question shattered me. Why?

"Because. You know why. You're the vampire king and I'm bound to my coven. There is no… this"—I drew an invisible line between us with my finger—"thing. Whatever it is. It ends now. There is no way this is going to happen. So, let's be real about it, okay?"

His jaw hardened. "This is realest thing I've felt in all my 200 years."

I pulled back, shaking my head. "Yeah, see that's crazy. I'm 18. You've been alive for 200 years. You… I'm a witch. I'm not going to live that long."

And he murdered all those people. Let his brother enslave more.

He kept moving toward me. My heart raced at his nearness. What was he doing?

"None of that matters to me. Why should it matter when we're in love?"

Love? My eyes bulged. He thought this was love? A nervous chuckle escaped me. *Oh, no. This is SO not happening.*

I held up a hand to stop him from getting any closer. "You're crazy. I know you were stuck in a coffin for two years, so it's probably screwed with your mind, but I promise you, you are not in love, Ryn."

His eyes burned into me. "I know what I feel, Kenzie. You can't tell me what I'm feeling—what you're feeling, isn't real."

I bit back a groan. He was insane. Gorgeous, unfairly, and ungodly so, but crazy as...

He leaned forward. I gasped as his lips caught mine. My body stiffened like a statue. I should have pushed away. Should have slapped him. But no, I didn't do any of that.

His lips were warm and soft, and the passion behind his kiss weakened me.

My mouth moved on its own accord, meeting his hungry kiss with all the desperation of someone starved of affection. As if knowing we were on stolen time and this was just a dream. Any moment and it would be over, gone forever.

Reason returned and shame flooded me. Using my magic, I pushed him away.

"What are you doing? What if someone saw us? Are you crazy?"

He was grinning, eyes sparkling with delight as if he'd just won a prize. I stilled. My stomach turned over in dread. Is that what this was? Some kind of sick competition with his brother?

Red spotted my vision. The simmering rage must have leaked through because his smile vanished.

He took a step back, mouth gaping and eyes blinking in confusion. Gorgeous even when he looked like a stupefied fish.

My hand shot out and before reason could take over, I let my magic fly. The pain was immediate as it tore through me and went wild.

Ryn's grunt of pain echoed in my ears. He clutched his chest and stared at me with such a wounded look, I paused. Was I wrong? Did it matter?

"I don't want any part of this, Ryn. You and your sick brother just leave me alone."

A tremor ran through me, but I stood strong. "I'll help you take down the barrier and you'll sign the covenant, find Julia's killer, set the humans free, but that's it. I am not your plaything. I'm the fucking queen of Savannah."

"I'm sorry. I'm sorry, Kenzie." He rubbed the spot where my magic had punched him.

The light in his eyes dimmed and the sorrowful look he gave me made me feel like I was the one who should be apologizing. He didn't seem like he was acting. The emotion in his voice sounded so real.

"I shouldn't have kissed you. I promise, it won't happen again."

My chest tightened. In a flash, he was gone, and I was left standing in the wake of his leave, the air grew chillier without him. I wrapped my arms around myself and took a deep breath. Guarding myself from him was for the better, but why did it feel wrong?

Unable to focus on the grimoire, I turned and stormed down the hall back toward my room.

A figure moved in the shadows, making me pause. Blue eyes blinked at me and I couldn't stop the outward groan as it rolled off my lips.

"Fane." I glared at him.

He emerged, looking just as elegant and sexy as his brother, but instead of the gentleness and kindness Ryn portrayed, Fane's lips were spread in a cold smile.

The bloody devil himself.

"Are you stalking me now?"

His eyes drank me in, making me bristle.

"You'd like that wouldn't you? For me to follow you like a lovesick puppy? Like that sappy-eyed henchman of yours."

My fists clenched. "Shut your mouth."

Egged on, he circled me, and I could tell he'd barely begun his harassment.

"Sorry to disappoint, but I'm not the lovesick type. Now sex on the other hand..." His voice was smooth.

I threw an arm up. "Get the hell out of my way, Fane. I've had enough of you bloodsuckers for one day."

His eyes narrowed. "You've seen my brother? I guess the early bird does get the worm, huh?"

"Go away." I pushed past him.

His hands whipped out and caged me. I gasped.

"Tell me you don't want this, and I'll stop." Fane's voice grew rough.

I swallowed. "I don't want this."

His eyes dipped to my lips. "Why don't I believe you?"

My heart pounded against my ribs and heat spread across my skin. I couldn't deny the pull he had, but I also couldn't let myself fall. I was the queen of the witches. *So, start acting like it.*

"McKenzie."

I shuddered at the sound of his voice. He moved closer and I should have fought him off, but I didn't.

In one swift movement, his lips captured mine, and I was lost.

Falling deeper and deeper.

His body pressed against mine and the heady scent of whisky and cologne—musky and woody—filled my senses. My skin was on fire. Somewhere in the back of my mind, my good senses were screaming at me.

What are you doing? Stop this. Stop it now. Stop it now before...

His tongue found mine and all rational thought ceased.

I let him press in closer, my back slamming against the wall.

He broke the kiss for a breath, his eyes still piercing me. I was vaguely aware of my labored breathing and the rise and fall of my chest. Why couldn't I stop? Why was my body betraying me?

My cheeks reddened. What had I done? The need to get away, far, far away filled me.

"Good night, Fane." I threw my magic at him, making him stagger back.

Lifting my chin, I marched out, not daring a glance in his direction. My heart thumped wildly in my ears.

I touched my trembling lips, wondering if I'd imagined it all. Had I really kissed not one, but *both* vampire princes and in one night? It couldn't be real. There had to be an explanation. Could it be compulsion? I shivered at the thought, but if it wasn't compulsion that made me do it... weariness filled me. I had to end this now.

Focus on the barrier and the curse. Don't let them trap you. You can do this.

21

VALERIA

The witches gave us a car to travel back to our camp. It was a super old, rust bucket of a car, but it was the first vehicle I'd ridden in since the curse and I was thankful we didn't have to walk. Though I worried all our movement was going to catch Diego's attention. Was he watching us, waiting for another chance to attack?

I leaned my head back against the seat and sighed.

Beside me, Elijah shifted and winced.

"Does it hurt? The hex they put on you?" I asked him.

My wolf snarled at the thought.

He glanced at me. "Only if I think about killing a witch. So, yes, it does."

"When does it wear off?"

He glared at the back of the driver's head. "They didn't share that information."

"I'm sorry."

Elijah looked away and didn't respond.

The gentle hum of the car filled the silence. Outside, the empty streets of Savannah swept by. Though the city hadn't changed much as far as appearance, I couldn't help but feel like I was somewhere completely foreign. It might as well have been because Savannah—the Savannah I knew—was gone forever.

When I looked up, the witch was staring at the road ahead as he drove and Drew sat in the passenger seat, looking out the window. Becca sat next to me, head resting against her window and I wasn't sure if she was awake or asleep.

Elijah turned to me. "Why do you care about the humans so much?"

I winced at his question. My eyes darted to Drew who was trying to pretend that he wasn't paying attention to us. "Because what Diego is doing is wrong, Elijah. Hasn't there been enough death already? Why can't we just... not kill each other?"

His eyes searched my face. "Humans have killed us for centuries."

"And we've killed them. The cycle goes on and on and I'm tired of it. I... I don't want any part of Diego's future."

"He's just scared. Scared of what the humans will do if they're in control again."

I met his gaze. "That's why this covenant is so important. Everyone would be equal. All of us would have a say and be in charge."

Elijah shook his head. "It will never work."

Anger sparked inside me. "If you don't believe in it, then why are you even here? Why don't you just tuck tail and run again?"

He flinched, making me almost regret my words.

"Where else would I go? The barrier is still sealed."

For now. If the queen was able to break the spell that held us trapped in Savannah, then what? Would he leave again?

We fell into silence, our inner wolves content just to be close. Drew and the witch didn't respond to our conversation, but I was curious to know what they were thinking. Visions of the fire and Diego's pack flashed in my mind. And Jen. They'd been through just as much grief and violence as we had. We had to help them with the covenant. It was the only way to salvage what was left of Savannah.

Before long we were driving up to our camp and I dismissed the thoughts.

Elijah stiffened. I'd already told him about the witch attack in the forest and how Drew and Becca had come to us. I even told him about what I'd said to Jay about him. Something I still hadn't apologized for.

Though I hated the idea of the witches hexing him, part of me was thankful he couldn't hurt them or anger them. He would be safe from them now and maybe he could let go of his obsession with avenging Rachel.

Two wolves appeared at the gate. Jay and Rob—armed with guns. My heart leapt into my throat. Where did the weapons come from? We only had two shotguns and no bullets in our supply.

The witch stopped the car and glanced back at us.

Elijah opened the door and stumbled out. I followed him.

Rob hurried to open the gate for us. I motioned for the others to drive in and turned my attention to my wolves.

"Elijah." Jay ran to him.

I watched as they embraced, my hurtful words about Elijah's true feelings at the forefront of my mind. Despite what I'd said, Jay was still happy to see his alpha.

Rob greeted him too and glanced at me.

"Alpha." He nodded at me.

I pointed to his handgun. "Where did the guns come from?"

He exchanged a look with Jay before meeting my gaze once more. "A gift. From Diego."

His words shook me. A gift? For what?

"You didn't give up the humans to him, did you?"

Rob shook his head emphatically. "No, Alpha. He didn't come into camp. Only met with Jay and Tati."

Elijah frowned at Jay. "What did he want?"

Jay glanced from me to Elijah. "Just to tell us that he was working with some of the rogue witches. They're working on a cure for the curse. He promised if we took his side, that he could help."

My wolf growled. I scowled at Jay. "And what did you tell him?"

His eyes narrowed on me. "That he would have to discuss it with our alphas when they returned."

"If you've been scheming behind my back, Jay—"

His eyes flashed silver. "I have never given you reason to doubt me."

Elijah stepped between us. "Enough. I know you wouldn't betray our pack. Thank you, Jay. Let's go. We'll gather everyone together and go over the plan."

Heat rushed through me. I hated that he could swoop in and take control so easily when it was a struggle for me. I hated that I'd let the distrust build up between me and my betas, but mostly I really hated the fact that Diego thought me a weak alpha. Thought he could sneak behind my back and take my pack.

We will kill him. Rip his throat open and watch while his blood soaks the earth.

My wolf's promise made a shiver run down my back.

Elijah turned to me. "Val?"

Straightening, I walked with him as we headed for the clubhouse. There were a lot of things we had to discuss with our pack. At least I wasn't the only one who had to call the shots.

Our alpha is back. My wolf's joy filled me.

Despite the anger at his leaving, I couldn't help but feel the same happiness at his return. I wouldn't have to do everything alone anymore. At least until he left again.

~

Back at camp, I let Elijah explain to everyone what was happening. Jealousy filled me at the easy way they accepted the plan when it came from him. The humans listened, eyes wide. Drew and Becca stood with them and I could hear Drew's reassuring words that we would get the others back.

Sensing my gaze, he turned to me and smiled. I nodded at him in acknowledgment and glanced at Elijah. He was watching the exchange with narrowed eyes.

There would be no hiding how we felt from Elijah and I wouldn't have wanted to, anyway. He was my best friend. He would understand, wouldn't he? We wouldn't be the first fated pair to explore other relationships in our human form.

"Elijah," I called him.

His head whipped toward me.

I motioned him over, ignoring Drew's intense stare.

Eyes followed us. My wolf sensed the pack's unease as they watched me escort him away from the humans. Jay's face split into a smug smile.

We left the clubhouse and walked along the sidewalk away from the others.

"You don't have to say anything. About the human." Elijah spoke first.

He didn't meet my gaze.

"That's not why I called you over."

His dark eyes bore into mine. "Then what?"

I scoffed. "This whole plan to capture Sylvie and ally with the others. I want to know that I can count on you. That we can count on you."

His face softened, and I turned away. I didn't want him to know how his leaving had cut me, but there was no hiding anything from him. He knew me too well. Knew my wolf too. In the way only he could.

Not your human.

I stared in the distance, trying to collect myself.

"I'm sorry and I know my apology isn't enough. But I'm here now. You're not alone, Val."

My fists clenched. How did he always know the words I needed to hear?

Because he's our mate.

"I was doing fine without you, you know. We all were."

He didn't say anything.

"I hope you didn't agree to come back for me."

His smile was sad. "I didn't."

I reeled. Even now, he wounded me. My wolf snarled within me.

"Then why are you here?" My words were strained.

He sighed. "I owe you my help. To get this covenant signed. Make sure Diego doesn't come after our pack."

"And then what, you just disappear again? Without a goodbye?"

"I said goodbye to you."

"But not to the others. You owe them that much too, Elijah. They're loyal to you. Even when you abandon them."

I started to walk away.

"Val."

The pain in his voice stopped me cold.

His eyes darkened. "The human."

I stilled, holding my breath. If he thought he had the right to tell me how to feel, he'd find my fist in his face.

"Why him?"

His question rocked me. Why? Thoughts raced in my mind.

Because... he was sweet, handsome, brave, but Elijah was all those things too.

But he left.

I lifted my chin. "He was here when I needed him."

Elijah's shoulders flinched, regret flickering in his eyes. I turned away, pretending his reaction didn't cut me in two.

The rest of the day we spent mapping out the city and coming up with a plan to get Sylvie away from her pack. We also needed to gather the other alphas. Convince them to side with us and not Diego.

Pulling my hair up and out of my face, I faced the others. "How are we going to do this? Take her right from under Diego's nose?"

Drew glanced at Becca and then back to me. "We lure her away from the pack."

Chills crawled up my spine. I didn't like where this conversation was heading. "Lure her with what?"

He met my gaze. "Me. I'll be the bait."

My eyebrows flew to my forehead. I looked to his twin, but she didn't seem surprised—pissed, yes, but not surprised. When I turned to Elijah, he seemed just as unmoved.

Anger stirred inside me. Had they already discussed this? Without me?

"That's the plan?" I whirled on Elijah.

His lip curled. "Don't look at me. It was his idea, not mine." He pointed a finger at Drew.

Turning back to Drew, I sucked in a ragged breath. "That's crazy. You can't offer yourself as bait. What if she catches you?"

He drew himself up. "Then you guys will swoop in and take her."

"Once we have her, we'll go to Taylor first. Her camp shouldn't be too far from Diego's." Elijah added.

"Uh... won't Diego be hot on our heels once he finds her missing? His wolf will alert him."

"We'll wait until he's distracted." Drew's voice was firm, determined.

There was no way he'd change his mind now, and as much as I hated it, Elijah was right, there weren't a lot of other options for us.

"You're not... we're not going to hurt her. Just hide her until the covenant is signed?" I looked from Drew to Elijah.

Becca stared off into the distance, not bothering to take part in the conversation. Elijah and Drew shared identical frowns.

"No."

"Of course not."

They spoke simultaneously.

I blew out a breath in relief, feeling better. Kidnapping was one thing, but hurting her, even if she did deserve it, that didn't feel right to me.

"Once we get her, we're going to have to be quick. Get away fast before Diego comes after us. You think you guys can keep up?" Elijah looked to Drew.

The human gave him a flat look. "Don't worry about us."

Elijah grunted, but before he could start another argument, I held my hand up for silence.

"Sylvie isn't stupid. She might not fall for the trap."

Drew's determined gaze flickered to me. "She will."

I didn't respond. My thoughts jumbled together as worry grew. This wouldn't be easy. It could end horribly, horribly bad.

Yes. My wolf's agreement did little to stop my fears.

"Are we really doing this?"

Elijah turned to me with a questioning look.

I shook my head at him and rubbed my arms. "Kidnapping Sylvie? Don't you think that's a little extreme."

His lips flattened. "Extreme? No. I think it's stupid."

Drew's head snapped towards him. "You're the one who suggested it."

Elijah stared at him coolly. "Yeah. Because no one else had an alternative. If you want to force Diego's hand, that's the only way. A wolf's bond can't be broken." His eyes narrowed to slits.

Drew met his accusatory glare with a face of stone. If he was scared of Elijah, he didn't show it.

Foolish human.

Brave, I countered.

Fool.

I shrugged off my wolf's words and stared out at the city. We were getting closer to Red wolf territory and soon, Diego would be alerted to our presence.

"Ready?" the witch asked, holding up the strange mixture the queen had given us.

My lip curled. "It smells horrible. I can't imagine what's in it."

He grunted. "I doubt you'd want to know, anyway." He held it out to us, and I went first.

I opened the lid and held my breath. It was supposed to keep the wolves from finding us right away. Some sort of cloaking potion, but like most of their magic, it was temporary.

Tossing the bottle back, I swallowed just a drop, wincing as the lukewarm liquid hit the back of my throat. I fought the urge to throw up.

It tasted like sea water with a dash of something spicy. Shaking off the strange sensation overcoming me, I handed the bottle to Elijah next. He took a sip, made a face, and gave it to Becca. Drew took his turn after her and we exchanged looks.

My body tingled, but other than that, I didn't feel changed. "Uh... I can still see you guys."

The witch smirked. "You'll still be able to see each other, but no one else can."

Elijah stared him down, body tense. If it weren't for the hex and the deal I'd made with the queen, he wouldn't have allowed the witch into our camp at all. Working with the enemy had to be eating him up inside and I hated that.

"Alright. Let's move," Elijah urged.

Becca and Drew had the guns, so they led the way. The street was quiet and empty. Right away, my wolf tensed.

"You said you know where they are?" Elijah looked to Drew.

The human nodded. "Yeah. Follow my lead."

Elijah frowned at him. I squeezed his arm in warning. Now was not the time to play the big, bad alpha card. We needed to work together to do this.

His dark eyes met mine and his lips quirked into a small smile. My heart warmed at the sight. I couldn't help but be comforted by his presence. I felt like I was whole again, but I hated that. That I needed him.

It's the bond. He needs you too.

I dismissed my wolf's words. We had other things to worry about than our bond or rocky relationship. There would be time to deal with all that later—hopefully. What we were about to do wasn't exactly a guaranteed success even with the witches' help.

22

VALERIA

Morning sunlight streamed in from the wide branches overhead and a warm breeze lapped at my clothes and hair. Perfect weather and, in the past, I would have spent it at the lake or in the woods, letting my wolf enjoy it as well. My eyes swept the empty streets of the wealthy district. Instead, I was about to go head-to-head with a dangerous alpha and help the humans and witches seal the covenant.

"Are we sure this is where he'll be?" I turned to Drew.

He gave me a solemn nod. "It's either here or back at our old camp dealing with the rogue witches."

The images of the burning theater filled my mind. I shuddered at the thought of the poor humans under Diego's control now. Would he give them over to the vampires? Let them put slave collars on them so they could feed from them whenever they wanted?

Mansions lined the wide street, each standing far from the next and boasting large overgrown yards and gardens that had probably once been a sight to see. Their colonial and Victorian style spoke of old money. They were built ages ago, in a time when humans didn't believe in our existence. I wondered what those long dead owners would have thought about a violent group of werewolves living there now and a world where everything they'd built had collapsed. Dismissing that depressing thought, I scanned the street.

Some newer mansions were scattered among the old ones. Would Diego have claimed one of those for his hideout? Why weren't his guards out patrolling? Were they that confident in their power?

My lip curled at the thought.

"That's it. That's the place." Drew's voice made me pause.

Elijah motioned for him to be quiet. Werewolves had excellent hearing. They could probably already hear us. So why weren't they coming out?

"That's where they had Jen," Becca whispered and used her gun to indicate the house.

It was an older one. A pretty, blue colonial with a wraparound porch. My stomach rolled. It looked like a grandmotherly house where you went to visit for tea and cake. Not a place where they caged and tortured humans.

"It's where they keep all the slaves," Drew added. Fury danced in his eyes.

"Not all of them. I saw some in another house they held me in." Elijah spoke.

I spun toward him. "What? Diego held you prisoner and you're just now telling me?"

My wolf snarled.

His gaze darted away from me. "I didn't think it was important."

"How did you get away?" Drew demanded.

Elijah's eyes narrowed on him. "Does it matter?"

I stepped between them. "How?"

He sighed and looked at me. "The queen stepped in. Then she held me prisoner in her coven. You know the rest."

Blinking, my mind was slow to register what he'd confessed. The queen of the witches saved him and in return he still wanted revenge for his sister's death. What else was he not telling me?

Drew stepped around me and jabbed a finger in the air at Elijah. "You were with other slaves and you just left them there?"

Elijah stood taller and returned his stare. "I couldn't do anything to help them."

"Couldn't or wouldn't?" Drew's face grew stormy.

Elijah stilled. I could feel his wolf rising to the surface—and he was pissed.

"Stop. We have a job to do," I interrupted.

Becca grunted. "She's right. Let's get this over with before those wolves come after us."

They continued their stare off, neither one wanting to back down.

"Elijah," I snapped.

He turned to me. "Yeah. I'm ready."

"Diego should be busy torturing slaves so we can hit his camp and lure Sylvie out." Becca spoke as she led the way.

I shuddered. The torturing slaves part made my stomach turn over. I didn't want to imagine what they were doing to the poor humans.

"Right there. That's the camp." Elijah nodded toward a small brick guest house in the yard next door to the blue mansion.

"The guest house? Are you sure?" Drew frowned.

Elijah's lip curled. "I know where I was held."

"Okay. Then lead the way. Let's go before the veiling spell wears off."

I turned to the witch. "How much time do we have?"

He shrugged. "Depends."

Elijah snorted. "That's helpful."

Drew waved us forward. "Come on. We have to go."

He turned and ran for the fence. We raced after him. I winced at the sound of our heavy footsteps. They had to have heard us coming. My eyes ran up and down the street, my senses alert.

We made it to the white picket fence without being spotted. My heart pounded in my ears and my wolf's warning rang clear. *Wolves. Everywhere.*

I snorted. That wasn't helpful news. We were right in the middle of their territory, and there were only five of us. Why did we think that a good idea?

Swallowing my fear, I followed the others to the back of the fence. Elijah stepped forward first and sprang for the top of the fence. He collided with something in the air and fell back. I gasped as he landed backwards on the ground.

"Elijah?" I whispered.

He groaned and shot back to his feet. "Barrier."

Becca swore.

Drew's eyes widened. "Magic?"

Elijah leveled him a cool gaze. "I didn't just fall for the fun of it."

I waved my hand for them to shut up. We were at the camp now and with that crash, someone was going to come.

"Can you take it down?" I asked the witch who'd come with us.

He nodded and waved his hand at the fence.

My mind raced. Had Diego forced the rogue witches to spell his camp or were they all working with him? Dread unfurled in my belly. The werewolves we could handle, but witches?

The plan was falling to pieces.

"Shh. Someone's coming." Elijah waved at us.

"But what if it's not Sylvie?" Becca whispered.

It is. Their alpha and a beta. Two others.

My eyes widened in surprise at my wolf's words. How could she tell all of that from their human footsteps?

I'm a smart wolf. Her smug tone made me smile.

"What do we do now?" Becca hissed.

Drew was staring at the fence, a determined look on his face. The witch's fingers flew, but was it fast enough? I glanced at Elijah. He looked just as lost as I was.

"We leave and come back with more back up. Let's go see Taylor's pack first." Elijah finally answered.

"No." Drew was shaking his head. He turned to us, "If that alpha's camp was near Diego's she's probably already taken his side or is dead."

His words filled me with horror. Diego was cruel, but he wouldn't kill a fellow wolf, would he? Though he did threaten me.

Elijah sneered at Drew. "So, what you want to just sit out here and wait for his pack to capture us?"

"I'm not getting taken." Becca lifted her gun, a fierce determination sparking in her eyes.

No, I believed that. She would go out with a bang, taking as many of her enemies as she could with her.

"Hurry up!" Drew urged the witch.

The boy grunted. "I'm trying."

"Go. They're coming. This way," Elijah urged.

We followed him as he ran past the fence and down the street. He was heading for Taylor's camp, I realized. Drew's words played back, and I really hoped he was wrong.

If Diego had Taylor's pack then we would be surrounded.

"Look! There!" a voice called behind us.

I didn't stop to glance back. Elijah and I exchanged worried looks. Our cloak was gone.

A gun fired at us and missed my arm by mere inches. My heart leapt into my throat and I pushed myself faster.

"I thought we were supposed to be catching Sylvie not running from her," Becca yelled at us.

"Up there. We'll set up an ambush." Elijah nodded at a house at the end of the street.

My mouth dropped open. "An ambush? Elijah, you know she sent one of those wolves to warn the others. They will all be coming after us."

"We just need to get a hold of Sylvie," Drew insisted.

"But what about her beta and the others?" I asked.

"We'll have to take them out," Elijah answered.

My eyes snapped to his. Take them out? Could he really do it? Kill another wolf? Uneasiness rolled through my gut.

"Don't look at me like that, Val. It's too late to choose a different path now. It's us or them."

I turned away, his words feeling like a slap. He was right, but I hated that he was right. Us or them.

Elijah led us into the giant house, and we paused to take a breath. I glanced around at the entry way and the staircase leading upstairs. Walking farther in, I realized the house was empty. No furniture or anything left behind from its previous owners. Robbed? Or had whoever lived there moved before the curse? A lot of people had fled the city when the kids started dying. In the hope that the disease wouldn't reach their families, but it didn't matter. All the children died. Everywhere.

"Spread out. Hide. We pick them off one by one and get Sylvie," Elijah instructed.

The door flung open before we could move. Sylvie led her beta and another wolf toward us. All of them were armed.

My blood turned to ice.

"What are you doing here, Elijah?" She glared at him.

Me, she purposefully ignored. My wolf growled at her insult.

His eyes darted from her to her pack members. He stood in front of me, shielding me from them.

"Sylvie. We just want to talk."

She issued a harsh laugh. "Yeah, right. Let's talk about why you brought two humans and a witch into our camp."

Her wolves smiled at Drew and Becca. Hungry—predatory smiles.

Elijah glanced at them and shrugged. "A gift. For Diego."

Drew's head whipped toward him, fire burning in his gaze. Becca's eyes held the same fire. She stepped away from Elijah, clutching her gun. I could see the calculation in her gaze. The witch's hands were raised, his eyes steady on Sylvie.

"What are you doing?" I hissed at my alpha.

Sylvie laughed at me. "I think they call it acting," She glanced back at Elijah. "Nice try, but you must think I'm pretty stupid to fall for that. You didn't bring them here for Diego. What are you doing here, Elijah?"

He returned her smile. "You caught me then. I'm here to see you."

His flippant grin made her pause. Her brow furrowed as her eyes swept the room. "Well, I'm here so now what?"

Elijah met my eyes with a silent message. My heart raced. This was it. It was our only chance before the others came. If we wanted to get out of there alive, we needed Sylvie.

A gun fired, making me jump. My wolf winced at the noise.

"Get her!" someone shouted.

"The guns! Watch out." Elijah pushed me out of the line of fire.

My head whipped back and forth. Becca had taken down one of the wolves. Drew stood beside her, drawing his own gun.

Elijah scrambled forward and grabbed the fallen weapon. The beta wolf returned fire, but his shots went astray. One caught the witch in the chest. He fell. Horror filled me.

Elijah raised his gun to strike the beta, but Becca was faster.

She fired a bullet through his head.

Bile rose in my throat as he collapsed atop the other wolf. Sylvie stared at them, mouth open in horror. She clutched her gun to her side with a trembling hand.

"Get her," Becca screamed.

Sylvie roared and lifted her gun. Elijah knocked it out of her hands before she could pull the trigger. Her eyes turned silver.

"I'm sorry." I grabbed her by the arms.

She fought against me, eyes murderous.

Before she could shift, Becca slammed the butt of her gun against her head. The loud crack made me wince. Sylvie's eyes rolled back, and her body fell limp.

"I had her. You didn't have to do that," I hissed at Becca.

The girl snorted. "Really? She was about to turn."

She tucked her gun back into the top of her jeans and grabbed the alpha's legs. I grabbed her top half, holding her beneath her arms and walking backwards towards the others.

"He's dead." Drew was kneeling beside the witch.

My gaze swept over his outstretched body. He'd only been trying to help us. I shuddered. Blood blossomed through his shirt.

What would happen now? I met Elijah's eyes and found concern written there. Concern for the witch or for what Diego would do if he caught us?

"Let's get her back. To the coven. He won't look for her there." Elijah motioned me forward.

I gaped at him. "The coven?"

"Come on."

"It's too far. We'll never make it back," I argued.

"Then Taylor's camp?" Elijah asked.

"What about him?" Drew asked.

"Leave him."

Drew frowned, eyes meeting mine. Waiting for me to agree with him? I looked away. Though I hated the cruelty of it, Elijah was right. We didn't have the time to worry about the poor witch right now.

Ignoring Drew's heavy stare, I handed Sylvie off to Elijah and took his gun. Shouts echoed in the distance driving fear through my heart. Diego.

We ran out of the back of the house and raced for Taylor's camp. Worry washed over me. What if Diego was already there? Waiting for us? What if Taylor was on his side? I pushed away the doubts and scanned the empty streets.

Howls filled the air, making me tremble. My wolf bristled. The Red Wolves. They were coming.

Pain jolted up my legs as we ran. My wolf begged to be freed, insisting she was faster than me, but I didn't let her loose. I needed to think clearly about our next step. We didn't know what we were heading into. It was already late afternoon. We were running out of time to get the alphas. Soon the blood moon would appear, and we had to make it back to sign the covenant.

"There. It's right there," Elijah gasped out.

I looked to where he indicated. Taylor's camp. It was an older street than the one Diego lived on. The old main street with outdated little shops and restaurants. Elijah led us toward a block of empty buildings.

He paused.

"What is it?" I asked.

His face turned grim. "There should be guards."

Drew swore and shook his head. "I told you."

Becca glanced around. "Where else can we go? We have to move now. They're right on top of us."

"Come with me. I know where to hide." Elijah led us through an alley.

I frowned at him. "How do you know this place?"

He looked away. "Taylor let me stay here for a bit. Right after I left our camp"—his gaze shot to Drew—"and she wasn't working with Diego then."

My wolf growled at his confession.

Taylor's mate turned twenty almost two months ago and died from the curse. I tried not to think about what Elijah had been doing in Taylor's camp. How could he have abandoned our pack to hang out with hers?

Storing away my hurt for later, I scanned the quiet street and bit my lip.

"Valeria," Elijah called.

I picked up my pace and followed as he led us into the back of a building.

23

VALERIA

A medicinal smell mixed with herbs and spices filled my nose. Some kind of health shop? I blinked against the darkness. The windows were boarded, and no light streamed through.

"Stay in here while I check it out." Elijah waved us in.

"What? No. You're not going out there." =

He sighed. "Val, I'm not going to argue with you. Just stay."

I bristled at his alpha tone.

"I'm going too. I don't trust you." Becca spoke up.

"Becca, no." Drew grabbed her arm.

Dim light shone from the window, highlighting the fear in his eyes.

"No one is coming with me. Just stay here." Elijah's words were steel. He set Sylvie down on the floor beside us and stood.

I wanted to laugh. His authority didn't work on the humans and I was his equal. If he thought, he could boss me around...

Listen to our mate, my wolf snapped.

Before I could argue, he was gone. Becca and I moved to follow him. Drew stepped in our path.

"What the hell, Drew?" His sister tried to shove by him.

He glared at us. "Can we just stop for a minute and think about this? You really want to follow him into danger?"

"I'm not staying here for them to find us," Becca argued.

Sylvie groaned. Becca moved toward her, the end of her gun raised.

"Stop. Don't hurt her."

I jumped between them and clenched my fists. "We said we weren't going to hurt her."

Becca's eyes were ablaze with anger. "I never agreed to that. She knew what was happening. To Jen and to the others. She probably took part herself."

Her words made me wince.

"I'm sorry," Sylvie gasped.

I turned to her. She struggled to sit up, holding her head with her hand.

"You're sorry?" Becca scoffed.

Sylvie flinched.

"Becca," her brother warned.

"No, Drew. I'm not going to listen to her BS apology. Not after what they've done." Her voice rose.

I glanced at the gun in her hand. Fear washed over me. This wasn't the plan. If she shot Sylvie... Diego would never sign the covenant. He'd kill us and everyone else.

"Think about the covenant," Drew told her.

A half-crazed laugh escaped her. "The covenant? You want me to think about the fucking covenant? After what they did, we're just going to sign a paper that says it's all okay?"

Her movements were jerky now.

Drew and I exchanged nervous glances. Sylvie watched us from the floor, her eyes darting back and forth.

"Yeah, I know, you think I'm crazy." Becca huffed. "Maybe I am. What they did to Ruby." She choked up.

She kept shaking her head, gun waving with the movement. "I can't stop seeing it. Seeing everything. I'm so fucking tired of seeing it." Her voice was strained.

I watched in horror as she held the gun to her own head.

"Becca, no!" Drew moved toward her.

She stepped away from him. "I just want it to end, Drew."

The defeat in her voice brought tears to my eyes. How had we ended up like this? We were just kids. This wasn't how things were supposed to be.

"Please, Becca. I'm sorry. I promise things are going to change. Please. God. Please. Don't do this." Drew's words were desperate.

The door flew open, making me jump. I turned to find Elijah storming in. He stopped in his tracks, eyes widening on Becca.

She glanced at him and Drew dove for her. They fell to the floor together with a loud crash. He wrestled the gun away from her and stood. She curled into herself and didn't move. Drew handed me the weapon and knelt beside her.

Sylvie's sniffles caught my ear. I turned to find her with her face buried in her hands.

"I don't know what the hell happened, but this is so not the time for... whatever this is." Elijah shook his head at us.

I frowned at him. "Just give them a moment."

He scoffed. "A moment? We don't have a moment. Diego's here."

Sylvie's head snapped up.

Fear spiked my blood. "He's here?"

Elijah nodded. "He's got her. He's got Taylor."

"Come out, Elijah. Valeria. I know you're there and I know you have Sylvie. Bring her to me unharmed and I won't kill you."

I glanced at her. She wiped her tears, her body still.

Drew looked to us. Becca was sitting up, but her eyes were focused elsewhere. Drew held her tight to him. Pity filled me at the scene. They'd been through so much and it still wasn't over.

Beads of sweat coated Elijah's forehead. I could feel my own palms growing clammy.

"You have exactly two minutes."

I bristled at Diego's calmness. How could he be so cold? Attacking other alphas? What had made him turn into such a monster?

"What's the plan?" Drew spoke first, his eyes shifting from me to Elijah.

"We have to do what he says. He'll kill Taylor," I answered first.

"Let me talk to him. Make a deal."

I frowned at Elijah. "Deal?"

"Maybe if we give up Sylvie and agree to leave the city and stay in our camp, he'll let us go. Won't come after us anymore."

Drew scowled at him. "What about the others? The humans? His slaves? What about us? You think he'll let us just go when they've taken everyone else?"

I shuddered. No. I didn't think Diego would just let the humans go and I couldn't give them up to him. To be tortured like Jen.

Elijah sighed and shook his head. He looked to me. "We never should have gotten involved in this."

My anger spiked at his attitude.

"If you let me talk to him..." Sylvie interrupted.

I whipped toward her. "How can we trust you?"

She flinched. "I don't want any more violence either."

"You bring Sylvie and I'll give you Taylor." Diego's voice echoed outside the shop.

My pulse quickened. He was right there.

I motioned for her to follow me.

"Val, what are you doing?" Elijah stopped us.

"I'm making the trade."

"It's okay. He won't hurt you. Let me talk to him," Sylvie pleaded.

Elijah growled and waved us forward. I glanced back at Drew and Becca before pulling the alpha outside. They stared at me with haunted eyes that filled me with resolve.

I would end Diego's terror. No one should have to live like they had. Like we were—in constant fear.

The street was filled with wolves—Taylor's pack and Diego's. And the sky was darkening.

Diego strode toward us, his eyes narrowed.

"Where is she?" I demanded.

He pushed a distraught Taylor forward.

Anger pulsed within me. "What happened to the other alphas? Did you kill them?"

"No. Vampires did that. I stopped them from killing the rest of their packs."

"What happened to their betas?"

Diego glanced away. "Vampires."

The hairs on my neck bristled. Did he expect me to believe that?

"The vampires killed the alphas and betas, but you just happened to be there to save the rest of the packs. Is that right?"

"That's right." He met my gaze, his eyebrow arched in challenge.

He didn't think I would call his bluff.

I blinked, still recovering from his admission. An icy fear crept up my spine. If he controlled all the packs, it was just me and my wolves left. We could never stand up to him. There weren't enough of us. What if he killed me and my betas next?

As if reading my thoughts, he smiled. "There's only one pack left now, and it's mine."

A growl escaped me, my wolf's fury rising to the surface.

"The Shadow Wolves still have an alpha. Me. Not you."

He shook his head. "Don't be stupid, Valeria. You know you don't stand a chance with me as your enemy."

Elijah growled at the threat. "Stand down, Diego. We have your mate. Let Taylor go, and I won't hurt her."

Diego laughed. "You won't hurt her, Elijah. I'm calling your bluff."

I bristled at the haughtiness in his voice.

He thinks us weak, my wolf snarled.

"Let her go and we'll let Sylvie go." I pulled Sylvie forward.

"Diego. Please. I'm fine. Let's just go home." Sylvie finally found her voice.

His gaze softened on his mate. "We will."

He glanced back at me and pushed Taylor toward us. She stumbled forward with a whimper.

Anger blazed within me as I spotted her bruises and scratches. Sylvie's eyes fell on her, sorrow flashing on her face.

"Go." I released the alpha.

She ran to Diego.

Before I could reach Taylor, a gunshot rang out. My wolf flinched at the sound.

Taylor fell limp to the ground. Shock coursed through me. No.

Her eyes stared up at the sky, blood pooling beneath her broken body.

My wolf howled with anger at the betrayal.

"Val. Get out of there!" Elijah's voice snapped me to attention.

Around me Taylor's pack shifted, howling with fury. Diego and Sylvie shifted in unison. His wolves circled us.

I stood to shift as well, but someone collided with me. We landed tangled together in the dirt.

Fury rushed through me.

"Val. No. Please. We have to get out of here." Elijah's eyes were wide with fear.

I struggled to push him off me.

"He killed her! We had a deal and he just killed her!" My voice cracked.

He pulled me up to a sitting position and shielded me with his body. "I know. I know. There's nothing we can do now. We have to go. We'll go back to the coven."

I gaped at him. "No. Elijah, we have to avenge her. Her pack... they can't beat Diego's."

Elijah held my face in his hands, forcing me to look into his dark eyes. "Listen to me, Val. We can't. Even with our whole pack, we wouldn't be able to stop him. We're leaving. Those who want to follow us, can."

"I can't. I can't just leave them."

He swore and shook his head.

"The covenant. We have to get back and make sure the covenant is signed. The witches. They can help," he insisted.

His words made sense, but my emotions were rolling like waves inside me. Pushing them back down, I let him lead me away. We raced back to the shop and found Drew and Becca waiting for us. Drew was armed with both their weapons.

"We have to get to the coven. Now," Elijah ordered.

They followed us outside with no argument. I glanced at Becca, worried for her. She didn't have her gun anymore and the lost look on her face twisted my heart. Would she recover from what she'd been through? Would any of us?

The sun was nearly gone when we made it to the coven. We were a hot, sweaty, dirty mess and my emotions clashed together in a continual wave. Anger turned to sorrow, and sorrow turned to anger.

Taylor's death replayed in my mind, stirring my wolf's anger along with my own. Diego was a traitor. A coward. Using a gun to take down the alpha. It was horrific.

Unforgivable. My wolf agreed.

Elijah was the first to make it to the porch. The door flung open and the witches poured out, ready for us.

"Diego," Elijah gasped.

We were all breathing heavily.

The witches talked all at once, their shock and fear echoing in their words.

"They're coming." Kohl's voice silenced everyone.

My eyes shot to him. "How do you know?"

He didn't look at me. "The queen is gone and so is Prince Ryn. There's no one here to stop them except us. Diego just took the city. This... is where they'll come next."

Fear spread through me. He was right. Diego would come for us now, but did he know about the covenant?

"Can you send word to the queen? To Prince Ryn? To my pack? They will come."

Elijah shook his head. "They won't get here in time."

Kohl turned to another witch. "Send someone to the vampires and to the wolves."

The girl nodded and scurried off. Another witch rubbed her arms. It was the redheaded one from before.

"I'll get a message to Deepa."

"Where is Wes?" the tall witch asked, his hazel eyes studying our faces.

The witch.

"He didn't make it." Elijah answered.

I exchanged a worried look with Drew. Everyone fell quiet, their sorrow and fear growing into a tangible thing.

"Come on. We have to prepare. Everyone find a weapon and help me barricade the coven. We can't let him get through," Kohl ordered.

I'm ready, my wolf assured me. I winced. I wasn't so sure I was.

24

MCKENZIE

I spent all day with my witches preparing for the barrier spell and looking through the grimoire for anything about the curse. By early evening, we'd finished scouring all the pages and tested some of the spells, but we found nothing about how to reverse the curse. Breaking the barrier spell first was still our best option.

Doubt and worry crowded my mind and though I should have been more concerned about how we were going to harness enough magic to do it, my mind kept drifting back to what I'd done.

Kissing the two vampire princes was high up there on my list of things I regretted. Thankfully, no one had seen me in my weak moment and it sure as hell wasn't happening again. So why couldn't I just let it go?

"I still don't get how she got all this stuff?" Deepa's question broke my thoughts.

I looked over at the table where they'd laid out the spell ingredients. The cursed key, hair from a dead queen, finger bone of a witch elder, and pure glass.

"I'm telling you. We have a mole," Blake answered her.

She scowled. "But if someone knew there was a spell to break the barrier why didn't they take it to the queen? Why side with the rogues and vampires?"

Fane's words replayed in my mind. *They think you are weak...*

Blake grunted. "I don't know. We've been busting our asses looking for a way to stop this curse and the barrier, and this witch just comes along and solves everything on her own?"

I shared his irritation. The rogue witches weren't supposed to have that much power or knowledge—it belonged to the coven.

"Let's go set this stuff up before sundown. We'll—"

Deepa screamed, cutting me off. Blake jumped back from her with a hand raised and ready to chant.

"What is—"

She rolled up her sleeve with a whimper, revealing her arm. My words died on my lips.

There carved into her skin was a message. *Diego. SOS.*

An icy fear rushed through me at the bloody words. Blake swore and quickly started a healing incantation. The doors flew open, making me flinch.

Ryn entered along with two of his vampires. His eyes widened on Deepa's wound. He tore his gaze away and looked to me. "What is it? What's happened?"

Dread unfurled inside me. "It's Diego. He's going after the coven. I have to go back."

He blinked and held a hand up to me as if he meant to calm me. "Back? You can't go back. We have to open the barrier. You said it has to be tonight. The blood moon."

My mind raced and my heart pounded. If someone had taken the time and energy to perform an incantation to message us this way, then it had to be serious. I glanced at my charm bracelet. Why hadn't Kohl warned me? Was he okay?

A thought flickered in my mind. What if Ryn and Fane had planned this? To get me away from the coven while Diego swooped in? They'd lost their rogue witch, so they thought to replace her with me—so I would do their bidding.

I whipped toward Ryn. "Did you know? Are you helping him?"

He gaped at me.

"Are you?"

He walked toward me, the movement slow and deadly. "You think I'm helping him?"

I refused to back down now. "Someone is."

Blake and Deepa stood beside me. I could feel the strength of their magic in the air.

Ryn only had eyes for me. "And you assume it's me?"

"I don't know, but the vampires in the city have been pretty cozy with Diego. If you forbid them to fraternize with his pack, why would they go against you?"

His nostrils flared. "Not everyone wants to see me become king. I'm just a prince. Some of them think they don't have to listen."

"Well then you have to make them listen."

"Like your witches listen to you? You know as well as I do the struggle with ruling over others."

Anger boiled deep inside me. I'd been doing a pretty good job of it considering our circumstances. Who was he to judge me?

"I swear to you, I had nothing to do with this. I would never help Diego. We should see to the barrier first and then, I promise you, I will help you go after him. Your coven is strong. They can hold him off long enough."

My stomach turned over. What if it was too late? Ryn's

words made sense—it was the logical thing, but I hated not knowing what was going on. My witches were strong though, and I trusted Kohl to protect them and the covenant.

"I swear, Kenzie. I would never help that wolf."

His eyes bore into me.

"Aww. Your first lover's quarrel. And lucky me, I get to witness it." Fane's voice startled me. I turned to see him stepping from the doorway.

I tore my gaze from Ryn and glared at Fane. "It's you, isn't it, Fane? You're helping Diego."

He frowned and splayed a hand over his chest. "Me? Why would I help the wolf? You know how I feel about you, *cariad*. About us."

His eyes slid to Ryn, who still stood fuming.

"Then how is he taking over the entire city?" I demanded.

Fane snorted. "That's what's got your panties in a bunch? You're jealous of a lowly werewolf alpha?"

My lip curled at him.

"Stop playing games, Fane. Answer her question. Did you do this?" Ryn snapped.

Fane's face darkened, but he didn't respond with his usual smugness.

He turned back to me. "I didn't help anyone. Like they say, *cariad*, I only care about myself."

I stiffened under his intense stare. Ryn stormed toward him and the other vampires skittered back.

"She needs a better healer," Blake spoke to my back.

I glanced at Deepa, who was still clutching at her arm though the blood had stopped spilling. My stomach churned. Why hadn't they chosen to send the message to me?

"We have a healer," Ryn answered, turning his attention back to us.

Blake scowled. "She needs a real healer. A witch. Not a vampire. We—"

"No. I'll be fine, Blake. Just need something to clean this and a bandage. Standard first aid is fine," Deepa interrupted him.

Ryn nodded. "Of course. Amos will take you."

The vampire glared at them and motioned for them to follow. Ryn waved the other one to leave as well. I stood alone in the room with the two brothers. Seeing them side by side was more than unnerving. Shame filled me as the memories of the night before came to me.

Fane picked at his fingernails and glanced at me. "So, anyway. I came in here to tell you I went to the woods to investigate the barrier and to see what spooked the wolves."

He paused, looking from me to Ryn.

"Okay, and?" I demanded.

Fane shrugged. "There's something there."

"Like what?"

He sniffed and frowned at something under his nails. "How should I know? I'm not a witch."

"You are so not helpful, brother." Ryn shook his head.

Fane shrugged again. "Didn't realize you two needed my help so badly." He flashed a smile at me. "I believe you told me earlier today that you *got this*? And that I should fuck off?"

I huffed. "Why are you so annoying?"

His smile grew. "Why does it bother you so much? Could it be because deep down you know you want me?"

I made a face. "Gross. Hell no."

"Fane," Ryn warned.

He turned to his brother, eyes narrowed. "Ryn."

The two brothers squared off, matching stares that made me want to skitter back. If a fight was about to break out, I wanted to be far away from it.

"Are you going to tell us what you saw in the forest?" I interrupted.

Fane turned back to me. "I can take you there. You should see it for yourself."

Ryn scoffed. "If you think I'm going to let you go anywhere with her on your own—"

"Then why don't you join us, brother?" Fane's smile grew tight, "The more the merrier, eh?"

His eyes shot to me. "Looks like you get a special treat. Two for one. I bet you'll just love that."

Heat flushed across my skin at his insinuation. "Shut up, Fane."

I turned to Ryn. "I'll tell Deepa and Blake to meet us there with the spell stuff. It's not that long until sundown. I want to get back to my coven as soon as possible."

He nodded. "First the barrier, and then we go to your coven. I promise."

Ignoring Fane's smug smile, I followed Ryn out and went to track down my witches.

The sun was lowering as we left the city behind. Instead of riding next to Fane in the carriage, I sat up front beside his brother. My heart pounded in my ears and worry gnawed at me. What if Diego had already destroyed the covenant and my coven? What if it was too late?

I pushed away the doubts. Kohl could handle him. Plus, the werewolves were gathering the other packs to face him.

We bumped along the road and I scanned the empty land as we went. We'd made it to the outskirts of Savannah and the woods were getting closer. The horses whinnied and stopped, refusing to enter.

"I guess we're walking from here." Fane sniffed.

My eyebrow rose as I followed him out of the carriage. Ryn jumped down from the driver's seat and landed beside us. I turned on my flashlight and swept it over the darkening trees. Where were all the animals? Why weren't they making any sounds?

"After you, Queen." Fane bowed.

I threw him an irritated look and walked past him. He and Ryn followed.

"Wait. I have to tie the horses somewhere."

Fane snorted. "Why? Just let them return to the mansion. They know the way."

Ryn frowned at him but listened, anyway. His eyes met mine and his gaze softened, making me flush. The memory of his kiss was still fresh in my mind.

Storing the details away to worry about at another date, I pressed forward. The air was colder and despite our loud footsteps, none of the animals appeared to watch us. As soon as Blake and Deepa were ready, they would come with the ingredients for the open the barrier.

I breathed in the fresh pine smell and fought the urge to shudder. The woods at night always gave me the creeps. My flashlight bounced from branch to branch.

"What is it you needed to show us, Fane?" Ryn broke the silence.

"Up there. In the clearing."

We walked to the edge of the tree line and paused. Chills crawled along my skin and my magic swirled around us. Holes and piles of upturned dirt dotted the grass.

"What is this?"

"Shouldn't you know? It's something witchy." Fane smirked.

I scowled at him. "This has nothing to do with my coven."

"They were rogue witches. The coven wouldn't bury them in the city."

My head snapped to Ryn. "How do you know?"

His solemn eyes met mine. "I'm the one who buried them here."

"And you're the one who killed them too, aren't you? The ones who didn't die from the curse?" Fane pressed.

Ryn looked away, falling silent.

Shock filled me.

I knew about Grace and all the humans he'd drained, but he was responsible for the death of rogue witches too? How many?

Fear crawled on my skin. The rumors of his past replayed in my mind. Prince of Darkness. Heartless Heir. It was so hard to reconcile the horrific truth with the boy I knew now. He was gentle, kind, nothing like the monster he'd been before.

I pushed away the thoughts and turned back to the clearing. "But where are the bodies? The ones you buried?"

Fane scoffed. "Gone. Obviously. You didn't think I brought you here to stare at some witch graves, did you?"

My eyes shot to Fane. "That is exactly what we're doing."

He snorted and pointed to the gaping holes in the earth. "Yes, but as you can see, they're empty. Graves aren't supposed to be empty."

"No shit, Sherlock," I snapped.

Ryn held up a hand. "Shh. Listen."

I stilled. Fane mumbled something under his breath and turned away. Branches snapped in the distance and leaves rustled behind us. The animals were silent, but something was moving in the forest, growing closer.

"What is it?" I asked Ryn.

Fane sneered at me. "Like he would know."

Irritation flared inside me, but I caught Ryn's serious look and bit back my retort.

"Can't you feel that? Something is off." His voice turned urgent.

Embarrassed that I hadn't, I licked my lips and focused my senses on the magic around us. It slammed into me full force. I winced as pain overtook me.

Ryn was right—something was wrong. Very, very wrong.

Before I could make sense of the alarms ringing through me, a powerful gust of wind enveloped us. It tore through the clearing and whooshed in my ears. Tree branches snapped and flew around, barely missing us.

Nature had chosen her side, and it wasn't with us.

"Run!" I screamed over the torrent of noise.

We turned in unison as the wind strengthened, battering us. I went down first and then Ryn. Fane was nowhere to be seen.

I gaped at the spot he'd been standing in. What the hell? What the hell was happening?

Ryn grabbed my hand and yanked me to my feet. He turned for his brother and swore.

His eyes shot to mine, wide and frantic. "Where is he?"

I could only shake my head.

"Fane!" he screamed above the roaring wind.

Voices echoed around us. I squinted against the strong wind and gasped as bodies—dead bodies—emerged from the forest. Some were whole while others had limbs and other parts missing. My stomach churned at the sight.

"What the hell? What is this?" Ryn asked.

I swallowed hard. "The rogue witches. There's so many of them."

"But how are they... alive?"

"I don't know."

"Is it the blood moon?"

My eyes shot to the sky where the red moon hung. Magic

swirled in the air, it pulled and tugged me in a heightened frenzy. I summoned it and let it rush through my body.

"This is our forest. Leave or die," one of the witches spoke.

I shuddered at her eyeless gaze. Movement startled me, making me skitter back against Ryn. His strong arms wrapped around me and pulled me back to his side. A thoughtful, protective gesture, but unnecessary.

I was the one with the magic.

The witches lumbered toward us, and I raised my hand to cast a protection spell. Something invisible hit me first. Pain ripped through me, making me gasp.

Ryn fell to his knees beside me. I blinked at the zombie witches in confusion. How could they cast? They were dead and cut off from magic. Was it because of the blood moon?

"I'm sorry about that, but you left us no choice." Fane's voice came the forest.

I whipped around to find him and a hooded figure standing in the clearing. A rogue witch?

Red spotted my vision. "What are you doing?"

"Fane. Why?" The pain in Ryn's voice cut me like a knife.

I glared at Fane.

He stood, emotionless. The red moon illuminated his beautiful face. So beautiful and so cold. He was the devil, and we'd both ignored our gut instincts.

25

MCKENZIE

Fane smiled coldly. "Why? Why do you think, Ryn? How can you still not see it after all these years? You never should have inherited the throne. You are weak. Pathetic. Too emotional. Honestly, it would have been better if you hadn't woken up at all."

Ryn stiffened.

"And you." Fane turned to me. "You aren't surprised at all are you, *cariad?*"

Anger burned through me—hot and fast.

I spat in his direction, the only retaliation I could manage under the invisible hold.

He smiled. "You knew what I was all this time, and yet you still wanted me?"

"I never wanted you!" I spat, glaring at his smirking face. "Don't do this, Fane. We can work something out."

A dark laugh escaped him. "As much as I love to hear you beg, I'm afraid everything's already been worked out. I keep you both here to stop you from signing the covenant and breaking the barrier while Diego kills the rest of the alphas and his witches take control of the coven."

My heart leapt into my throat. *Kohl.*

Ryn scowled at him. "But, why, Fane? What is in it for you? You want the werewolf in charge?"

"In charge? No, don't you see. I'm the one in charge. I've always been the one in charge, pulling the strings."

His words struck me like an arrow. Why didn't I see it before? How could we have been so blinded and stupid?

"Unlike you, I'm not against sharing power. It could have been us, brother." Fane's face hardened. "It should have been us. I was hopeful that after your brief confinement, you'd see the errors of your way and join me. But you decided you wanted to play the savior." His gaze flicked to me. "I blame you for that."

I summoned more magic, trying to free myself from their spell. "Diego won't share his power, Fane. He'll stake you the first chance he gets. You were just a means to an end."

He held up a hand to me. "No, sweet Kenzie, it's the other way around. I'm using him. If his ego gets too big, well, I can kill him. Otherwise, I'm fine waiting for the curse to take him."

"And what will you do once the curse takes everyone else? It will be just you and the other vampires, and you think they'll accept you after what you've done to their king? Your own brother?"

Fane was in my face in a heartbeat. His icy, blue eyes pierced into me. I fought the urge to shrink back and escape that penetrating gaze.

"Well, I'm hoping you'll find the answers to that. Stop the curse, remember?"

"You think I'm going to help you after this?" I struggled against the invisible bonds.

Magic thrummed around me and I wanted so desperately to

grab hold of it and unleash it on Fane. Make him fall. Make him bleed.

As if reading my violent thoughts, his lips quirked into a smirk. "You will."

I spat at him, but he moved out of reach.

"Allison. Did you kill her?" Ryn's voice was hard.

Fane stilled. A flash of regret crossed his face before the coldness returned.

"She was supposed to be working on a cure for the curse." He turned to me. "I didn't want her to open the barrier, but I didn't kill her. She died before I could. Past her expiration date, unfortunately. The work of the coven since it was your kind who cast the curse to begin with."

Heat filled me.

I glanced at the hooded figure next to him. Was it the mole? Whoever it was, they obviously had a lot of power. To keep me and Ryn in their hold for so long.

They think you're weak...

Pushing away Fane's words, I focused on a way to free myself.

Fane circled us. "You two will stay here. Until everything is over. You, I have no use for anymore, brother. You've failed me again and again. But you..." He turned his attention to me.

I shuddered under his gaze.

He smiled. "I still have a use for you."

My stomach churned. I didn't want to know what kind of sick plan he had for me. I forced my power out, trying to break the frozen spell his witch had cast.

"Let the rogues have their fun, Blake, but make sure they don't kill the queen. I need her."

I gasped. My eyes shot to the hooded figure who visibly flinched.

Fane's smile widened. "Oops. Guess it doesn't matter now, huh?"

Anger rolled in thick waves inside me. "Blake? How could you betray the coven?"

He didn't respond.

I whipped toward Fane. "Did you compel him?"

He leaned toward me. "No. Didn't need to. As much as I'd love to stay and watch the show, I have other things to do. Try not to miss me too much. Goodbye."

With that he was gone. I stood, fuming at the spot he'd occupied.

"Fane! Get back here. Fane!" Ryn's voice echoed through the trees.

That was it. We were trapped.

I shared a look with Ryn. Worry swam in his eyes and a rush of fear swept over me. The witches' power leaked in the air and I wasn't so sure Blake or Fane could control them. A chill crawled up my spine. It had to be the blood moon.

Despite his insistence that I live, these rogue witches wanted blood—my blood.

If I didn't come up with something, we would be joining them in death. Only we didn't have the option to return as easily as they had. Our end would be final.

I glared at Blake as he stood between us and the wavering witches. "Why are you doing this? You're not a rogue, Blake."

"I'm sorry, Kenzie. It's nothing personal, but I won't let the humans take control again. If we open that barrier, more of them could come. They nearly destroyed us in the beginning. I'm not giving them a second chance to do it, and I'm not the only one who feels this way."

My skin prickled with anger and hurt. Is this what it all led back to? Revenge? The wolves wanted revenge, the humans wanted revenge, and now the witches too?

"What about Julia, huh? What about the other witches the vampires have hurt in the past? You forgot about that when you switched teams?" My words came out fast and sharp.

"Julia was an unfortunate casualty. She saw me talking to Fane. She would have gone to you."

A numbness filled me. Witches turning on each other? The world really had gone to hell.

"You will pay for this, Blake."

"Your friend. What did you do to her? Was she in on this too?" Ryn's question made me flush with shame.

Deepa. How could I have forgotten about her?

Blake shook his head. "No. I put a sleeping spell on her. She won't wake up until it's over."

My lip curled. "Until what's over? The zombies over there killing us?"

"Not you. Just him." Blake's voice was steel.

The bodies had stilled and were watching us with their creepy, eyeless sockets. Some of them wore dirt spattered, torn clothes, while others were in rags.

As if on cue, the witches started moving in unison. A shudder escaped me as they surrounded us. No. It was not going down like this.

Drawing more magic into myself, I let it rip through my body. Pain washed over me as it raged within. I hissed and bit my lip, waiting for it to settle.

It rolled off my skin and before Blake could start another chant, I sent it barreling into him. His hold broke, and he stumbled back with a grunt.

"How's that for a weak queen?" I threw my arm up and let another burst of power fly.

It hit him in the chest, forcing him back. Ryn guarded my back as the witch zombies advanced. Their high-pitched screeches filled the air.

"How are we going to stop these witches?" Ryn's question made me pause.

My eyes narrowed on Blake. "If I stop him, they won't be under his control."

Blake threw up a barrier between us and scoffed. "They're not under my control."

"Only magic rules us," one of the dead witches spoke.

Under the light of the blood moon they were terrifying. Icy fear gripped me. Because of the lunar eclipse, the magic was heightened—for all of us. Even the dead.

"So, what you were just going to watch while they killed us?" I snapped at Blake.

He threw his hand up to cast, but I was faster. My magic shot out, breaking his wrist. His pained cry echoed in the forest. Grim satisfaction filled me at the sound.

Try casting now, asshole.

"Kenzie, we have to get out of here." Ryn was beside me.

"But the barrier. We need the blood moon."

The witches had us completely surrounded now. My stomach dipped. How were we going to stop them?

"Whatever your quarrel is, it's with me. She's done nothing. I'm the one you want." Ryn's words rattled me.

They looked at him.

"You? You who laid us to rest here? It was by your brother's compulsion that you let your bloodlust take control. Our flesh is long gone so we have no fight with you. That is, if you leave."

Ryn gaped at them. Shock ran through me as well. Fane? Fane compelled him to kill the humans and witches in the past? Why? Was it to make Ryn look unfit for the throne?

Anger flashed on Ryn's face.

I turned to the one who'd spoken. "Please, we don't want to hurt you. We just want to break the spell."

A worm crawled through her exposed skull and I grimaced. Nausea rolled through my gut.

"Leave the forest or die." Her voice was cold and determined.

"No. Wait. Please. I'm a friend of... Allison's. I think she resurrected you?"

Blake scoffed behind me. "Liar. You're a liar."

Heat rushed across my skin. I couldn't wait to unleash more magic on him, but first, I had to deal with the dead rogues.

"She was trying to open the barrier. That's all I want and then I'll leave. I swear. Please."

"The forest is ours," she repeated.

"Yes. I know. It's all yours. Just let us open the barrier, please and then we'll go. And we'll make sure no one disturbs you again."

"You can't promise that. If the barrier is opened, more people will come. Humans. Humans destroy everything." Blake's voice rose.

He held his injured hand, fingers slowly flexing. He'd healed himself too quickly.

I turned back to the witches. "Please. Tell me what you want, and I'll help you."

"Don't listen to her. She's the queen of the coven. The same coven that murdered your ancestors."

My eyes widened. It couldn't be true. There was nothing in our history about that.

The zombies hissed, their anger and power growing around them. Wind whipped through the tree branches—nature raging on their behalf.

"Kenzie. We have to go," Ryn insisted.

"I don't know what he's talking about. I swear. If there are any wrongs, I will right them. I swear. I will make a covenant with you."

The head witch cocked her head at me, eyeless sockets staring into my soul. "There are many wrongs to right, queen of the coven. How will you right them?"

My heart pounded. "I will do whatever you ask. Please. Just let me break the spell that is holding us trapped here."

"A blood oath then. Signed under the power of the blood moon. You will free our souls."

I gaped at her. "Your souls?"

She pointed a bony finger at me. "The souls your ancestors hide within the coven. Our souls that give you the magic."

My head spun at her words. The souls that gave us the magic? What was she talking about?

"Yes. I promise," I blurted.

Ryn exchanged a worried look with me.

"Swear it then," she demanded.

Before I could move, she sliced my wrist with her sharp nail, making me gasp.

I made the promise and held my bleeding wrist up to her. She placed her wrist on top of mine and I clenched my mouth shut, fighting the urge to puke as her decayed bone brushed against my skin. Her stench filled my nose, so strong it felt as if it was going to burn my nose hairs. Bile rose in my throat.

"How are you going to open the barrier without the ingredients?" Blake's voice cut into the silence.

My heart sank. He was right—we had nothing.

"Finger bone of a witch elder. Strand of hair of a witch queen. Those combined with the blood moon should be adequate," the witch spoke.

"A dead witch queen."

She cocked her head at Blake. "All witches are fated to die. The hair can be taken any time."

Shock filled me. Did that mean I could use my own?

"But what about the other stuff?" Blake demanded.

I could feel his magic stirring in the air around him. As if he was strong enough to take on all the dead witches and myself.

He'd lost, and he knew it.

"Useless. For any spell all you need is the bare bones," the witch's disembodied voice echoed through the clearing.

The other witches jerked and twitched, the sound of the wind rattling through their bodies made me shudder.

Ryn glanced at me. "I can't tell if she's making a pun or—"

Blake's magic cut him off. He toppled over, clutching his chest. His eyes shot to Blake and the fury I saw in them chilled me.

With a roar, Ryn whipped around, moving too fast to see. He was behind Blake now. Ryn was fast and fierce, but Blake's magic was at full power.

Before the vampire could strike, Blake unleashed another chant. Ryn was tossed into the air, his body flying into a tree with an echoing crunch.

I ran to him.

A branch snapped off and hovered in the air. My blood ran cold. Blake was going to stake him. I threw my hand up and tried to break the wood, but Blake had created a barrier to protect it.

Ryn's head whipped from side to side, but his body remained stuck against the tree. A holding spell? My eyes widened in surprise. How was Blake able to use so much?

"It's the blood moon, child. Don't be afraid of the magic. Let it in," the dead witch whispered in my ear.

Ignoring the chill racing along my back, I did what she said. The magic rammed through me and I could barely stand under the onslaught. Pain filled all my senses. I couldn't see. I couldn't hear.

There was only pain—hot, icy, burning, shredding pain.

My head spun.

"No!" Ryn's voice called out.

I ran towards the sound. Blinking, I tried to focus under the pain.

The branch was sharpened to a point and glowing red. It was a permanency spell.

A permanent stake—permanent death.

It flew towards Ryn.

Air rushed out of my lungs. No.

My hand shot out, and I chanted the first thing that came to me. I watched, breathlessly, as my spell unfolded.

The stake meant for Ryn jerked backwards. It landed with a sickening thud and squelch squarely through Blake's heart.

I fell to my knees in horror. A reversal spell. What had I done?

Ryn leapt over Blake's fallen body and stood in front of me. He pulled me to my feet and wrapped his arms around me. "It's alright. It's alright, Kenzie."

My body was numb. As hard as I tried not to picture it, I saw it replay again and again. The branch. Blake. The blood. Nausea rolled inside me.

"The barrier." The witch's voice made me cringe.

"Your coven still needs you," Ryn reminded me.

Right. Diego. I sucked in a breath and nodded.

"Yes. Let's do this."

"Are you sure you're up to this, Kenzie? Won't it take a lot out of you to do this spell?" Ryn whispered.

Worry flashed in his golden eyes.

My body protested the thought of another spell. I was still recovering from what I'd just cast.

"I'll be fine."

He didn't look convinced, but I didn't have a choice. We needed to do the spell before the blood moon was gone.

"Come," the witch called.

I glanced back at Blake.

Ryn shook his head. "Leave him for now. We can bury him later."

Bury. His words made me shiver. Pushing away my guilt, I turned and followed him and the witches farther into the woods.

26

MCKENZIE

I tugged a strand of my hair and laid it against the stone alongside the finger bone the dead witch had placed there. My body still thrummed with magic, magic that was ready to be unleashed once more.

The power behind my cast was intoxicating. I'd never felt my magic come so easily—or so painfully before. I felt invincible. Too bad Fane and Diego were too far for me to reach.

"We will help you break the spell and in return you will release our souls," the witch spoke.

I nodded at her. "Yes."

"Why didn't you help Allison break the barrier when she resurrected you?" Ryn interrupted.

My eyes widened in surprise at him. It was a good question. One I should have thought of myself.

The witch turned her eyeless, decomposing face toward him. "We had no magic at our disposal. There was no blood moon."

"Why did she raise you? Did she tell you?" I asked.

"No, but I believe she meant to bring someone else back. Someone she loved."

"Someone who died from the curse, probably," Ryn spoke.

A lump grew in my throat. I was so tired of death and all the grief. We'd lost so much and if I couldn't find a way to stop the spell, we'd lose more.

"Are you ready?" The rogue witch's question brought me back.

I nodded and flinched as she gripped my hand in her bony appendage. A shudder ran down my spine at the touch. Another dead witch grabbed my other hand and squeezed it in her icy, cold grip.

Together we chanted, and the magic swirled around us in a frenzy. I winced as it shot through me, the pain double what it usually was.

"Step back," I instructed Ryn.

I couldn't look back to see if he listened. Our voices grew, and the magic rolled through the forest, ripping right through us.

It was sharp and demanding, filling me to the point of bursting. My skin felt paper thin as if any moment it would be shredded to pieces. Something warm trickled down my lips and tickled my chin. Was I bleeding?

My heart slammed against my ribs and my body shook. I was vaguely aware of Ryn's panicked voice calling my name. The sound of bones rattling together filled the air. We were all shaking, I realized—shaking and floating in the air.

Fear struck me. It was too much power. Too much. I couldn't handle it.

My ears popped and a scream tore from my throat. I was falling.

Too fast.

I tried to summon more power to stop myself. Instead, only

pain filled my senses. I screamed again and closed my eyes, waiting for the crash.

Strong arms caught me. I trembled and gasped. For a minute I lay there, my body worn past exhaustion and my mind a scrambled mess.

Where were the witches? Had we done it?

Struggling to sit up, I blinked and looked around. The magic spun around the air. It was just as strong and powerful, but I couldn't call it to me.

"Kenzie, are you okay?" Ryn's voice woke me from the stupor.

I could only nod. *Yes.*

"The barrier?" Ryn asked.

I swallowed the lump in my throat and stretched my hand toward it. "It's open. We did it."

My magic thrummed inside me, but it would be awhile before I'd be able to cast again. I bit back a groan as pain sliced through my head.

The ground swayed and spots dotted my vision. I could barely make out the dead witches as they disappeared into the forest. I glanced at the spot Blake had fallen. He wasn't there. Did they take him?

"Kenzie." Ryn's concerned voice echoed in my ear.

He sounded so far away.

I winced as the ache in my head grew. My whole body burned, and it was all I could do to keep my head up.

"Kenzie, what is it?"

Ryn held me tight, anchoring me in place.

"We have to get back to the coven. Stop Diego. Fane." My voice came out in gasps.

"Are you sure I shouldn't take you back to my house? Can you make it to the coven?"

I groaned. "First the covenant. I'll be okay."

His golden eyes swam in and out of focus and his arms wrapped around me, the only thing keeping me from collapsing.

"Fane? Did he come back?"

Ryn shook his head. "I don't know where he went. But I swear, when I find him, he will pay."

A tremor ran through me. Pain filled my senses and I couldn't respond.

"Hold on. We're almost there." Ryn's voice was warm and soothing.

I reached out for him, grasping at air.

"Hold on, Kenzie."

My head spun as we arrived at the giant house. I blinked in confusion. This wasn't my coven. We were back at Ryn's palace.

I whipped toward him as he reached for me. "I said to take me back to my witches."

His face was like stone. "You need a healer, Kenzie. Then I'll take you. I promise."

Fear spiked my blood. "We don't have time. Ryn, they need us."

"We'll be there. Just hold on."

My body protested as he carried me up the driveway. Confusion filled me. Where was the carriage? Had Fane taken it? Had Ryn carried me all the way?

Pain overwhelmed my senses, and I gave up on trying to keep my head up. I let it loll against his broad chest as he carried me. His warmth surrounded me and the realization that I heard nothing but silence where his heart would beat made me shiver. Mistaking my movement for cold, Ryn held me tighter.

Once inside, he lay me on a couch and demanded a healer. Deepa came with the vampire healer, their eyes widened at me.

"What happened?" Deepa asked.

"The barrier. I opened it." My voice was hoarse.

She gaped at me. "By yourself? How?"

I grunted. "I had help. Rogue witches."

She frowned, but I didn't explain further. I knew she would ask about Blake, and I didn't want to have to tell her what I'd done. The image of his slackened face made me shudder. He'd left me no choice, but the memory still filled me with nausea.

"Blake is gone. I woke up and he wasn't here. I think he went back to help the coven, but I don't know why he didn't leave me a note."

Her words made me wince. Ryn met my gaze, a silent question in his eyes. I turned away from him. Though I appreciated his willingness to tell her, I had to be the one to do it. I was the queen after all.

I sucked in a breath. "Blake didn't go to the coven. He was the mole. He tried to attack us, so I had to stop him."

Deepa reeled back. "Blake? No. He can't be the mole."

My fist clenched. "He was. He was working with Fane. He admitted to killing Julia too."

Anguish flashed on her face. "No. But she was drained. It couldn't be him."

"He led her to Fane."

She shook her head, mouth opening and closing in disbelief. I tore my gaze away from her. The pain in her eyes too raw.

I'd killed Blake. He'd been guilty of betraying us first, but that didn't change the fact that I'd killed him, and not out of self-defense like I'd told her. He wasn't trying to kill me—it was Ryn that he was after and I'd stepped in.

But I couldn't tell Deepa that. I couldn't tell any of them that. They wouldn't understand. How could I choose a vampire over one of my own witches? Even with his betrayal, they wouldn't understand.

I winced. The pain spread through my limbs and I could barely keep my eyes open. It felt as if I was breaking apart from within.

Cold dread swirled within me. I couldn't die. Not yet. Not when I was so close to fixing the curse.

Deepa helped the vampire with the healing ointment and gave me a pill to stop the pain. I shut my eyes, shutting the world out as they worked.

Hurry. Please. My thoughts bounced in my head.

What if we were too late when we arrived? A lump grew in my throat. Kohl was there. And Val and all my witches. We had to make it back in time.

Voices drifted around me. I stirred, pain shooting to my head. My eyes opened, and I found myself on a couch. I blinked against the darkness. A couch, but, where was I?

"Kenzie." Ryn's voice startled me.

I glanced in his direction. Candles lit to reveal his worried face. Deepa was there with him and some other vampires I didn't recognize.

"The coven," I coughed.

"I've sent my vampires to help. We'll leave at once. Are you sure you can make it?"

I struggled to sit up. "Yes. We have to go now."

"Kohl would want me to keep you here. To keep you safe," Deepa interrupted.

My eyes shot to her. "Kohl isn't in charge. We're going to the coven. We have to make sure the covenant gets signed."

Ryn turned to his vampires. "If you see Fane, send me word at once."

They glanced at each other. One spoke up, "Your highness, your brother has already come and gone. He went to the city."

To the coven? My stomach turned in dread.

Ryn slammed his fist onto the table, knocking over a chalice. Wine spilled from it and rose petals shook loose and flew, scattering to the ground.

"What are you going to do about your brother?"

He turned to me. "Let me deal with him. First, we have to make sure the covenant gets signed."

I nodded and let Deepa help me to my feet. Pain sliced through me, but I pushed it away. Pain or no pain, the fight wasn't over yet.

27

VALERIA

Diego came, but he didn't come alone. Vampires and rogue witches followed him and all his wolves. His full force against us.

It was war.

The sun had set, and the blood moon lit up the sky. I couldn't help but think it was fitting. A red moon for what was sure to be a bloody night. Even if the other rogue witches and my wolves came, it wouldn't be enough.

Our only hope was the covenant. But how would we get Diego to sign it now? I watched from the window as Diego and his minions filled the streets, surrounding us. Their howls echoed in the night.

Elijah stood beside me and shook his head. "This isn't going to end well."

I didn't answer.

Kohl and the other witches were at the front door, chanting another protection spell. Drew and Becca were nowhere to be seen, but I knew they were there. But I doubted they were in any state to fight. Not after what I'd witnessed at the health shop.

"The queen and Prince Ryn will come back," I finally answered Elijah.

He leaned toward me. "It's not too late. We could make a run for it."

I stared at him in shock. Anger slithered in my chest. He wanted to run away again?

"We can't survive this, Val."

"I'm not abandoning them."

I turned away from him. Hot tears filled my eyes. How could he even ask me to do that? Pushing away my emotions, I headed for Kohl and the other witches.

Something is wrong.

I frowned at my wolf's words and scanned the room. Five witches walked up behind Kohl and the others. I frowned. What were they doing?

Traitors.

I gasped. I opened my mouth to warn Kohl, but a loud boom echoed and shook the house. Kohl and his witches flew back as the doors burst open.

Screams erupted. Witches moved, their hands flying and mouths chanting.

"Val!" Elijah called.

I leapt out of the way as the witches sent spells flying at each other.

Kohl shot to his feet, his eyes briefly meeting mine. He turned to the tall witch behind them and shot out his magic. "What are you doing?"

"We won't let the covenant be signed," she replied.

Howls and shouts echoed from outside.

Kohl's eyes widened in panic. "Reset the ward. Now," he yelled at the remaining witches.

I leapt to the front. Elijah was close behind me.

He pulled at my arm. "What are you doing?"

"We can't let them in," I screamed above their roars.

Elijah yanked me out of the doorway and dragged me back inside. I struggled against him. Another set of howls echoed. My wolf perked up.

Our pack.

They were coming. Dread unfurled inside me. Diego would kill them all.

No. What was happening? What had I done? Led them straight into a trap.

Numbness filled me. I let Elijah pull me past the front room and into the back. Into a coat closet. We stood pressed together, his sweat and the faint scent of candles and soap filed my senses.

"Valeria!" I heard Drew calling me.

His voice snapped me into action. They needed me.

"I'm not hiding in here while our pack fights, Elijah. If you want to stay here like a coward, fine. But I can't." I yanked myself out of his grasp and went for the door.

"No, Val!"

My leg kicked out behind me, connecting with him. I flung the closet open and stepped out before he could grab me.

I glanced around the crowded room. The Red Wolves and vampires were attacking the coven.

Diego's eyes met mine. The smugness I saw on his face made my anger swirl within me. He'd won, and he knew it.

Elijah jumped out behind me.

Diego's eyes narrowed. "I didn't want it to come to this, Val. But you've chosen the humans over us. You are a disgrace to all alphas. All wolf kind. You should be glad your parents and all your elders are dead."

Anger spiked my blood. His words struck like arrows. How

could he say that when he was the one who killed the other alphas?

My wolf growled, straining against the barrier. *Free me.*

I obeyed.

Diego shifted at the same time. His wolf was bigger and darker, yellow eyes filled with savage bloodlust.

I snarled at him. He circled me, trying to dominate. I held my ground.

My eyes stayed on him, watching, and waiting.

Elijah shifted and leapt for Diego, but Diego's betas blocked him. His angry howl echoed around us. My mate promised blood.

I glanced around. Diego's pack had us surrounded, but my wolves were close. My eyes focused on the giant alpha. If I could bring him down, I could end it.

He dove first. I skittered back, but not fast enough.

Sharp teeth cut into my fur and flesh right below my neck, drawing a yelp from me. I struggled against his hold. He lifted me from the ground. The pain speared through me, sharp and hot.

Elijah howled in fury.

I turned my head to bite Diego. His jaws sank deeper into me and I couldn't reach him. Couldn't stop him.

He slammed me into the floor, my head spinning as it connected with the cold, hard tiles. My body spasmed as he released me. I whimpered.

Excruciating pain radiated from my wound. He stood over me, blood dripping from his massive jaws. My blood.

Get up.

I struggled to my feet. Diego watched patiently. He wasn't done with me.

Before he could attack, I shifted back.

Kill him.

Diego growled at me. Pain washed over me as I staggered back. The wound would have to wait. Once I could shift back into wolf form, I could let it start healing, but for now it had to wait.

I searched the room for a weapon.

"Valeria!" Drew voice called from far away.

A dagger flew toward me, and I wasn't sure if it came from Drew or one of the witches trying to kill me, but I grabbed the hilt and whipped toward Diego.

He shifted, body transforming before me.

"Couldn't even stay in wolf form. Coward," he spat at me.

I stood before him, holding my weapon between us. He had some nerve calling me a coward when he'd shot down Taylor.

Noises erupted from the other room. Snarls and screams. The fight had started.

"Val!" Elijah's desperate voice called. He sounded weakened and in pain.

My wolf rose to the surface.

Diego smiled. "After I kill you. I'll kill him next."

My wolf growled.

Standing there stark naked, my blood dripping from his mouth, he looked fierce. He was fierce. He was everything the humans feared of us—strong, brutal, wild.

But so was I.

His eyes shot to silver and before he could shift, I moved forward. My knife sliced through his side.

"No!" Sylvie's cry bounced off the walls.

Diego reeled, clutching his wound. His eyes were wide with shock.

My wolf howled in victory.

I blinked at the blood blossoming from his skin. An injury in human form was much harder to heal. We both stood in shock at what I'd done. It happened too fast. Too easy. Was it over? It couldn't be over already.

Diego roared. His wolf was filled with fury. He punched me. I reeled back with the force of it, pain spearing through my jaw.

"Val!" Elijah pushed his way to the front.

"Don't. Don't shift." Sylvie was at Diego's side. Her eyes were shining with fear. "Don't shift. Your human side won't be able to heal in time."

Diego hissed in pain, his eyes shooting me daggers.

His wolves howled around us. My wolves burst through and descended on them. The humans we'd saved were with them—turning the guns Diego had gifted us on his pack.

Elijah pulled me into him. His shirt, unlike mine, hadn't been torn when he shifted. The rough material rubbed against my bare skin. I stood, numb, as Diego's blood dripped from my knife.

"Call off your wolves." My voice was hoarse.

Sylvie sobbed by his side, trying to stop his bleeding with a kitchen towel. Diego's eyes narrowed on me. The look he leveled me said it all. This wasn't over. It was far, far from over.

28

MCKENZIE

The streets were filled with werewolves and vampires. I could barely make out my coven past the crowds. Dread coiled in my gut. Ryn stopped the carriage and we hopped out.

Deepa stood beside me, mouth open in horror.

"Come on," I urged her.

Ryn ordered his vampires into the fray. He turned and gave me a curt nod.

I stumbled forward as they descended on the wolves and other vamps. Ryn's vampires against those loyal to Fane. Diego's army was bigger than I'd ever imagined. How could I have not seen it?

Blake's words came back to me. *There are others...*

More rogue witches right within our coven. Guilt pricked at me. I should have seen it. I should have known.

Vampires, witches, and werewolves all on the same side and against us. It would be a bloody mess once it was over. The only ones not there... humans. Where were all the humans?

I turned to Ryn. "The humans and the other wolves. The slaves. Free them. I'm going to help my coven."

Ryn nodded and commanded his vampires to follow my orders. They disappeared down the street.

Deepa and I went ahead, racing for the coven. She and Ryn shielded me from the rogue witches that came out of nowhere, blasting magic at us.

I leapt through the doorway and let Deepa use her magic to seal the doors. It wasn't a permanent fix, but it would help.

Inside there was chaos. Spells flying through the air, wolves tearing into each other, and vampires whooshing here and there.

"I'll deal with the vampires. You two go after Diego." Ryn's voice hardened.

I looked back and nearly stumbled. His brow was furrowed, and he looked exactly like the portrait I'd seen. Harsh. Unrelenting... and magnificent. He glanced at me before disappearing.

Snapping my mouth closed, I motioned for Deepa to follow me. I had to get to Diego. Make sure Kohl was okay.

"Kenzie!" Kohl called from the back.

Deepa moved with me, shielding us both with her power. Irritation burned inside me. I needed my magic, but it was still too soon to cast.

"Kohl!" My voice rang out.

Heads turned to us. Deepa swore behind me and I realized too late, my mistake. The rogue witches came for me and some of the familiar faces I saw cut me to the core. How could I have been so blind?

Kohl and my faithful witches cut them off before they could make it to me. They formed a circle around me and cast a barrier around us. A lick of anger curled inside me.

I didn't want to be stuck in the protection ring like a weakling. I should have been there on the front lines, striking them all down.

The blood moon was still in the sky so why wasn't I healing faster?

"Kohl, where is he? Where is Diego?" I yelled over the noise.

"He's with Valeria."

"The covenant?"

"It's safe." Kohl glanced at me.

Relief flooded me. I smiled at him. Concern shone on his face as he took in my appearance.

Someone screamed. I turned to see the candles knocked over, fire racing along the wooden floor.

Trying to burn down my coven? Fury sparked inside me.

"Deepa, Kohl, come with me. The rest of you put out that fire and end those witches."

They scattered immediately, ready to fulfill my command. Deepa and Kohl moved with me and kept the barrier strong.

We made it to the back room. I reeled at the sight before us. Valeria stood, naked, over Diego. A bloodied knife hung from her hand. Elijah, Drew, and her wolves were by her side.

They'd done it. They had stopped him. I stared at them, stunned.

Sylvie was beside her fallen alpha, blocking Valeria's path.

"Stop. I'll sign it." Sylvie's shrill voice echoed in the room.

I threw a hand up to silence everyone. "Enough. Stop. Diego, call off your wolves. It's over."

They all turned to me.

"Stand down." It was Sylvie who spoke.

Diego's eyes were narrowed on his mate, but he said nothing. He was too busy bleeding out on the floor.

Marching forward, I went to Sylvie. "You said you'll sign the covenant?"

She nodded.

"With his blood." I pointed at Diego.

She glared at me. "My blood works just as good."

"No. I want his."

He struggled to his feet. "No, Sylvie. Remember what they did. You sign that and we'll lose everything."

Her eyes filled with tears. "We already have, Diego. I can't lose you. You'd do the same if it were me."

Before he could argue, I took the knife from Valeria and swiped it along his cut. He hissed with pain, eyes flashing silver.

"Don't even think about it," I warned.

Trusting Kohl to have my back, I turned back to his mate and offered her the end of my blade. She leveled me a look of pure hatred as she took it.

"Kohl."

He pulled out the scroll and hovered it in the air before Sylvie.

"Sign it. Your name with his blood," I demanded.

With a trembling hand she did what she was told. Shock ran through me. Was it over? Was it really over? It couldn't be that easy.

Sylvie's shoulders slumped as she finished. She gripped the knife in her hand.

I held my palm out to her. "Give it back. I don't trust you with it."

Her eyes were silver. Kohl edged closer to me. Elijah moved first. He yanked the knife out of her grasp, and she skittered back.

Val was standing with a blanket wrapped around her shoulders now. Her face was scrunched in pain, but she was alive. Her and Elijah and Kohl.

"He needs a healer."

I glanced at the injured alpha. His face was murderous.

I smiled. "All our healers are busy. Taking care of our own injured."

Diego's pack growled. Kohl stepped closer to me, hands ready to cast.

"Fine. Are we free to go now?" Sylvie's voice was small and subdued.

She crouched beside Diego, her gaze on him. His eyes were clenched shut now.

It was only a matter of time before one of his rogue friends healed him.

Silence filled the room. Everyone stopped fighting and gathered around to watch what would happen next.

All eyes turned to me. I squared my shoulders back. "Yes. For now. Take your pack with you." I turned to face the others. "The covenant is sealed. Signed by the humans, the wolves, the witches, and vampires."

Or it would be once Ryn signed it. But they didn't need to know that.

"You don't speak for all witches," one of the rogues interrupted.

A harsh laugh escaped me. "Actually, I do. That's what being queen means. You can try to defy me if you want, but trust me, you won't win."

Ryn and his vampires came up behind the witches, their presence drawing gasps and stares. He met my look and nodded in assurance.

I marched up to the rogue witch. "Get out of my coven. Before I decide to strike you all down here and now."

Never mind that I couldn't use any magic yet.

She flinched at my words and that made me smile. They wouldn't think me so weak now.

The rogues exchanged nervous looks and one by one, turned for the door. A sigh of relief escaped me as they left. Sylvie and the other wolves trailed them. Diego, hobbled between his mate and beta, eyes raging as they landed on me.

He motioned for them to stop.

I steeled myself as he stood in front of me. "This isn't over, McKenzie. I won't let you destroy what we've built."

"Get out of my face, Diego," I snapped.

He glared at me as the others led him away. Back to whatever hole they'd crawled out of. I watched him go, his threat echoing around me.

Not over...

I knew it wasn't over, but at least we'd come to a stand-still. We could figure out our next steps as we went.

Once they were gone, I instructed the healers to make use of the last of the blood moon and tend to everyone. There was a tangible relief as everyone moved about. We'd done it.

Surprise and joy showed on everyone's faces, but the moment didn't last long. A loud, slow clap sounded from somewhere. Everyone paused.

I frowned, scanning the shadows for the source.

Fane emerged.

His cold, blue eyes pierced me. A smug smile spread on his face. "Well done, everyone. Cheers. Sorry to have missed the excitement."

My mouth dropped open. Was he for real?

Ryn marched toward him. "Fane," He growled.

Fane's eyes flicked to him. "Prince Fane, please."

"What are you doing here? You dare show your face again after what you've done? You helped Diego." Ryn's voice rose and bounced off the walls.

Fane only smiled. "Yes. I'm sorry about that too. My humblest apologies. But looks like you're no worse for the wear so all's well that ends well."

Ryn took a step closer to him, fury in his eyes.

"Did she tell you she kissed me?"

Ryn reeled.

My eyes snapped to Fane's. His smile grew triumphant. *Bastard.*

"Get out." Ryn's voice hardened.

"I just thought you'd like to know."

Ryn stilled, his fangs out. "Leave, Fane. Now. Before I do something, I regret."

Fane's gaze flickered to me. "Haven't you already done that?"

Ryn leapt at him with a snarl and threw him against the wall. I flinched as his head collided with it, the sound echoing in the silence.

Fane's eyes narrowed. "You never could master your emotions. Weak just like before."

Ryn recoiled, anguish flashing across his face. His hands dropped to his sides as Fane straightened his shirt and sneered at me.

Everyone watched us. I didn't dare look at Kohl. My humiliation and Ryn's anger weren't enough for Fane. He stopped in front of Kohl and I sucked in a breath.

"Did she tell *you* about our kiss? She was practically begging me to take her."

Fury built inside me. "Shut your mouth, Fane."

"That's not what you were saying that night."

Kohl's fists clenched, knuckles whitening. His mask of coolness slipped, and the shock and hurt I saw written behind it made my stomach clench.

"But I guess one vampire wasn't enough for her." His eyes slid to me and back to Kohl. "I saw her sucking face with my brother. You should have heard her moaning. She ever moan for you, witch?"

A blast of magic flew from Kohl's palm, sending the vampire stumbling back.

Fane laughed.

I could feel the magic between my witches rise and fall. I didn't need to turn to see their shock and disgust.

My chin lifted. It was a kiss. Nothing more. It didn't mean anything.

Kohl didn't meet my eyes. His anger stung worse than the others. I swallowed hard. There was nothing I could say to make things better.

The truth was out.

"Get out, Fane." I strode forward.

He bowed and flashed me a smile before disappearing in a flurry.

"Are we seriously going to let him walk away? Just like that? His name isn't in the covenant. Doesn't that mean he can do whatever the hell he wants?" Drew's voice broke the silence.

No one answered him.

Fane was a traitor. We couldn't trust him. Ryn's signature wouldn't matter now. Not unless he took his place as King.

I turned to Kohl. Anguish flashed in his eyes, but his face was a mask of calm.

He didn't look at me.

Guilt flooded me, but I couldn't change what I'd done,

I cleared my throat. "Are the others okay?"

Kohl stared at Ryn. Ryn returned the silent glare.

"Kohl?"

He turned to me, the look of betrayal on his face like a punch to my gut. "Yes."

All eyes were on us, but no one spoke.

"Is there anything else? Kenzie?"

My heart twisted at the sound of my nickname and the sorrow in his eyes. He wanted an explanation for what I'd done, but I had none.

I wrapped my arms around myself and averted my gaze.

How could he expect me to talk about something I didn't even understand myself?

He stiffened, reading my silence as an answer. Then he walked away. I knew in that moment, I'd broken our friendship beyond repair. There was no going back now.

Whispers echoed around us. I could feel all their eyes on me. Their judging, harsh eyes.

They think you are weak...

Kohl disappeared into the crowd and I followed. He stepped outside and stood on the front porch, hands gripping the rails. Diego's army had fled and now only Ryn's vampires milled about.

"Kohl."

His shoulders stiffened. "Yes, My Queen?"

Shame and guilt crashed into me at the pain in his voice. Why didn't he turn and look at me?

"I... it was only a kiss."

"What you do is your own business."

Warmth flooded my face. "I haven't done anything, Kohl. Kohl, look at me."

He flinched. "I can't. Please, Kenzie. I can't." His voice was barely more than a whisper.

My heart twisted. I'd done this to him. To my best friend. I swallowed the lump in my throat, wishing I could rewind time and stop myself. I didn't want to lose Kohl.

"Why him?"

His question cut me. Which one, I wanted to say, but stopped myself.

"I don't know. I think I was compelled."

Kohl whipped toward me, his eyes studying me. "Compelled?"

I hated the hopefulness in his voice. My mind was

screaming at me to just go with it, but I couldn't. He was my best friend. He would see through the lie.

"Maybe." I looked away.

He issued a harsh laugh. "Right."

"It was a mistake. It's never going to happen again."

"May I go now?" His voice hardened.

I cringed. He was shielding himself from me, erecting a barrier to protect his wounded heart.

Tears filled my eyes. "Kohl. This changes nothing."

He sucked in a breath, my eyes tracking the movement as he squared his shoulders back. "What do you want me to say, Kenzie?"

"That we're okay. That you forgive me. That you don't hate me for this."

Slowly, he turned and the anguish I saw in his hazel eyes struck me like lightening.

"Hate you? I have loved you since you walked into Miss Evan's fifth grade class with your fake rose tattoo and that girly giggle."

My fists clenched by my side. A numbness filled me as he stared, that hopeful look on his face. My heart pounded against my ribs. He'd said it. He'd never spoken it out loud before.

Say something. Tell him you love him. But I didn't love him. Not like that.

"I'm sorry," I blurted instead.

Immediately, I wished I'd lied. His face crumpled and before I could take back my words, the stony mask was back.

"No reason to apologize, My Queen. You've made your feelings clear."

"Kohl, no. I do care about you. You know that. You're my best—"

"Don't, Kenzie. Don't say it. Please." His eyes clenched shut.

The pain I saw written on his face made me pause. There was nothing else I could say. I wrapped my arms around myself and watched as he marched back inside.

Blinking away the tears, I sucked in a long breath and followed. Maybe in time, he would forgive me.

29

VALERIA

I scanned the room. There were so many of us. All the humans they'd enslaved and the witches and wolves who hadn't submitted to Diego were freed. The ones who were still alive that was. My chest tightened as I watched a group of humans embrace each other with joyful sobs.

A loud sigh escaped me. It was done.

"Come. We need to get your wolf to Cruz." Elijah's tone was stern.

I let him lead me away. The wound was already starting to heal and though it hurt like hell, it was worth it.

Words my father taught me echoed in my mind. *Most risks worth taking are painful, Val. If it were easy, everyone would do it and it wouldn't be a risk.*

I swallowed the lump in my throat at the memory. Diego's insults were still fresh in my mind as well. Was he right? Would Dad have been ashamed of me siding with humans after what they'd done to us?

The fact that the alpha wolf's words made me question my

choices and question my own father's feelings toward me made me want to stab him all over again.

"Valeria." Drew's voice cut through my thoughts.

Elijah's grip tightened on my wrist. His body stilled and I could tell right away he was fighting his wolf's urge to keep me from the human.

I turned to face Drew, offering him a weak smile. My eyes flickered to Elijah. I gave his large hand wrapped around me a pointed look.

His lip curled, but he withdrew his hold.

"Are you okay?" Drew's gaze roamed over me, and the concern I saw written there made me flush.

"I'm fine. Just going to find the healer."

Drew's eyes shot to Elijah and back to me. "I want to come with you. Make sure you're okay."

Elijah scowled at him. "That's not necessary."

"Elijah," I warned.

His face softened and he looked away. We moved toward the corner of the room where Cruz and the other healers were tending to the injured. Drew and Elijah stood by my side.

"We did it. We actually did it." Queen McKenzie's voice rose above the noise.

Everyone quieted and turned to her. She held up the signed paper and ran her fingers across the lettering. It shook in her grasp, the edges glowing a bright yellow.

My eyes widened. Magic?

"We still have a lot to figure out. As far as the rules we want to make. How the housing and food situation is going to be handled. There's so much." She shook her head as she spoke.

"But there's time for all that. Tonight, we celebrate." The vampire prince smiled.

His fangs stuck out making my inner wolf's hackles rise. The declaration Prince Fane had made still hung in the air. The witch queen and the vampire prince—both of them, apparently. It was hard to wrap my head around.

Unnatural. My wolf offered her opinion.

Not our business, I reminded her.

"Yes. We have good news. The barrier spell is broken. We—"

An uproar of cheers and gasps cut off the queen's words. I reeled at the confession. My gaze fell on Elijah. The barrier was open. Would he still stay?

My wolf whimpered.

The queen held up a hand and everyone shut up. Irritation filled me at how easily she commanded attention. Even after her public embarrassment she acted as if nothing had happened and the others followed her lead. What did she have that I didn't?

"We don't know what's out there or if it's safe. So, we will be sending out a group to scout... and to guard it. We have to be careful about this. We also need to set up a meeting where we can all decide on the rules for the covenant."

"But I thought the rules were already made? What did everyone sign their name for?" a human spoke up.

The queen glanced at her. "The signing was just to establish the covenant. To establish order. From there, we'll have to come up with the rules we want our society to run on."

"How about no more slavery," another human growled.

Others murmured their agreement.

"Yes. We will go over all that, but not now. Right now, we should regroup. Everyone's been through a lot. Everyone goes back to their... groups and you can discuss what you want to see in the rules and protocols. Then we'll pick a day to meet."

I nodded along with the others.

Diego was still alive, and he still had many on his side, but we were unified now, and there were more of us. We would keep the covenant. He would either have to accept defeat or we would have no choice but to lock him away.

Or kill him, my wolf offered.

I shuddered at the idea, though I'd come close to doing just that. I didn't want it to come to murder, but my gut told me it wasn't over. He would fight back.

Cruz dipped his head in acknowledgment as I stepped in front of him for healing. With a pained smile, I shifted. The blanket fell from my shoulders.

Pain hammered into me. A pitiful whine escaped me. I glanced up to find Elijah staring at me, his eyes turned to silver.

I called to his wolf, but he didn't come. Instead, Elijah landed a gentle hand on my head, his eyes shut. He was holding his wolf in. Sorrow filled me. Why wouldn't he come?

The healer worked quickly to lessen my pain. I curled myself on the cold floor and shut my eyes, letting my body do the rest of its healing. Voices drifted above me, and people moved around noisily. The room was too crowded, but the presence of my mate calmed me.

When I woke up, I found myself back in human form and covered with a heavy blanket. I was in a bed and it was too dark to make out anything else. Was I in a guest room? My body tensed as I tried to sit up. The wolf part of me was still recovering.

Something rustled at the end of the bed. I shot up.

Our mate.

I blew out my breath in relief. Elijah. I leaned forward to find him sprawled at the foot of my bed, a gentle snore coming from him.

How long had he been watching over me? My heart

warmed at his concern, but another part of me was still sour about the fight. The scene replayed in my mind. Why was it so easy for him to walk away?

He is part human. Sometimes humans are weak.

But was that all it was? He let his fear control him? I wanted to trust him again, but how could I? It wouldn't matter anyway once he left Savannah. My chest tightened.

Pushing away the thoughts, I lay back down and tried to sleep before morning came. Diego's face followed me in my dreams, his wolf's attack played on repeat. I saw it unfold over and over, and each time it felt as if I was dying again.

When sunlight woke me, I sat up to find Elijah gone. My wolf assured me he was still in the building and as much as I told myself it didn't matter—it did.

He was still there.

A knock sounded on my door and I sprang to my feet to see who it was. I looked down and stopped, realizing I was still naked.

"Hold on." I turned to scan the room for clothes.

Someone had left an outfit for me on the side table. Dressing quickly, I stretched and went for the door.

Surprise filled me as I opened it to find Drew there.

His eyes took me in, and I couldn't imagine what a mess I probably was.

A small smile spread on his face. "How are you feeling?"

"Better," I croaked.

"Here. I brought you some water." He handed me a bottle.

I took it and guzzled it down gratefully. Screwing the lid back on, I smiled. "Thanks. How is Becca?"

Sorrow flickered in his eyes. "She's... better. Quieter. I don't know."

Pity filled me. I didn't know what to say to that. The poor

girl needed help. We all did after the trauma we'd been through. But who could help her?

Drew shifted on his feet and changed the subject. "Are you hungry? I wanted to wait for you before I went down for breakfast."

My eyebrow arched. "Down for breakfast? What is this? A hotel?"

He chuckled. "Everyone's eating together. I think that's a good sign, don't you?"

"I guess."

Drew's eyes darted to the bed behind me and back to me. "Elijah wouldn't let me check on you last night. Did he... never mind?" He shook his head. "Not my business."

I folded my arms across my chest and frowned at him. "What's not your business?"

He flushed and looked at the floor. "Nothing. I'm sorry. I'm sure you're happy to have your alpha back. Your mate."

Yes. Our mate. Walk away, human.

My cheeks flamed at my inner wolf's words, thankful Drew couldn't hear them. I bit my lip and shook my head. What was I supposed to say? Telling him it was complicated... a short laugh escaped me.

It was way, way more than complicated.

His brows knitted together. "What?"

I sighed. "I am happy to have him back, but I don't think he's staying."

Drew's eyes widened. "Not staying?"

"Yeah. The barrier is open, and he told me before he was going to leave. Again."

"But why? Isn't he still alpha? How can he just walk away?"

Rubbing my arms, I glanced away. I didn't know what to answer. It was the same question I had.

"Hey." Drew's lowered voice brought my head up.

His brown eyes met mine. "Like I said before. He's an idiot to leave you."

My wolf growled, but his words made me flush. I looked past him and into the hall to make sure no one had heard him.

He lingered near my door and we stood in awkward silence. What did he expect from me? It wasn't like I was exactly available, but I did like him. I snorted at myself. I barely knew him and there were way more important things to focus on like my pack and the covenant. So, why couldn't I just end it—whatever *it* was—and move on?

"Drew, I—"

Before I could finish, his mouth was on mine. My eyes bulged. Soft, pliant lips moved slowly, the sensation stirring a fire in my belly.

My wolf raged in fury, eager to be unleashed. I shoved down her emotions. The last thing I wanted was her distress to reach Elijah's wolf.

Drew tasted like coffee and cream and instead of releasing me, he deepened the kiss and I moved with him, returning it.

I called our mate. My wolf's smug voice echoed in my mind.

What? I shook my head as her words registered. Elijah. My hand flew up between Drew and I, and I stepped back.

His eyes were still hooded, and his face looked flushed. Heat spread up my neck. This was a dangerous game. Before anything could happen—anything else—I needed to talk to Elijah. To set things right?

"What's wrong? What is it?" Drew's eyebrows furrowed in concern.

"You should go. If Elijah—"

"I thought you said it was over with him. That he was leaving again?" He scowled.

I glanced around the hall, worried any moment my alpha would be bounding down it. My eyes met Drew's.

"That's not what I said. It's just... even if he does go, I'm not sure this is a good idea right now. My pack needs me, and with the new covenant and everything, it's better if I just focus on that."

Drew's jaw hardened. Guilt needled me. Why did I let him kiss me?

"I'm sorry, Drew. I do... like you. I do, it's just complicated." I winced as the words tumbled out of me.

He sighed. "I know. I'm sorry. I don't want to make things more difficult for you. Just know... I'm here. I'm not leaving."

My cheeks flamed at his intensity. Footsteps sounded, and I turned to see Elijah standing at the end of the hall.

His fists were clenched, and his eyes narrowed on us. Drew stiffened beside me. I moved toward Elijah, worried his wolf would lash out.

"Elijah. We were just heading down to eat with everyone."

He glanced at me and the hurt I saw flickering in his dark eyes made me flinch.

I paused and turned to Drew. "We'll meet you downstairs."

Drew frowned and looked from me to Elijah but nodded and walked away. Elijah's stare bore a hole into my back. I steeled myself before turning to face him.

"It was just a kiss, Elijah."

A low growl escaped him. His eyes flashed silver and his nostrils flared. He stormed after Drew, but I blocked his path.

"Don't." I laid my hand on his chest. "You said you wanted to leave. You don't get to be the jealous boyfriend now."

He met my gaze, and I could see the emotions warring on his face—anger, regret, and sorrow. The sight of my strong alpha so broken made my heart twist.

"Do you want me to go?" His question pierced me.

"How can you ask me that? I never wanted you to leave in

the first place, Elijah, but I'm not going to stop you. You have to make the choice. Are you staying or leaving?"

Elijah flinched and looked away. His silence cut through me like a knife, the rejection more than I could bare. Recovering quickly, I sucked in a breath and started to walk away.

My heart pounded as I went. Wasn't he going to try to stop me? I fought the urge to look back. Tears threatened to spill. Blinking them away, I pushed myself forward. As much as I wanted him to stay, I didn't want him there out of obligation—because of the bond.

You can't stop the bond. My wolf's wounded tone filled me with guilt.

It was too complicated, and I didn't have the energy to deal with it. There were other concerns. Queen McKenzie was right. Even with the barrier open and covenant signed, there was still a lot of work left to do. The curse was still in effect and if we didn't find a way to stop it, my bonding wouldn't matter anyway—we'd all be dead.

A shudder ran through me at the thought. I pushed away grim images and Elijah's shattered face. Whatever his decision was, I had to be strong. I was still alpha.

He won't leave. He's our mate.

I didn't argue with my wolf, but I didn't have her confidence. The old Elijah would never have left me, but the curse, the new world, had changed all of us.

30

MCKENZIE

The sun was setting, and the view over the balcony was beautiful. Beneath me, the city was quiet as if holding its breath. We were still recovering from everything we'd endured. I could hardly believe our success myself. We'd actually broken the barrier and signed the covenant.

Though victory didn't come without a steep price. Kohl's look of betrayal flashed in my mind. I'd lost my best friend possibly forever, and it hurt just as bad as I knew it would and yet...

I couldn't bring myself to regret kissing Ryn as selfish of me as it was. My chest tightened as I imagined what the rest of the coven thought of me now. What would my parents have thought? Mel?

Tears burned my eyes as I imagined what my sister would have said.

Movement caught my attention, and I turned to see Ryn in the doorway. I tensed. Glancing behind him, I didn't see anyone else. Voices drifted from downstairs and I was pretty sure Kohl was still holed up in his room. Still hurt—still angry.

"May I join you?" Ryn's words were gentle and unsure.

My heart raced at his presence.

"Sure." I shrugged a shoulder.

He swept a curl out of his face and moved toward me. I looked past him, worry crawling over my skin. Us being alone together was risky. Especially with the other witches downstairs, but I didn't want him to leave.

I didn't want to be alone.

"Are you alright, Kenzie?" he asked.

Concern was written on his handsome face. I looked over the balcony and stared at the tops of the buildings.

"I'm fine."

Ryn stood beside me at the rail. "Are you certain?"

I nodded. "Yes. I'm just... recovering. After everything."

He gripped the metal, eyes scanning the city below. "Yes. It was a lot. I'm sure my brother will be back. The covenant won't stop him from causing trouble."

I sighed. "I figured as much. How are we going to deal with him?"

Ryn grunted. "Don't worry about Fane. Let me handle him. We have other things to worry about."

His smoldering eyes roamed over me and I fought the urge to blush. How was it that he could level me so with just a glance? It wasn't fair.

"And whatever you need, I'm here to help."

"The curse. We still have to figure out a way to reverse it or end it. Even with the barriers open, there's no guarantee that I can harness enough magic to..."

He grabbed my hands, making me pause.

"We'll figure it out. Together."

Heat rushed through me. *Together*. I hated how the word made me shiver. There wasn't supposed to be a together for us.

He was the vampire king, and I was queen of the witches. Something I had to keep reminding myself of.

Yet, here we were. Guilt filled me. If it weren't for the curse, we would never have become allies. Kohl would still be my best friend. As horrible as it was, I couldn't help the sliver of sadness that wormed its way inside me at the thought of never knowing Ryn—knowing the real him.

What was happening to me?

"I think we should celebrate. Hold a ball or something. To celebrate the signing of the covenant. This is a big deal for Savannah." His words shook me from my thoughts.

My eyebrows shot up. "A ball?"

He smiled sheepishly. "What? It's still a thing."

I bit back a laugh. "No. It's definitely not. Maybe like a party or something, but fancy gowns and stuff? No."

A frown marred his perfect face. "But I like all the fancy stuff." His eyes lit with excitement, "We could have a masked ball."

I gaped at him. He liked balls? The notorious prince of darkness? The more he spoke about it, the more I could picture him on the dance floor, moving gracefully. He could definitely pull off a tux, I'd give him that.

"What do you think?" His question snapped me back to the present.

"About a ball?"

He nodded, "Masked ball, yes."

I didn't have the heart to tell him no, but the absurdity of it made me shake my head. How could he expect everyone to dress up and dance like everything was fine? Like we weren't all cursed on the edge of death and living in a world gone to hell?

The covenant was only the first step. We had a lot more work ahead of us.

"Uh... maybe? Let's worry about the curse first."

Seeming satisfied with this, he smiled and glanced away. He had a dreamy look in his eyes, and I wondered if he was still picturing the old timey balls he'd been to before. Had there been anyone special in his past? Fane's words came to me.

Isabel.

My face warmed. What the hell did I care? I dismissed the thoughts and drew myself taller. It didn't matter. Everything I did now would determine everyone's future, and there was simply no time for any more games. The clock was ticking.

"We will have order now." Ryn's voice snapped me to attention.

I scoffed. "Yeah. We'll see."

Order. What did that even mean? More responsibility. More work. I sighed.

Ryn turned to me, face serious. "I know you probably think the worst of Fane, but he's not... completely unchangeable."

My eyebrow arched. "He tried to kill you."

"Just let me worry about him. Please."

Instead of answering, I just stared at him. It was clear Ryn still loved him despite the betrayal, despite common sense that said to deal with him quickly and permanently.

"Okay. But I have to do what's best for the coven. For everyone now."

Ryn didn't answer. His face looked troubled, and I fought the urge to comfort him. Everyone would be watching us now and I couldn't screw up.

They were all counting on me to get it right.

"I should go check on the others." I turned to go.

Ryn moved with me. "Kenzie... are we okay?"

A bitter laugh escaped me. "We? There's no we, Ryn. The kiss was a mistake. You know that. Just let it go. Let's just... work on the curse and work on setting up the covenant rules."

His face hardened. "What if I can't just let it go?"

I shook my head at him. "We have to. We have to, Ryn. Please. Give me space. I can't do this right now."

Worry creased his brow. "Okay." His voice sounded so small and unsure.

Guilt flooded me, but before I could let it take root, I turned to leave. My chest tightened. It was the right decision, I knew, but why did it have to hurt so bad? Is this what it meant to be queen? I blinked back angry tears.

No. I would not cry. Queens didn't cry.

Valeria

I stood by the lake staring out at the smooth surface. It was the same place I'd been countless times as a girl. I could still picture Jaime skipping rocks and practicing his shifting by the giant oak. My fist clenched, nails digging into my palm as I pushed the memories aside.

Today wasn't for grieving. There'd been plenty of those days and there would be plenty more, but today was for us survivors—for hope and a future where we could carry on our families' legacies.

A trio of ducks called in the distance. I watched as they floated along the edge of the water. The sun was lowering and the air growing chillier. Did McKenzie and the others set a date for the first covenant meeting? I wanted to be there for it, but I couldn't pull myself away from the idyllic scene.

There was something magical about untouched nature. I snorted at myself. For all I knew, there probably was magic involved, but it wasn't something I could sense.

Footsteps sounded behind me, bringing my head around.

"Elijah."

He smiled. It was the small, sad smile he'd carried since the beginning of the end. I missed the face splitting one that used to be there. Would it ever return?

"Nice out here." He nodded toward the lake.

"Yeah."

His arms stretched above his head, broad chest jutting out. The ducks glanced our way and flew off to the opposite side of the lake.

"You're scaring the wildlife."

He smirked and stepped closer to me. "I am the wildlife."

"I haven't seen your wolf loose for hunting since…" I snapped my mouth shut quickly.

Our last hunt. When his kin died, my wolf reminded me.

Idiot. Why would I say that? I mentally kicked myself.

His gaze dipped to the ground, pain lighting his features. "The more I shift… sometimes, I don't know if I could turn back."

My body stiffened. "Couldn't or wouldn't?"

He didn't meet my gaze.

"It's easier, you know. As a wolf. I can't remember them as well. I still miss them, but it isn't an all-consuming type of pain you know?"

The sorrow in his eyes struck me like an arrow. The pain was unbearable for me too, but I couldn't run from it. It was the price we paid for loving them despite the little time that we had with them. With them gone there was a piece missing and it felt wrong to pretend that there wasn't. As if they hadn't left an impact—an imprint—on us and the world. I knew they would want us to be happy, but not to grieve them at all—it would be like they hadn't mattered.

"None of it is easy, Elijah."

He blew out a breath and shoved his hands into his pockets. My wolf urged me closer, to offer him my comfort.

I wrapped my arms around him, the top of my head brushing his chin. He returned the hug, drawing me in close. I could smell the woods on his clothes and the faint fresh scent of soap. His warmth radiated through me and made me want to nestle closer.

My inner wolf was more than happy to oblige.

Our mate.

Her words made me shiver. The bond was terrifying to me. If I gave in to it and something happened... if I lost him like the others, it would be a loss I wouldn't survive. Didn't he realize that?

His strong hands rubbed my back, the touch electrifying. My cheeks flamed. What would Drew think if he saw us like that? I cared about him and I didn't want to hurt him, but Elijah was familiar and warm. It didn't feel wrong to be intimate with him.

Because he's our mate.

It was the one thing I didn't like about being a werewolf. That bond that would shackle me for the rest of my life. I'd seen bonded pairs who couldn't stand each other while in their human form. Pairs who betrayed each other. Elijah had already left once.

I pulled back at the same time he glanced down, his lips brushing my forehead. Fire lit inside me.

His eyes widened, and I knew he'd felt it too. Our bond kindling. I recoiled, needing space between us.

My heart thumped, the beat too erratic. Inside, my wolf was howling with need, and no, just no that was not happening.

I made the mistake of looking at Elijah. His dark eyes were narrowed, and his nostrils flared. It wasn't just my wolf who was ready for action.

He blinked and looked away, body visibly relaxing as if

nothing had happened. I shook off the unease and matched his steely exterior.

"You should get moving soon. The sun is already setting." I cringed at the roughness of my voice.

"Moving?"

"Yeah. Past the barriers to wherever you're going."

Elijah's eyes drilled into me. "I'm not going anywhere."

I gaped at him. "I thought..."

"Trust me, I'm not leaving again."

"Trust you? How am I supposed to trust you? That you won't run away again?"

His hand reached for mine, but I dodged it, not ready to feel the sparks again.

"I'm not going anywhere, Val."

Idiot, that I was, I believed him.

"What changed your mind?" I asked.

He licked his lips and met my gaze. "You. You showed me what a true alpha looks like."

My face reddened at his compliment, though I secretly wondered if it had more to do with Drew's interest in me. Our wolves were horribly possessive and jealous creatures.

Protective and loyal, my wolf argued.

Drew's face flashed in my mind. Sweet, innocent Drew. What was I supposed to do about him now? I couldn't deny my feelings for him, but I couldn't exactly be with him in front of the pack. What would they think of me? Elijah was back and they would expect us to perform the bond.

Heat spread up my neck and nausea rolled in my gut. I couldn't do it. My wolf was howling with joy at the prospect of it. She was more than willing to claim him and be claimed in return.

The thought made me turn crimson.

"Val."

I turned to meet Elijah's eyes. His smile made my heart flip flop, but I was still wary. It was up to me to keep my heart guarded. Him staying produced a multitude of problems and emotions. I drummed up my courage and steeled myself.

I wouldn't let him hurt me this time.

"Yes?" I finally answered.

"I never said thank you."

I frowned. "For what?"

He squeezed my hand. "For being the alpha our pack needed. For staying strong even when I couldn't. I wish..." He swallowed hard. "I wish your father could see you now."

Tears sprang into my eyes. "Do you think... he'd be angry about what I've done?"

He frowned. "About Diego? Hell no. He'd be proud of you. They all would."

I swiped the tears away. "He wouldn't approve of Drew, I know that."

Elijah stiffened. I watched him carefully, wondering what he'd do. He surprised me by squeezing my hand and falling silent. The touch warmed me though it also made me nervous. There was only so much I could do to fight our bond.

Maybe we could all still be friends after everything. If the witches found a way to save us and the covenant held, maybe there could be a future for all of us—wolf, human, witch, and vampire.

Nothing like what we'd ever pictured, but it was a start.

"Should we go back? The others will be looking for us."

I smiled at Elijah. "In a minute."

He returned the smile and let go of my hand. We stood together staring at the lake and I couldn't help but revel in the harmony. Despite everything we'd been through and the dark future ahead of us there was a surreal solace in that moment, and I didn't want to leave. With the blood moon covenant in place there was hope. Tomorrow there would be new problems and old hurts would remain, but that was something to worry about on another day. For now, everything was okay.

Calm before the storm, my wolf warned.

I shook off her worry, refusing to be swept up in it. I would prepare my pack as best as I could and enjoy what little pockets of peace there were. This wasn't the end.

It was just the beginning.

The story continues in book two, *Allegiance...* coming 2021

ACKNOWLEDGMENTS

Once again, I have to thank my editor at Cate Edits for her help and Maria Spada who did fantastic job on the cover!

Also a big thank you to my family for their never ending support and all the readers who have inspired me with their kind words and loyalty. If you enjoyed the story, please consider leaving a review and if you didn't enjoy it, I'd still love to know your thoughts. Thank you!

ALSO BY R. L. MEDINA

The Inner World Series

Book 1: Princess of the Elves

Book 2: Goblin King

Book 3: Fae War

Prequel: Feylin

GRIMM Academy Series

Book 1: Shifters and Secrets

Book 2: Vampires and Werewolves

Book 3: Witches and Wizards

Summer Bites: A Limited Edition Collection of Summer Vampire Tales

Short Story: A Summer Night Stroll

Blood Moon Covenant Series

Book 1: Order

Coming soon...

Book 2: Allegiance

Book 3: Betrayal

ABOUT THE AUTHOR

R. L. Medina was born in the Amazon, adopted and raised by two upstate New Yorkers. At age six, she vowed to hate reading forever. That hate quickly turned to love (or obsession) and by age eight she was filling every notebook with story after story. Now a mother herself, she juggles her time between a busy five year old and the stubborn characters that demand her time. When she's not exploring all the Sci-fi/Fantasy worlds in her head, she enjoys life with her family in Florida.

Check out her website at www.rlmedina.com for a free story, giveaways, and updates!

You can also find herself embarrassing herself on TikTok @thecrazybookdragon